We were so good together, how could he do this to me?

"She's not leaving me much to live on," Isaac said after hearing his wife's terms for a divorce. "We'll have to economize in lots of ways."

"We don't need to belong to the country club."

"I forgot to mention—"

"Let me guess. She gets the country club membership and you get the dues."

"We'll have some pretty lean years to start."

"I don't mind. I'm used to not having anything. Now I've got you. That's enough." *Guess I'll have to put off starting a family.*

He smiled. "You really mean it?"

"Kiss me." *I have you. That's enough for now. I've got lots of time to have a baby.*

I felt especially close to Isaac that night. No man had ever sacrificed for me before. Our lovemaking was the best ever. He made my kitty purr quick, long, and loud. It was so good we were late getting up and had to hurry through breakfast to get out the door on time. It was a particularly busy day at work, even for a Thursday. After work, I hurried home.

He must be working late. Is that a note? It's his key. Oh shit!

He'd scribbled something on a sheet of yellow tablet paper and left it on the kitchen table. It read, *Tookie, You're a great girl but I*—and nothing else.

He had gone back to his wife. I couldn't believe it. We were in such perfect harmony. He was so attuned to my feelings. He always said exactly what I needed to hear. How could he have left me so easily? The cold shock of reality struck me in the face when I opened his empty closet. Convincing myself that this was an aberration, I opened his dresser drawers. Empty, too.

Mary Louise, a bookish, redheaded, freckle-faced, eighteen-year-old virgin, who is unaware she has Asperger's Syndrome, dispenses with Tim, her loving but far too serious and conventional high school boyfriend, then thrusts herself, groin first, into the 1960s sexual revolution, pioneering concepts such as friends with benefits and serial monogamy, while earning two college degrees in statistics. Nicknamed Tookie by her doting father, she engages in often humorous escapades with innumerable unsuitable lovers, whom she seduces with her oral virtuosity. But through it all, the one thing she really wants escapes her—a man who will truly love her, despite her faults, and give her a daughter.

ONLY TIM SENT FLOWERS

REVISED EDITION

George Kaplan

A Black Opal Books Publication

GENRE: NEW ADULT/HUMOROUS FICTION/MAINSTREAM

ONLY TIM SENT FLOWERS ~ Revised Edition
Copyright © 2015 by George Kaplan
Cover Design by Jackson Cover Designs
All cover art copyright © 2017
All Rights Reserved
Print ISBN: 978-1-626947-29-0

First Publication: DECEMBER 2015

Published by Black Opal Books **http://www.blackopalbooks.com**

DEDICATION

*To the several editors who have guided
my work to the point it is today.*

CHAPTER 1

Invisible

Tookie

I discovered boys in kindergarten. They still hadn't discovered me in high school. Not one flirt, no pat on the ass, and not even one attempted to look up my skirt when I walked down the stairs. How insulting! I was invisible. I even overheard them standing in a stairwell joke about other girls but not me. Once, I flounced up and down the stairs sans panties after gym class. Even that didn't get me noticed.

At least I had one good friend here. Sue sat with me on the bus. She was blonde, pretty, perky, outgoing, and had a boyfriend. I think she befriended me at first because I was new in school and could help her with homework. I never made a friend like this at my previous schools. This time, Daddy's job brought us to a place in Illinois near St. Louis called Milltown. It was a misnamed blue-collar bedroom community without any industries or the tax base they provide. I so hoped Daddy's project would last long enough for me to finish high school here. Starting over at yet another place would be awful.

One typical 1965 late-November day after school, like usual, I babysat the little girl who lived next door with her parents in a modest new three-bedroom, single bath, red brick veneer ranch house with a one-car garage virtually identical to the others in this recently developed corn field on the edge of town. Our house was the mirror image of hers except that it had several rows of white bricks on the front. It wasn't clear if the bricks were intended to serve as an accent or if they ran short of red ones. After supper, I trudged past my parents' bedroom on the way to the kitchen to do my homework when their dial phone rang. Hoping it was Sue calling, I answered it on their extension.

"Hello. May I speak to Tookie, please," a nervous-sounding boy's voice said.

A boy? For me? I hope he doesn't want help with his homework. That'd give me an opening but I want some-one smart.

"Don't like Tookie. My name's Mary Louise."

"I—I'm sorry, Mary Louise. This's Tim Burgess. We met—"

He's kinda cute. Why's he calling me? "I know." *What should I say to a boy I hardly know?*

"Would you like to go to the movies on Saturday, Mary Louise?" he asked after several seconds.

A boy with his own car just asked me out. How can I get them to let me go?

"I'll check." I put the phone down and floated to the living room of the rented house. "Mother, Daddy, Tim Burgess, a boy who lives on the corner, wants to take me to the movies Saturday. May I go?" I tried not to sound excited.

Daddy lowered the newspaper he was reading, revealing his mostly bald head. "You're awfully young to be going on car dates." He'd become very cautious about everything after his heart attack a year earlier and had put on some weight because he was afraid to stress his heart by exercising.

"But all the other girls do."

"If all the other girls jumped off a bridge—" was his stock response.

"Dear, kids start dating younger than we did in our day." Mother always tried to be supportive.

My sister and I began calling her mother when we were well into puberty. It sounded lame to us for nearly grown women to continue calling their mother mommy. She was the apple of Daddy's eye. He wouldn't have chosen to live a second longer if anything ever happened to her.

"Beth's a year and a half older and she hasn't gone on any dates." Overprotective Daddy could be a pain at times because I was his favorite. I still remember what he said upon seeing me in my First Communion dress. "You look like an angel about to ascend to heaven you're so beautiful."

"She's barely a year older than me and nobody's asked her."

"Watch it." Daddy got that stern look on his face he got when we argued with him too much. He was always kind and loving but didn't like backtalk.

"But—but—"

"No buts. You're not going and that's final. You're too young and inexperienced to sit in a dark movie theater with a boy." He raised his newspaper and started reading again, signaling the end of the conversation.

Think, Mary Louise, think. It's taken so long to get asked out. Don't want to miss this chance. It might be the last. Maybe we could do something else. I slowly walked back to their bedroom and picked up the phone.

"I can't go to the *movies* with you." *Please don't give up on me.*

After a long silence, he tried again. "Could you go to the basketball game on Friday?"

Full of hope, I trotted back to the living room. "How about the basketball game at school on Friday?" *They can't object to this.*

Daddy looked displeased with me for still trying. "You're awfully young to be dating, Tookie."

"*Daaaadddy.*" Whining usually worked with Mother.

"Dear, there will be hundreds of people around. It couldn't be a more public place. I went to games when I was her age." Mother, who Daddy nicknamed Chunkin' or Mother Chunkin' for reasons known only to him, no longer had her girlish figure but, after having five children, was hardly plump and her dark hair had no gray.

"You did?" Daddy seemed genuinely surprised.

"You didn't know me then. I always had dates to football and basketball games. You may go, Mary Louise."

"But—"

"She's not retarded, dear."

I raced away to accept before Daddy could object but paused in the hall where they couldn't see me so I could hear what they were saying about me. "She's very smart but naïve and her relationships with girls are a challenge," he said. "She's got a lot to learn before she's ready to date. Even though Tookie's not nearly as pretty as you, boys will want to…ah…you know."

"And she needs to learn to fight them off—soon. This boy seems safer than most but I'll ask around to be sure."

He may have to fight me off.

Trying not to sound too excited, I said, "Pick me up at six thirty."

"Uh o-okay."

I'm becoming a woman now.

Lifting my breasts to little effect, I looked at my profile in the mirror. *More boys may find me attractive when they grow some more. Sue'll be shocked when she hears this.*

I busied myself the days leading up to my date by doing the usual things, babysitting, teaching the neighborhood children how to roller skate, and dreaming about what it would be like to be out on a real car date.

When the clock hit six twenty-five on Friday, I fluffed my hair in the mirror in the bedroom I shared with my Irish-twin sister, put on my coat, and went into the kitchen.

Mother perched on the picnic table, the only table we owned, guzzling an over-sized bottle of Falstaff.

Did I just hear someone pull into the driveway? I put my hand on Mother's hand that held the beer. "Mother, please?"

"Toookie, your date's here," bellowed thirteen-year-old Daniel from the living room.

Better get Tim out of here before they embarrass me.

I grabbed my knitted hat and gloves and hurried into the adjoining living room where Daddy waited to interrogate Tim. Dark Daniel buried his face in a chess book oblivious to my auburn-haired younger brothers Mike and Jake, aged seven and five, respectively, who wrestled on the floor.

I let Tim answer a few of Daddy's questions then stepped around the grapplers and grabbed him by the arm. I glared at Daddy. "We better go. Don't want to be late."

Jake glued himself to my leg "Stay home with us, Tookie," he begged.

I signaled Daniel, who then pried him loose. As soon

as I was freed, I pulled Tim out the door, closing it tightly behind us.

He didn't have that coat on before. It looked new and the color matched my slacks. He was a couple of inches taller than me with blondish flyaway hair and sexy blue eyes.

He opened the passenger door of his cute little classic Thunderbird for me. Even though I was wearing my favorite wool slacks because it was cold, I got into his car ladylike just like the nuns taught us. I sat down backwards on the seat ducking my head with my feet flat on the ground then, with knees together, I pivoted to my left, gracefully bringing my feet into the car under the dog leg. I wiggled my way into a respectable position—not too close to him but not hugging the door—while he walked around the car.

Tim handed me a blanket. "You might need this. The heater works fine but the blower motor that's supposed to circulate the warm air needs to be replaced."

Whatever. It's awfully cold in here.

Tim alternated between scanning the various gauges and instruments, half of which didn't work, and looking at me while he drove the mile through Milltown, smiling all the while.

Strange. No boy's ever looked at me like this before.

"What time do you have to be in by?" he asked.

Since neither Beth nor I had been on a date before, it hadn't been discussed. My parents had been so focused on whether I should be allowed to go or not, the topic of a curfew didn't arise. "No set time."

"Why do they call you Tookie?"

"Don't remember." I turned away to cut off that topic.

At the gym, the dean of boys recognized Tim and gave me a friendly grin, "You better watch him."

Tim just smiled. Since we were both students who had earned good grades and didn't attract trouble—Mother had asked around about Tim before our date—I took this to mean he approved of our dating each other.

We climbed to an open spot in the bleachers where no one would be sitting close to us. When Tim helped me off with my coat, I set my purse on a seat from where it fell through the gap below the boards all the way to the floor below.

Tim saw a ten-year-old boy chuckling and reached into his pocket. "Here's a quarter to get her purse."

The boy quickly crawled down through the cobwebs and dust bunnies and handed my purse up to me. Tim handed him the promised coin.

"Thank you," I said, blushing for my awkwardness and focused on watching the game, or pretending to.

"Number thirty-two is in my English class," I said, exhausting my sharable thoughts.

"Most of the starters were sophomores when I was a senior," he replied.

Neither of us said anything of note the rest of the game. He seemed shy and I didn't want to say anything that might spoil the date.

"Would you like to go to Tony's and get something to eat?" he asked when the buzzer sounded.

"Okay." It was too early to go home. It was fun being on a date, especially when you can tell the guy really wants to be with you.

We went to Tony's in a nearby town and shared a square-cut pepperoni pizza. Between bites, Tim grilled me. "Where did you live before here?"

"Ohio."

"How long did you live there?"

"Two years." Conversing with Tim stressed me. I'd never before talked with a boy remotely interested in me.

"How long do you expect to live here?" Tim looked confused.

"Two, maybe three, years."

I was too embarrassed to tell him I needed to pee. I tried giving him short answers to end the questioning so we could leave. It was flattering, him wanting to know more about me.

"Where will you go from here?"

"Don't know. We never do."

Maybe he ran out of questions or got my hint. Regardless, he drove me home, ignoring the gauges and staring at me more than at the road.

When Tim opened my door to let me out, he reached out his hand to help me out of his car.

No boy had ever held my hand before—dance class didn't count. Those boys didn't even want me as their partner. I kept hold of him even after we were on my stoop.

He stood there mooning at me. I desperately needed to relieve myself, but I didn't want to let go of his hand. It seemed like an eternity but couldn't have been ten seconds.

"Would you like to go out next Saturday?"

"Yes," I answered without thinking.

He put his arms around me and kissed me.

Please don't stop. I tingle. Wish I didn't have to pee so badly. I barely kissed back but didn't pull away until he did. When he did, I jetted into the house, throwing my coat to Mother and racing to the toilet. My parents met me when I emerged.

"Did you have a nice time, dear," asked Mother.

I nodded in the affirmative.

"Did he ask you for another date," asked Daddy.

"Yes. He's nice. Good night."

"Wait a minute. Did you say 'yes'?"

"Of course, Daddy."

He seemed perturbed that I accepted a date without getting permission to go. I'd deal with that later.

I went to bed, fantasizing about my future dates.

After the next date, I yanked him into the house where I could smooch him in private. Not only did I enjoy kissing, I loved feeling his body wrapped against mine. He made me feel desirable. I enthusiastically looked forward to the last act of each date, hoping each kiss would last longer than the previous one. I practiced gently breathing through my nose so I wouldn't have to stop a kiss because I ran out of breath.

Smitten, he asked me out week after week. Daydreaming about my upcoming dates got me through the school week.

"You're so beautiful. I've never seen such dark red hair. It's gorgeous."

Very awkward. At least he means it. "Please don't call me those things. I'm not pretty at all."

"You're prettier without any makeup than the cheerleaders are with it."

He wanted me badly and I enjoyed his touching me—most of the time. As soon as spring broke, we went to a drive-in movie and necked up a storm. I soaked in all the attention. Midway through the feature, he undid a button on my blouse and tentatively slid his hand in partway. It must have been a new experience for him because he seemed unsure of what he should do next.

Ooohh. My breasts wanted to be fondled so much but I dared not let him find out how little I had.

"Do you want me to be one of those girls who panic every time their periods are a day late?"

"No," he answered sheepishly and removed his hand.

"It looks like I'll have to wear anti-attack clothes in the future."

"I'm sorry." Penitent, he pulled back and watched the movie.

After too long with no contact, I said, "I didn't say to stop kissing me. I just want you to keep your mitts outside my clothes."

He wrapped his arms around me and kissed me more passionately than before.

❦

Sue told me about make-out parties where girls and boys from our class would pair off in Cindi's basement rec room when her parents weren't around.

"Sam and Gail neck and a lot more with the lights low, but bright enough for others to know what they're doing."

"Doesn't she worry about getting pregnant?"

Sue squirmed. "Yes. But not enough to keep her knees together."

"I can't respect girls who risk their entire futures."

I liked it when Tim rested his hand on my leg when he was driving—I sat next to him in his pre-seatbelt car and rested my head on his shoulder. One time, he put his hand on the uppermost part of my inner thigh, firing an electric bolt through my body.

Whooo. Now I know how it feels to want to have sex, and I want it NOW. I've always wanted it an abstract sort of way but, right now, I want him to pull down my pants and have his way with me.

I didn't act on that impulse because I was way too smart to do anything so stupid and risk ruining both our lives.

Another time, when Tim helped me down from my perch on the younger boys' bunk beds, he held me tightly against him, my pubis pressed firmly against his chest.

No lightning bolts but nice, very nice. I said nothing to discourage him and let him hold me like that until his arms tired.

We saw a lot of each other. Tim would come over to my house to watch *Batman* on TV just to be with me. I even convinced my mother I was struggling with geometry and needed him to tutor me as a ruse to get extra time with him. I got to play footsies with Tim under the kitchen table away from prying eyes except when Mother came in to get another Falstaff out of the fridge. I was the happiest I'd ever been—until my parents tried to end it.

"Mary Louise, your father and I think you're seeing too much of Tim."

"From now on, you may go on one date on the weekend, but that's all."

"But—but—"

"No buts. Your mother and I have thought this through and this is what's best for you."

I cried uncontrollably. The thought of having Tim taken away from me was unbearable. I ran to my bedroom and threw myself on my bed.

Mother sat on the edge of my bed and rubbed my back. "Don't cry, dear. It's not as bad as all that."

"She's so sensitive," Daddy said, "and smart. She won't do anything stupid."

I continued to sob as I felt like my world had been crushed.

"Okay, Mary Louise," Mother warbled. "You may see him more often than that but not too much."

Tim was my rock in those uncertain times. He worshipped me like Daddy worshipped Mother. Perhaps because his parents were alcoholics, he understood me better than anyone. I had a good mother until four p.m. when she uncapped her first of several beers for the evening. Daddy was great most of the time because he only drank good whiskey and could only afford it on pay days. I hated it when they were drunk and prayed, to no effect, that Mother would stop. I tried being the best child I could, but even that didn't help.

My bliss with Tim ended in May 1966. He joined the air force to avoid being drafted and sent to fight in Vietnam. I cried when he was reclassified 1-A, but held back the tears most of the six weeks before he left for boot camp—in front of him, at least. He wrote often and I answered many of his cards and letters. For fun, I doused some of them with perfume. He came home on leave twice before being sent overseas. I got annoyed with him in the middle of both visits. I thought it was because he got too serious but, looking back on it, I couldn't stand the pain of not knowing if I'd ever see him again. I broke up with him but, each time, kept his air force bus driver's hat so he'd have to stop by before leaving. With no other boys interested in me, only his letters kept me from feeling unlovable.

While Tim was away, my parents became friendly with his mother, Gin. Daddy addressed her as "Mother-in-Law" and Mother went out drinking with her whenever Daddy was out of town on business. I hated it when she came home drunk and disheveled. They generally walked to a bar a few blocks away but sometimes she didn't walk home. One night—I've been unable to erase from my memory—I was awakened by the sound of a car making an abrupt stop. I looked out the window to see Mother crawl out of a strange car driven by a man I didn't recognize. I cried myself to sleep.

In the fall of 1967, Daddy was transferred to North Jersey, where I struggled to finish my senior year. Not only were my classes harder, the kids were much more sophisticated—and snobbier than any I'd seen before.

The clique sneered at me from a distance at first but

when the weather turned cool, they attacked. "Is that a *cotton* sweater," asked Deidre, the stylishly-dressed ringleader whose daring miniskirt showed off her legs.

"Yes." I looked for an escape path but saw none.

"Don't you have any cashmere?"

"No." I was panicking.

"The girls on Bandstand wear them. Don't you want to be on Bandstand?

"I've never given it any thought."

The other girls sniggled.

The bell rang signifying the start of class. We all took our seats—them to avoid detention, me to escape them.

I'll never forget one particular morning. After making snide remarks about my few outfits, some girls in my home room cornered me before the teacher arrived.

"Why do you have two names," asked Deidre, seeing an opportunity to attack me again.

Having never been confronted like this before, I cowered. "I like my names. My mother thinks they're pretty."

"Where were you born—Mississippi," asked her sidekick whose cashmere sweater emphasized her only assets.

"No, Arkansas." I didn't expect the response or I would've lied and said Ohio. After living in so many different states in my early life, I had no discernible accent.

Both girls emoted nasty laughs. "You're not just Southern. You're a Southern hick," said the sidekick.

Thinking everything up was down here, I tried to deflect that insult. "Friends call me Tookie."

The pack of hyenas sneered.

A trashy girl with big hair and the miniest of miniskirts, muscled her way through the huddle. "Tookie. Hmmm. That's a good name for a Jersey girl." Raquel, a biker chick who went by Rockie, put her arm around my shoulders and guided me away from the inquisition and back to my seat. Raising her voice, she announced, "Tookie here's my friend. Anybody have trouble with that?"

The room went silent. The preppies weren't about to cross Rockie. We rode different buses, so didn't see each other outside of school, but we ate together and often talked on the phone.

She got her pick of the hoody boys but, because she was smart enough to be in my classes, she didn't have other girlfriends at school. My parents would have fainted if they'd seen her. Rockie educated me in the ways of this brave, new world daily over lunch.

"If you're plannin' on stayin' here, you gotta learn to be a Jersey girl."

"Don't think I'm tough enough."

"It's not muscles, it's inner toughness. First thing, stop takin' crap off people."

"I could never beat up Deidre and her gang of snobs."

"Of course, you can. She's a bully and bullies're weak. Next time she tries somethin', punch her lights out. You won't hear another peep outta any of them after that."

"That's pretty much what Tim told me. He was always about the smallest one in his class and some bigger boys—not the really tough guys, just bullies—would pick on him until they pushed him into a fight. He always beat the bullies and learned they were bullies because they were weak."

"He's right. Punch those bitches one time, and that'll be the end of their shit. We're eatin' lunch in the gym tomorrow. I'll show you a few things they won't expect. Kicks in the groin aren't only for boys."

❧❧

Strawberry blonde Beth, whom I'd never gotten along with, had graduated the spring before we moved and enrolled in college shortly after we arrived in New Jersey. Her derelict boyfriend from Milltown followed her east and sniffed around like a tomcat looking for a queen in heat and a free meal. Apparently wanting to get out of the house and not enjoying school, she agreed to marry him in late June and took a clerical job to support them. My parents despised him but Beth was of age and didn't need their permission. Mother and Beth picked out a dress for me to wear as her only bridesmaid. She hadn't made any friends here and didn't leave any behind when we moved. I didn't go along because I hated shopping and disapproved of Beth's marriage.

One spring evening, Rockie shocked me with an offer.

"Wanna double-date for the prom?"

"It's kind of you to offer, but nobody's asked me." The Jersey boys ignored me even more than the hicks had.

"You have a date if you want one. Vinnie's buddy, Sal, thinks you're hot."

"How could he? I barely know who he is." *How bad do I want to go to the prom?*

"Want a date or not?"

"Why doesn't he take his girlfriend?" *He must be some sort of loser.*

"Her father's in the air force and they got transferred to North Dakota."

I can wear the bridesmaid dress, so it won't cost my parents anything. "Okay."

"I'll show you the latest dances from *Bandstand.* We'll have fun."

I wore the sky-blue floor-length A-line, which was the first of many ugly bridesmaid dresses I'd wear over my single years. Rockie's dress was the complete opposite. Where mine was conservative in the extreme, hers brushed against every one of the school's limits. Her strapless white organza tutu-like mini-dress—trimmed with a wide turquoise band to accentuate her more-than-ample breasts—looked cute until she moved, especially if she bent over or kicked, both of which she did frequently when she danced. She wore matching turquoise bikini panties to give the preppies and the chaperones something to talk about—and they did. I danced crazier than ever before or since because nobody noticed what I was doing. Their eyes were glued on Rockie.

When the band started playing "In The Still of the Night," Sal and Vinnie, in their matching powder-blue-pastel tuxes, jumped out of their seats.

"Mona, let's trip the light fantastic," Vinnie said.

"Mona?"

"Tell you later."

Sal clamped onto me. "You got some good moves," the lanky Sicilian whispered in my ear.

He was so tall I could barely reach high enough to clasp my hands around his neck. Midway through the second verse, I felt something I hadn't felt since Tim left. However, Sal's poked under my sternum. It was comforting that another boy found me fuckworthy but I wasn't ready for that, especially with some jerk I didn't know.

When he cupped my butt cheeks, I pulled his hands away. "Don't be fresh," I said and shifted into the position the gym teacher showed us in dance class.

"Don't worry. Got lots of protection." He patted his jacket pocket.

"I'm not an easy girl like the ones you must be used to going out with. Get it?"

"So, you're gonna make me work for it?" He grinned. "That makes it all the better."

On the way back to our table, Rockie pulled me aside. "Let's go to the sandbox. You're blowin' it."

"I'm not sleeping with him, if that's what you're talking about."

Rockie took me by the hands and stared me in the eyes. "You're not still a virgin, are you?" She looked astonished when I nodded.

"And I'm going to be one when I walk through graduation. I promised myself years ago I wouldn't risk my future. I'm not taking chances of getting knocked up."

"Can't you just whack him off or somethin'?"

Not him. "Can't risk staining the dress. Have to wear it in my sister's wedding."

After the dance, I climbed over the folded down passenger's seat to get into Vinnie's hot rod, paying close attention to keep well on my side of the hump. Sal got in the other side while Rockie slid across the front seat. When Vinnie got in, he draped his right arm around her, twirled the steering wheel with his left hand using the spinner knob with a picture of a naked woman, and tore out in reverse. He slammed on the brakes, spun the wheel the other way, threw the car into low gear, and peeled out. While Vinnie drove us to the restaurant, Sal slid over to me, pinning my head against the window, and kissed me. Before I could push him away, his tongue probed my throat, inciting me to gag. When I bent over to get my breath, he assaulted my zipper.

I slapped his face, hard. "Keep your hands to yourself."

Hearing the smack, Rockie turned around to see what was going on in the back seat. She looked perturbed. "What gives?"

"He's an animal."

Rockie glared at Vinnie when he laughed.

"I never begged a girl for nothing," Sal snapped, "especially one like her."

Get me out of here. "You can surely find someone to give you what you want for a little money."

Sal slid back to his side and pouted. "I'm not buyin' her dinner."

Vinnie raced to my house in total silence. Rockie got out and pulled the seatback down for me. As I struggled to get my balance, Sal pushed me out with his foot, launching me into Rockie. She helped me get my balance and squeezed my hand. "I'll call you tomorrow."

"Good riddance," Vinnie hollered, as he squealed his tires, punctuating the end of my first and only formal dance.

Rockie and I talked about the prom at lunch the next Monday.

"Tooks, have you heard the rumor Sal's been spreadin' about you blowin' him?"

"Nobody's paying any attention because I'm inconsequential."

"You can't let things like that stand. I knew you wouldn't say nothin' so I said, 'Sal was so hot for Tookie he came in his pants. She wants a man not a boy.'"

"Thanks for standing up for me. Also for catching me. I'll be able to wear the dress in Beth's wedding thanks to you."

"Why's your sister gettin' hitched? She ain't pregnant."

"She wants out of the house? She wants to have sex? I'm not really sure. Can't imagine anyone wanting to marry the slug she's marrying."

"She's got a job doesn't she?"

I nodded as I ate the detested egg salad sandwich Mother packed me.

"She can get her own apartment. It wouldn't be much but she'd be out of the house."

"It must be for security. That cockroach'd skip the state if he got her pregnant."

Rockie narrowed her left eye. "I thought you said he doesn't work? Tyin' herself to this boat anchor just to soil some sheets doesn't make sense."

"I never said she was smart or logical." I finished my milk and bit into my apple."

"She's fuckin' nuts. Time for a smoke. Call me to-night." She left for her after-lunch cigarette in the toilet stall nearest the window the smokers kept perpetually cracked open.

Almost overnight, it had become acceptable for un-married girls to have sex—and talk about it. My chats with Rockie also served as an education for a sheltered girl who never heard a swear word or sex mentioned at home. She could have written a slang dictionary. I had no idea there were so many words for doing it. I was often confused when trying to figure out which act she was talking about because several had nothing to do with pe-nis in vagina. I was pleased to hear so many for using my mouth. I've always had an oral fixation because, since the first time I felt Tim's rub against me, I wondered what it'd taste like.

Soon, high school was mercifully over and Beth got married, leaving me a bedroom of my own for the first time since I was an infant. Every day, I searched want ads for jobs and filed applications, but got no offers, not even an interview, probably because I was too young.

Rockie called me early on a mid-July morning. "Where'd you like to have lunch, birthday girl?"

"It's a Monday. Lots of places aren't open today. How about Luigi's?" It reminded me of the place Tim and I went on our dates. He would be back soon.

"I'm pickin' you up at a quarter to twelve. I've got you all afternoon. Remember?"

"I've been looking forward to it since graduation."

I hung up and looked for Daniel, finding him where he always was, at his chessboard.

"Daniel, you've got to hang around the house today. I'm going out for the afternoon and you've got to watch the boys."

"You never go out to lunch. What's up? You sneaking off to see some guy?"

"No! It's my birthday and Rockie's treating me."

"Why's Mom have to work and push babysitting off onto us?"

"Us? This's the first time you've had to watch them."

"No, it isn't."

"That was when I had a dentist appointment. I'm sorry I burden you so much. She'll be home by three thirty. I might be later."

"Why does she have to work now?"

"It's a lot more expensive here and we're barely getting by. You're old enough to do something."

"You're older."

"I'm going to take the first job I find. Somebody might hire me now that I'm eighteen. Then you'll learn what it's like to babysit."

☙❧

Rockie's demeanor changed from flippant to dramatic as soon as we placed our orders. She looked guilty about something as her eyes darted around the room. Seeing no one watching us, she handed me a plain box from her purse. "Happy birthday, Tooks."

"Thanks." I started to open it but Rockie grabbed my hand and pushed it toward my chest.

She lowered her voice. "Put it on your lap where no-body can see it."

She wouldn't give me a joke gift. "Is this a condom," I asked as I showed her my present.

"No. Put it back in the box." She leaned over to me and whispered, "It's a diaphragm. You put it inside you to keep from gettin' knocked up."

It looked too big to go in there. "How do I do that?"

"You have a two o'clock appointment to get fitted properly. She'll show you everything you need to know."

"Wouldn't condoms be easier? I might like to put them on."

"You'd have to buy them and carry them in your purse. Do you want your mother to see them?"

"Or my brothers. No way. I can hide this in my room and put it in before dates."

"Don't worry about condoms. Lots of guys carry them all the time."

I'd never seen one. "How do you know that?"

"Easy. Their wallets have a circle."

"I always thought that was a logo or something." Tears came to my eyes.

"What's the matter? Have I hurt you?"

"I've had friends before but no one who's been as kind to me as you. Thank you so very much."

"Quit cryin' and eat. Don't want to miss your appointment."

"You've got to go in with me. I can't do this alone."

"I'll hold your hand but you won't need that."

Rockie and I played a little game to pass the time waiting to see the doctor. We called it Wishing, Wanting, or Hoping, We evaluated each patient as she walked in as to whether she was wishing to get pregnant, wanting to get rid of one, or hoping she wasn't—WAH for short. We could reevaluate for half score when they left.

Finally, a nurse ushered us into an examining room. "Take off your clothes and put this on, Mrs. Lotte," said Nurse Hatchett, handing me an open-back hospital gown. "Then hop up here." She tapped the examination table then pointed at the stirrups. "And assume the position." She left us to ourselves.

"What's with this Mrs. Lotte stuff?" I asked Rockie.

"You don't wanna use your real name, do you?"

"No, but why that name?"

"Mona Lotte's Vinnie's nickname for me."

"I get it now. I hope I moan a lot, too. But not now. Do I have to do this? I hate being poked and prodded," I said with my feet in the stirrups and my privates exposed to anyone who walked in.

She rubbed my arm to comfort me. "I thought you came here so you could be poked and prodded to your heart's content without puttin' a bun in the oven."

"Definitely don't want that but the thought of having a woman's hand up there's creepy."

"I thought you'd be more comfortable with a woman doctor. Don't you want Tim to be the first man to explore you?"

He'd blush if he knew what I have in mind for him. "I'm looking forward to it."

A six-foot tall not-so-pretty version of Twiggy wearing a white coat sauntered in.

At least she had skinny fingers.

I tried to imagine I was doing something more pleasant like cleaning an oven or defrosting a refrigerator while she fitted my diaphragm. After more than a few test tries, she left one inside me.

"That should do it. Hop down and walk around the room to make sure it stays in place." She concentrated on something about my walk. "Squat a couple of times."

I did as she asked, looking at her the whole time.

"Feel anything odd?"

I shook my head.

She handed me a brochure. "This explains almost everything you need to know about it. Now take it out. You only want to have it in a couple of hours before you have sex."

Hooking my finger into it to get it out was easy.

She took the diaphragm from me and inspected it for breaks. She then inspected my right hand. "You've got sharp nails. Be careful not to puncture it. You don't want it to fail or have to buy new ones all the time, do you?"

"You got that right."

"Always keep a spare one of these in your purse." She held up a tube of spermicidal jelly. "You'll need to send in reinforcements three hours after insertion, regardless of whether you've been exposed or not unless you know for sure you're done for the night. Have my secretary make an appointment for a follow up a month from now."

"I probably won't have sex by then."

Rockie jumped in to save me. "Her husband won't be back from Vietnam for six weeks."

The doctor looked at my chart and frowned. "Just how old were you when you married him?"

"Oh, I'm not married yet. I just don't want to get pregnant on my wedding night."

"Amen to that. Practice putting it in and taking it out until it feels right. Once you think you've mastered that, keep it in all day. See how it feels when you exercise strenuously. Sleep with it in sometimes to see how well that works. Better to have this down pat. Who knows what a crazed Vietnam vet will want to do."

"Tim's not like that. He—"

Rockie cut me off. "Is there anything else she needs to know, Doc?"

"Have him wear a condom during the middle of your cycle for extra protection. See you in a month. You may want a refitting after your honeymoon. Activity changes things, especially in young girls."

∾∾

"Mary Louise. Mary Louise," shouted my Mother from downstairs, jolting me away from the detective mystery I was reading. "You've got a call—from California."

Why's she so excited? It must be Tim. My heart skipped a tiny beat, so tiny I almost didn't notice it but I did.

Mother handed me the phone, saying, "Tell him he can stay with us for a while."

"Hello?"

"I'm back and want to see you. Do you want to see me?" He said in his familiar young voice, sounding nervous and excited.

"I—I guess."

"It's so nice to hear your voice again."

"It's nice to hear yours, too."

"I have to visit my folks and buy a car. Look for me on Labor Day."

"Deposit one dollar and thirty-five cents for one more minute," said the disembodied operator's voice.

"I'm really looking forward to seeing you. Bye." He hung up.

I've been signing my letters "Young and Innocent." That's going to change.

CHAPTER 2

His Vision

Tim

Did a new family move in?" I asked my eleven-year-younger brother Jim, hoping he wouldn't figure out what I was about and tell Mom.

A half hour earlier that dreary November afternoon, a redhead I'd never seen before strolled past our house with a little girl in tow.

I'd waited, silently gazing out the picture window at the treeless former-prairie-cornfield-turned-housing-development-for-factory-workers in the off chance she'd prove not to be a mirage.

"Woodstreams." He pointed down the street of new, nearly identical, smallish tract houses. "They live next to Orzags."

"You know them?" No one had said anything but they never told me anything.

"Just Mike and Tookie. She babysits Cathy Orzag." He moved away.

She must be the little girl who was with her. "How do you know all this?"

"Joey plays with her. I havta get him in twenty

minutes," he said over his shoulder as he headed for the kitchen.

Be casual. "Don't bother. I'll pick him up when I go out." *Great!* I knew her name, where she lived, where she was then, but I had to concoct a way to meet her without looking too obvious.

"Okay," he said, looking surprised. "Why today?"

"I have Sweet Tarts for him." *Hope this doesn't seem too out of character for me.*

"Oh." Jim shrugged and left.

I hurried to the bathroom as quickly as possible without arousing suspicion to scrub my face and hands, brush my teeth again, and comb my hair. Done primping, I surreptitiously slunk down to my basement bedroom to wait and change my shirt.

When I returned from college six months earlier, I found my family living in a small, red brick ranch house with no place for me to sleep. So, I set up my old bed in a corner of the basement and built a simple room around it. Mom wasn't pleased because she'd figured I'd never return. Clark Gable I wasn't, so she had nothing for me except for those times I gave her something to brag about to her barfly friends by winning awards.

What should I wear? How about the plaid shirt Grandma said looked good on me because the blue in it matches my cornflower eyes? Isn't it time to go yet? The minutes passed like a century. Better not wear the coat. It looks too shabby and it'll be easier to slip out of the house without being noticed.

I shivered on the Orszag's stoop, shifting my weight from foot to foot waiting for Tookie to answer. The front door opened and she appeared not three feet away with just the thickness of the storm door glass between us. I was often disappointed when I saw a woman's face up close. Not this time. We stood looking at each other but not speaking. Eyes the color of young soy bean leaves, red hair darker than any I'd ever seen before, including the wig the bald donut shop lady wore. Cute little freckles all over her blemish-free skin the color of cream. No makeup, not even lipstick. She was even prettier up close than I imagined.

She cracked the storm door open, saying, "Hello?" She looked anxious to stop letting the cold air in.

Such a sweet voice; she has to be older than she sounds. Not too tall. If she had been taller, she wouldn't have gone out with me. Not then. Girls treated short boys as if we carried some sort of disease.

C'mon, brain, come up with something witty. Her tortoiseshell glasses look studious. They go with her coloring and eyes. Perfect teeth that don't look like an orthodontist's handiwork. Hope she doesn't notice the space between mine.

Her expression changed from curious to impatient, probably because cold air rushed in the open door.

"I'm Joey's brother, Tim."

"I'll get him." She closed the storm door and disappeared, giving me a clear view of the living room.

Quit churning, stomach. At least she didn't acknowledge hearing it. What to say when she returns? Damn, she's back already.

She knelt on the floor in front of Joey to put his coat on him. She quickly finished and opened the door.

I still didn't know what to say.

She smiled as she put his little hand in mine. "Bye, Joey."

"Bye." He smiled back. "Tomorrow?"

"We'll see." She closed the storm door and waved goodbye to him.

"C'mon, Joey, I'm freezing." *Didn't notice before how cold I am, but my teeth are chattering. Darn. I missed my chance. At least she knows who I am now.*

Back at home I wracked my brain for ideas to "accidentally" see her again. Nothing realistic materialized. *Why not call her and ask her out on a date? She's new in town and might not have a boyfriend yet. Better hurry before somebody scoops her up.*

I perused the phone book for her number, but found no Woodstreams. They must have been too new in town to be in the book.

I pulled on my ratty coat and slipped unnoticed out of the house, then trotted the two blocks to the phone booth in the Dairy Palace parking lot to call Information in private.

"Do you have a new listing for the Woodstream family? They've only lived here a few months."

"The number is 555-6687. Do you wish for me to connect you to that number now?"

I didn't know what to say to her. "No thanks," I replied and hung up.

My pencil apparently dropped out of the hole in my coat pocket on the way over leaving me nothing to write with. So, I scratched her number in the stones with my foot in case I forgot it before I got home.

I'd had the odd date or two with a few girls but never had a girlfriend. Where other boys had the opportunity to casually converse with girls at the malt shop after school, I was stuck working in the bike shop. I hadn't chatted with girls, even with ones I wasn't interested in, except for buddies' kid sisters, and they didn't count. With all my friends away at college, in the military or married and working at one mill or another, I was lonely. Being cooped up in a little house with ten other members of my dysfunctional family increased my isolation all the more.

That evening, after everyone else drifted out of the kitchen to another part of the house to watch TV, I found my chance to call her without trekking back out in the cold to use the pay phone again. *Better be quick and quiet so no one notices.*

Clack, clack, clack, clack, clack, clack, clack. An hour of silence, followed by a ring; another hour of silence and another ring. "Hello."

My heart skipped. It was her voice. No reprieve waiting for someone to fetch her. "May I speak to Tookie, please."

"Don't like Tookie. My name is Mary Louise. I don't like the other one."

Doesn't sound very friendly. "I'm sorry, Mary Louise. This is Tim Burgess. We met this afternoon."

Still don't have anything not stupid to say. Gotta say something. Here goes. "Would you like to go to the movies on Saturday, Mary Louise?"

"I'll ask," she said in a more encouraging tone.

I heard her footsteps as she left the room, but could make out nothing from the garbled voices I barely heard. *Is that sound someone heading this way? Not her yet.* Time passed slower than watching water boil in a submarine until she finally picked up the phone.

"I can't go to the *movies* with you," she said, sounding sad.

Damn, I'm sunk—Wait, there's hope. The way she said movies might mean she can go somewhere else. "Could you go to the basketball game Friday night?"

"I'll see."

Quit churning, stomach. I'm glad I knew there was a game. Don't know anything about this year's team. Can't be much worse than usual.

After another long wait, she said, "Pick me up at six thirty," with no inflection in her voice.

Stunned at my success, I barely got out, "Uh o-okay."

Great! I never wanted a date with anyone as much as I wanted this one and I hardly knew her. She was no movie star, but I sure liked how she looked. Such a sweet voice, too. I needed a better coat. I could get one now that I was working. I knew exactly what I'd get. The forest green car-coat in Barleff's window with leather hooks and wood buttons would go perfectly with her beautiful dark red hair. Had to be quiet about her or Mom would ridicule me. She despised me even more now that I didn't give her anything to brag about to her barfly friends.

I altered my course home after work the next day to pass her house because it was unseasonably warm and I thought I might catch a glimpse of her outdoors. Sure enough, she was. Mary Louise sat cross-legged on the Orzags' driveway tightening little Cathy's skates with the key that hung from a rawhide strip around her lovely freckled neck. Several other children huddled around her, including my two youngest brothers. Apparently, she was teaching the little kids in the neighborhood to roller skate. I tried not to stare, but she was too busy with the kids to notice.

✃✂✃

"Get her home at a decent time. She's a young girl," Dad—who was called "Shorty" by his and Mom's boozer friends more for ordering short beers than for his diminutive height—admonished from the kitchen as I tried to slip out unnoticed Friday night.

Someone had filled them in. I couldn't worry about that now. Didn't want to be late. They never knew when I get in. They were still out in a bar.

I drove down the treeless street, past Orszag's and pulled into the driveway of a house the mirror image of my parents', except for a few rows of white bricks on the front. I quickly got out of the car and, with butterflies in my stomach, walked the few steps to her stoop, where I took a deep breath before knocking on the door.

"Toookie!" A studious-looking early-teenage boy with straight dark hair and black glasses opened the door and called out for everyone in the house to hear as he opened the front door. "He's here."

Through the glass storm door, I saw a slightly over-weight, balding man in his mid-forties reading the evening news in the easy chair in the far right corner of the modestly furnished living room. He put down his paper, saying, "Let him in, Daniel. It's cold outside and I want to meet him."

Just inside the door, two younger, auburn-haired, freckle-faced boys wrestled on the floor. I gingerly stepped over them.

"Don't mind them. Black Bart—er—Bad Jake, is on the top. Good Mike's on the bottom," said the man as he looked me over. "Tookie, introduce your young man to me."

I hadn't seen her enter from my left with her coat already on. I turned to see her. She was more beautiful than I remembered.

"Daddy, this is Tim," said Tookie, shooting daggers at her younger brothers.

"Glad to meet you, Jim," he said warmly while looking me at me skeptically.

She gave him the evil eye. "It's Tim, Daddy."

'Er—Tim, is that your car?" He looked doubtful.

"Mine and the Credit Union's."

He raised his eyebrows. "So you work then?"

"I operate a grinder in the machine shop at the bullet works."

"You look like an intelligent young man. Why aren't you in college?"

"I haven't saved up enough money."

"It's time to go. Don't want to be late." Tookie interrupted her father's interrogation and motioned toward the door.

Just then, I noticed a fleshy, fortyish dark-haired woman holding an over-sized bottle of Falstaff silently poke her head out of the kitchen doorway behind Tookie.

"Drive safely," said the woman.

"We will, Mother," she said with a hint of irritation in her voice.

Her father smiled and waved to her but gave me the "you'd better not touch her if you expect to see my daughter again" look.

Before she took two steps, Jake clamped onto her, pleading, "Are you going to tuck me in tonight?"

"Tomorrow night. I promise." Daniel pried him off her leg and we dashed out the door.

I opened the door of my rustbucket '56 T-bird for Mary Louise and cautioned, "Watch your head. It's pretty low." She hesitated just long enough to figure out how to get in gracefully. She turned, placed her well-shaped derriere on the seat, and pivoted her body to the left, bringing her feet into the car under the dogleg on which people often banged their knees. I closed her door and walked around the car, ecstatic our first date was underway. My butterflies settled a bit.

"Unusual car. Do you like your job?" Although her voice had a sweet timbre, its flatness gave me no feedback about her level of interest.

"I want to get back to school, probably at Southwestern State."

"Flunk out?" Her deadpan lightly freckled face and matter-of-fact tone gave away nothing about her intent.

"Didn't do well enough to keep the scholarship. I wasn't prepared to compete with prep school kids." It was good it was dark so she couldn't see how ashamed I was for doing so poorly.

"Where do you work?

"The machine shop at the bullet works. What time do you have to be in by?"

"No set time."

Better to be quiet than babble and look stupid.

We drove in silence through the three blocks that passed for the downtown of Milltown, a town misnamed because it had no mills—or the tax base they provided neighboring communities. I didn't point out the former bike shop turned empty storefront in which my parents had indentured me during high school. They and my older brother started it then dumped it on me when he left for the Air Force right after graduation. I felt sad it was closed, but was grateful to finally have been released from my indenture after working there summers, weekends, and afternoons the last three years of high school. While schoolmates socialized after school or worked part-time jobs, I ran a business for no pay. I learned things not taught in school but didn't learn social skills and didn't have a clue how to converse with girls. What self-confidence I gained running the bike shop evaporated the first week of college and hadn't reappeared.

At the school, the Dean of Boys smiled when he recognized us while taking our tickets at the entrance to the gym. I guess he approved.

"Ooh!" Tookie's purse slid off the seat as I helped her with her coat and fell to the floor below the pull-out wooden bleachers in the gym was so small that it had no permanent seating. A boy sitting nearby chuckled.

"Can you get it for her?" I handed him a quarter to crawl under the bleachers to retrieve it.

"Thanks," she turned to the boy when he handed her the purse up through the opening between the boards behind us, giving me my first chance to see her full length. She wore green wool hounds tooth slacks with a solid dark-green sweater.

Very modest. Not a lot on top. Nice bottom. Perfect complexion.

After the game, I took her to a moderately-priced Italian restaurant in a nearby town. I sat across from her at a table in the middle of the room—I noticed nothing else about the place because I was focused entirely on her—so I could see her face better. Waiting for our pizza provided an opportunity to learn more about her, but conversing with this sphinx posed quite a challenge.

"Why's your dad call you Tookie?"

Her look told me I'd said something wrong. *Better not do that again.*

"Don't know. Always has. I don't like it." She didn't appear angry exactly, but her closed body language broadcasted that she wanted to drop the subject.

"What should *I* call you?" *Okay. This should be a safe question.*

"She looked into my eyes. "Mary Louise. It's my name," she said with a lilt in her voice.

"It's a pretty name." Getting no response, I shifted subjects. "Where'd you live before, Mary?"

"Mary Louise, please. Ohio."

I tried to find a subject more to her liking.

"Jake seems very attached to you."

"I probably mother him too much. My right hip sticks out too far because I carried him all the time when he was a baby."

That's why all the kids in the neighborhood flock around her.

"What's your dad do, Mary Louise?"

"He's a cost engineer for a company that's rebuilding a blast furnace at the steel mill."

That's a little better. "How long's that take?"

"Two or three years usually." Her expression never changed. She remained deadpan regardless of the question and her responses didn't keep a conversation going. She didn't encourage me, but didn't do anything that indicated she wanted to be somewhere else.

Having read articles in which women complained about men never calling again after a date, I made it a policy to always ask a woman out again on the few dates I'd had, even if it was obvious she didn't want another one.

At date's end on her stoop and having thought of nothing specifically to do, I offered, "Would you like to go out next weekend?"

"Yes," she said flatly with no noticeable emotion.

With that tiny bit of encouragement, I gathered the courage to take her in my arms and kissed her goodnight. She didn't kiss back, but didn't pull away.

Confused by her demeanor, I engaged a friend's sister who was in her class to gather some intelligence. She attempted to strike up conversations with ML, but met with worse results than I had. She reported that ML was intelligent, an excellent student, quiet, well behaved, but couldn't get a conversation going with her either.

She seemed slightly more comfortable conversing on our second date. After a movie and pizza, I walked her to her stoop. This time, she didn't slow down. In one continuous motion, she swung the storm door wide, pushed in the unlocked front door and stepped inside.

Darn. She's not giving me a chance to kiss her goodnight.

"Come in. It's cold out there."

I took two steps in to where she was waiting for me and, sensing this was an invitation, took her into my arms. This time she kissed back.

Over time, ML warmed up with me and laughed easily—provided she wasn't the butt of the joke. We saw each other exclusively, with me spending much time at her house evenings and Sunday afternoons because her parents allowed us just one real date per week. She convinced her mother that she needed help with geometry when she actually wanted to play footsies with me under the picnic table in their kitchen. I didn't mind being with other people most of the time; just being with her was enough. I was smitten and she wanted me in her life. This was the happiest period of my young life.

"'Baciami,'" she blurted out one evening when we were alone on the couch.

I peered into her eyes, searching unsuccessfully for clues as to what she meant when I should've been looking at her lips.

"Kiss me, you fool," she flirted. "It's a Robert Goulet song."

I responded enthusiastically and she reciprocated with gusto. "Baciami" became our little game. My favorite. She also enjoyed necking at the drive-in—up to a point.

When we sat on her couch, she plastered the side of her body against the side of mine, welded together shoulder to knee. Her youngest brothers, Mike and Jake, competed with me for the attention of their favorite sister by wedging themselves between us and punching me when she wasn't looking. Jake, especially, would flop down on us and wriggle his way in to separate us. Mike, her protector who feared I would take his beloved sister away from them, was more subtle. He would position himself between us before we had a chance to get closer. Daniel, the oldest of her three younger brothers, liked me and was always pleasant except when he gloated over beating me at chess. About the only contact I had with Beth, ML's year-older sister with whom she shared a bedroom and a hair dryer but little else, was fixing her up with double-dates with a buddy to give us extra nights out of the house.

Not having had an actual girlfriend before, lacking parenting and never able to communicate well with words, I was often at a loss as to what to say. I couldn't resist complimenting Mary Louise, although I was a total flop at it, because I wanted her to know how much I cared for her.

"I can't keep my eyes off you, you're so beautiful."

She blushed. "That's not true. Stop it."

"You're beautiful to me."

"Don't say things like that. It embarrasses me," she said, sounding irritated.

So uncomfortable with compliments was she that she never complimented me, not even once. She did enjoy physical contact, holding hands being her favorite, but her comfort zone ended at her clothing's protective edge.

"Do you want me to be like those other girls?" she said when I slid my hand up under her blouse, making me feel like a louse. "I don't want to worry about getting pregnant like some other girls do."

I've never desired a woman nearly as much as I desired her but the fear of losing her love kept my hands under control.

I soon felt as if ML was part of me. We almost never argued. At the least hint of her being annoyed I backed away, not wanting to risk losing her. Much later I learned we were both INTJs, an uncommon introverted Myers-Briggs Personality type typical of intelligent people who don't grasp social rituals well. Both our families considered us "high strung" and well-suited for each other. In a rare statement of approval, my mother once said, "You'll never meet a nicer girl."

ML's hypersensitivity made her extremely uncomfortable in unfamiliar situations. I adjusted by shifting plans immediately whenever I detected the first sign of discomfort on her part. One night after a movie, *Doctor Zhivago* maybe, I tried to treat her to a highly regarded St. Louis restaurant that stretched my budget to its limits. We didn't make it past the lobby.

"I don't want to stay here," she said, in her quietest voice, almost quivering. The woeful look on her face and the way she shrank and looked helpless told me I had to do something in a hurry.

"Let's go." I walked her by the hand out of the building at a slower than usual pace so she wouldn't trip. As we pulled out of the parking lot, I asked her why she didn't want to stay. I couldn't imagine why she didn't like it. It was a beautiful building, in Tudor style, with an interior like an English castle.

"It's too fancy. I don't feel right here." She pulled the blanket I kept in the car up to her chin. The heater, like most things in that car, didn't work well. We drove to a Steak 'n Shake where we dined on more plebeian fare delivered by a carhop not by a waiter in a tuxedo. I never fully understood what would make her uncomfortable, but immediately changed plans whenever she was. I did everything in my very limited power to make her happy.

We never talked about drinking. Our parents' alcoholism was a festering sore for both of us. Where my parents hung out in bars most nights, hers drank at home. I noticed that her father only drank on payday weekends. I remember one time in particular when they had another couple over to play cards how ML's body language and temperament changed.

"Let's watch TV in the basement," she said in a hushed tone, ushering her little brothers and me downstairs. She sat stiffly like a whitetail alert for danger. I heard nothing but pleasant chatter but she was clearly concerned about something.

A few weeks later, a terrifying, but not totally unexpected, piece of mail from the local draft board arrived. Knees buckling, I sat down to open it. They'd reclassified me 1-A, ready for active duty. I couldn't deny it any longer. I wouldn't ingest olive pits, wear a dress, or run off to Canada, and I had no hope of flunking the physical. I knew I'd be sent to war as several of my friends had already.

Tears streamed down ML's cheeks when I gave her the bad news that evening. "When will you leave me?"

I willed my tears back into their ducts. "Too soon."

I wished she wouldn't cry so much; it made it harder for me not to. I didn't want to go, but I wouldn't do something dishonorable to avoid it. The government devastated me when they tore me from her. The only pain I felt previously that compared to this came in the fourth grade when my grandfather died. He was the only person who really cared about me before I met ML. His loss left a huge hole in me because he had made me feel special. My parents didn't have the capacity to love the brood of children they brought into the world; they blamed us for their woes. My mother enjoyed having babies, but not raising them. We grew up like weeds. Richard—my older brother—and Kate, the oldest of my two sisters, who was two years younger than me—were her favorites. The rest of us rose or fell in her esteem according to our accomplishments. I was at the bottom then for not doing well enough at college to keep the scholarship. My father worked lots of overtime to keep food on the table and to pay the bar bills they ran up every night. About the only time I saw him in high school was on weekends, much of which I spent working in the bike shop. Now that I finally had someone who loved me, I was being ripped from her.

Fearful I'd never see her again if I was drafted into the army and sent to Vietnam, I followed some rare advice from my father and signed up with the Air Force for four years rather than let the army take me for two. I signed up for the Delayed Enlistment Program, the only option available because their regular quotas were filled, just days before my draft notice would've arrived.

ML's letters kept me going while I was away: first in Texas for basic training, next in Colorado for tech school in electronics, and then overseas to maintain radar on fighter planes in The Philippines, Vietnam, and Thailand. Lonely doesn't begin to describe how I felt, to me it was like being in prison. I made some friends, a few with whom I still communicate, and saved as much of my pay as possible. I took correspondence courses to reduce the time I'd take to finish my degree when I got out. I'd need a good job to support ML and the children she'd surely want. I avoided the whoring, drugs, and gambling that beckoned from just outside the air base gates because I wanted to be worthy of her and didn't want to risk losing her by contracting one of the incurable venereal diseases that ran rampant in the Far East. I didn't "go to town," to use the GI's euphemism. For a treat, I'd reread and smell her perfumed letters.

Near the end of my eighteen-month tour of duty overseas, I requested locations in the northeast to be as close to Mary Louise as I could on my "Dream Sheet." I was ecstatic when they gave me orders for an air base only a four-hour drive from her.

I landed in San Francisco, Travis Air Force Base actually, at ten thirty at night, an hour and a half before I left the Philippines thanks to crossing the International Date Line. It was one thirty in the morning in New Jersey. I got her new number from Information and called he in the morning before my flight took off.

"Hello?"

"Is this Tim," Mrs. Woodstream asked. Without waiting for a response, she shouted off phone, "Mary Louise, Mary Louise, you have a phone call—from California."

"Yes, it is," I said. "Is Mary Louise home?" Having thought of nothing to say to anyone but my beloved, I acted as if I hadn't heard her mother yell.

"Hello?"

Mary Louise's sweet, high-pitched voice sounded as young as it did the first time I called her two and a half years before.

"I'm in California and I want to see you as soon as I can."

"Okay."

"I have to visit my folks and get a car that'll make it that far. Should be there around Labor Day."

"Okay."

"Deposit one dollar and seventy cents for the next three minutes, please," said the nasal voice of the operator.

Didn't have that much change. "I'm really looking forward to seeing you, Mary Louise."

Click. The line went dead when the operator disconnected us.

CHAPTER 3

Tim's Return

Tookie

Mother ran to the front door, carrying flowers she had just cut. "Mary Louise, someone just pulled up. I don't recognize the car but it must be Tim."

"He said he picked up an old Plymouth Valiant, whatever that is." I checked my hair in the mirror and headed outside not knowing what to expect. He'd gotten too serious in his letters but nobody else expressed interest.

Fatigued, Tim held onto the door of his car to steady himself from his overnight cross-country drive as he watched me walk down from the house.

His tired eyes told me he loved me more than ever.

"Hello, blondy," I said, trying to be casual. He looked handsome—more handsome than he realized—with sun-bleached hair and trim but not muscular—jocks don't appeal to me. I'd only seen him when his hair was dishpan blond. His eyes were bluer than I remember. He was still short but a little taller than me.

"It's from working outside on the airplanes," he said,

telegraphing his fear that I wasn't excited to see him.

I just stood there, expressionless, trying to figure out how I felt. I still liked his body and hoped he was ready for the new me.

"I've got something for you," he said, reaching into the back seat. "Here." He handed me a bag containing presents.

"It's hot in the sun," Mother said. "Let's go in and have some lemonade."

Tim retrieved his gym bag from the trunk and followed us in.

Mother led us in the front door and into the room to the right of the stairs. "You can sleep in here. Daniel will sleep upstairs in the boys' room. The bathroom is at the head of the stairs, Tim. You're not to go farther than that."

He nodded.

"Let's have that lemonade now." Mother led us into the breakfast nook through Tim's bedroom. "Sit down, children, while I get the drinks."

Without taking his eyes off me, Tim slid into the nook. I slid in next to him.

He loved me more than ever. Having him back was comforting.

After quenching his thirst, he pulled a small package out of the bag and handed it to me. "Open it. It's for you."

I took out a woman's Seiko watch in silver and put it on my left wrist. "Thanks."

"You said you don't like yellow gold, so I got a silver one."

I smiled and set my new watch to EDT.

Tim handed me a tiny box. "This may require a little explanation."

Oh shit! It's a ring. Be calm. He wouldn't be that stupid. I unwrapped it as if it was nitroglycerin. Happy it wasn't what I feared but unsure what it was, I showed the stone to Mother.

"What kind is it," she asked while rotating the dark-colored oblong gem to get a better look at it.

"It's a star sapphire from Thailand. Turn it so the light catches it just right and you'll see the star."

Mother fiddled with the stone then handed it me, smiling. "See, Mary Louise, see the star."

"It's pretty." I didn't know anyone who had one of these.

"I know a jeweler in town who can put it in a set-ting," Mother said. "A ring would be nice."

Tim handed me some white cloth with embroidery in a pattern like wallpaper. "It's Thai silk—the only thing with green they had. It's only two yards. I hope you can make something nice out of it."

Mother looked it over, feeling the texture. Her body language told me she thought it was nice. "It'll have to be sleeveless but I can make you a dress." She held the cloth up to me. "It'll look nice on you."

Tim set aside the empty bag and yawned.

"You should rest for a while," Mother said, pointing toward Daniel's bed in the room between the breakfast nook and living room. "Mary Louise, you can help me with the flowers."

He was still out like a light some hours later when I woke him for dinner. After doing the dishes, we watched TV until everyone else went to bed then had a pleasant make-out session until my bedtime.

He sure hadn't forgotten how to kiss. Tim desired me as much as always but, probably thinking I was still the virtuous girl he left behind, he was hesitant to make ad-vances. I dawdled in the kitchen waiting for him to strip down to briefs and a t-shirt for bed.

Nice body. Not overly muscular, not puny. Sure

would like to pull down his pants to see a hard on up close. Better not. He'd faint.

"Tuck me in?" Tim's eyes pleaded for my love as he got into bed.

"Okay." I couldn't wait. Never had a boy this available to me. I pulled back the sheet and pushed up his t-shirt to get a better view. I lightly ran my fingertips across his belly along the top edge of the elastic waistband. His abs spasmed.

"Ooooohhh." He fought with himself to keep his body still while the bulge in his briefs got bigger.

I'd only dreamed of having such power over a man but didn't dare do anything with everyone in the house. I treated myself a couple more times and Frenched him goodnight. Audibly panting, he held onto me tightly.

"Sssh, they'll hear us." I pulled away, feeling guilty for leaving him in this condition but fearing I'd get caught if I did something about it. "Sweet dreams," I said, throwing him a kiss as I left for my bed and pleasant fantasies.

I woke up with a tingly sensation all over, desperately wanting to be touched. Knowing I'd have the house to myself with Tim all day, I stayed in my room until I heard the boys' school bus pull away. *Mother and Daddy are already gone. Now's my chance.* I tore off my pajamas and retrieved my diaphragm out of its hiding place. I liberally lubricated it with spermicidal jelly as instructed and propped my left heel on the footboard of Beth's bed—Mother wouldn't let me move it out of my room because she and Daddy held out hope she'd wise up and come home.

I spread my legs wider by stepping to my right. Now in position for my first live run, I smeared jelly on the diaphragm, folded it in half and stuffed it up inside me. Thinking I had hooked it in place, I pulled my fingers out. *Sprong!* It sprang out of me and sailed across the room, landing under my bed. "Shit." I threw on a translucent bathrobe, grabbed a bra and panties, gathered up my diaphragm paraphernalia, and zipped into the bathroom. After cleaning it and preparing it for reinsertion, I positioned myself with my left foot on the commode. After a few more unintentional Frisbee launches, I got it to stay in place and sashayed downstairs.

Tim opened his eyes as I walked into his room wearing just a bra and panties only partially covered by the open translucent bathrobe. He'd never seen me close to this before, not even in my bathing suit. He jumped out of bed, stiffening rapidly in front of my eyes.

I didn't need glasses to see he was aroused but they gave me a better view. Sure would've liked to pull down his drawers.

I walked over to him and he hugged me. Feeling his erection against my clit made it itch. I pressed myself against him, pulling him to me with my hands around his waist. He pulled me even tighter. *My pulse's racing through my vagina. Do I dare grind? Keep calm.* We stood like this for a long time, him wanting me, me wanting to be had, until the phone rang. *Shit! It might be Mother checking up.* As I pulled away to answer it, he sheepishly asked, "How did it feel?"

"Good." *Why'd it have to ring now?*

"You bowlegged this mornin'," Rockie asked when I answered the phone.

"Working on it but the phone rang." *Got to stop rubbing myself. It feels so good right now I won't be able to stop.*

"He tried to waltz your Matilda yet?"

"No." I lowered my voice so Tim couldn't hear me in the other room. "My body's never acted this way before. It's demanding it. Can't say more now."

"I'm really lookin' forward to *that* conversation. What're you doin' today?"

I raised my voice to its normal level. "Going to the beach."

Tim was too shy or fearful to push for more, and I didn't want him to think I was a loose woman by being too aggressive. We never had the house to ourselves again, so I had to keep my desire under control. Each night at bedtime, I explored and experimented on Tim's body. It was much safer but left my hymen intact.

No man has ever wanted me as much as he did. He reacted strongly to my every touch but he was so cautious he didn't feel me up, even from the outside. I so wanted to wrap my lips around his erection but I was afraid he'd have a heart attack. Worst of all, I failed to get my diaphragm field tested.

Mother and Daddy were glad to see Tim. From the beginning, they'd liked him and would've been pleased if I'd married him. Whenever I criticized him, they defended him. "He's so much like you: smart, sensitive, and gentle. On top of that, he loves you deeply and would kill himself making you happy."

"He has no social skills," I countered.

"You're one to talk, Mary Louise. Maybe you two can work together on that one."

Mike and Jake, however, were still jealous of him and punched him when no one was looking. One day, I posed for a nice photo sitting on Tim's lap but Jake spoiled it by hopping up on mine with the result of us looking like a totem pole. The boys thought he'd take me away from them. Their fears weren't unfounded because Tim very much wanted me to marry him. However, I wanted no part of a life like my mother's. Tim's adoration of me was very much like Daddy's love for Mother—and that didn't turn out well for her.

Not long after Tim left for his new air force assignment—he had a year and a half left on his enlistment—I landed a clerical job at Carver-Watkins, a local pharmaceutical company. Most of the young girls were made typists because they'd learned office skills in high school. I only took academic courses, so they assigned me to work with statisticians and programmers. My first tasks were keypunching data cards for medical studies. Before long, they put my brain to use writing simple FØRTRAN programs. I fantasized being a sexstatician, statistician by day and woman of intrigue by night, but nobody asked me out.

Tim drove down to visit me whenever he had a free weekend, enough gas, and money for tolls and dates— and when his clunker was running well enough to make the trip. He averaged one visit a month. Tired of dateless weekends, I flew up to visit him once that fall. My parents let me go but they insisted I not stay in a motel. A married couple Tim had met put me up.

Not knowing if and when I'd be alone with Tim long enough to have sex with him presented a quandary.

Should I insert the diaphragm before I catch the plane—or, maybe, in the airport after I land—and keep it in all day? But what if he wants to do it? Can't say stop and wait for me to insert my diaphragm. Might botch the insertion. That'd be awful. Better get a fallback. I pulled into a drug store where nobody knew me and paid cash for a box of a dozen Trojans. I hid several in the lining of my purse.

We had a nice visit but no sex, not even a good make-out session. The highlight of the trip was climbing into his barracks window so I could see his Spartan room. Doing something forbidden for once in my life electrified me but terrified Tim.

His head darted back and forth as he looked up and

down the hall and out the window, fearing someone might see us. He pulled me into his room and locked the door behind us.

His room was pretty basic but better than what he had at home. "Can I sleep on the other cot tonight?"

"No."

Never heard him be so stern before. "You don't have a new roommate, do you?"

"Not yet."

We hadn't been this alone since summer and better not waste it. I clutched his shirt and pulled him to me, kissing him the most passionately I had ever kissed him up to that point.

He barely responded, seeming nervous, almost petrified.

What's wrong with him? "I've never known you not to want to make out with me."

He looked extremely uncomfortable. "If we get caught, I'll be in big trouble and you'll be smeared."

"It's Saturday. Who could catch us?" *What a wimp.*

He pulled down the blinds so no one could see in. "Anybody could turn me in."

"So what if they kick you out? You hate the air force." *Let's get naked.*

"It's hard to get a decent job with a bad discharge."

The longer I stayed in his room, the more frightened he became.

∞

A dreary, rainy Thursday night in November when I had my hair in curlers, I received an unexpected phone call.

"I'm at the Port Authority Bus Terminal. Which bus should I take to get to your house?"

My hair was sopping wet, I have trouble driving on rainy nights, and he arrives unannounced, expecting me to pick him up.

"Catch bus one thirty-nine toward Marlboro Union Hill. Get off at Fairway Lane on Route nine. Somebody'll pick you up at the bus stop."

"The commander surprised us by giving us the entire Veterans Day weekend off. A guy in my shop from Long Island offered to drop me at the Port Authority if I came immediately."

Not exactly pleased and looking a fright, I trudged into the living room. "Daddy, will you pick up Tim at the bus stop?"

"I think it's a good idea for you to get him. If he's serious, he won't mind seeing you in curlers."

"*Mooother*?"

"Your father's right. He's your boyfriend. You pick him up."

I covered my curlers with a headscarf, something girls avoided doing except in the absolute worst emergencies in those pre-blow-dryer stone-age days, and drove the miles to the bus stop blinded by the glare from headlights, grumbling all the way.

"Thanks for picking me up." He leaned over to me but I turned my head causing him to kiss my cheek.

I simmered. "I didn't expect you."

"I didn't expect to be able to come but, at shift change, the commander gave us a three-day weekend off and a guy in my shop who was heading to Long Island offered me a ride to the Port Authority station. He gave me no time to call and I wanted to see you."

Tim was more cautious than usual during our late-night make out sessions that weekend and I, still irritated, probably wasn't my usual vivacious self. To make matters worse, I got a personal call at work. My boss frowned at me as I walked to my desk to take the call.

"I know I'm not to call you at work but this's differ-ent," Rockie said, sounding very serious.

"It better be. My boss's watching me."

"Vinnie and I are taking his bike south to get away from this weather for a while."

"When're you coming back?"

"Don't know yet."

A shiver ran up my back. "I'm not going to see you again, am I?"

"Sure you will. We'll be back sooner'n you expect."

I'll never see Rockie again. Better make friends with the girls at work.

Christmas night after everyone went up to bed, I shifted over to the couch next to Tim. The glow of the multi-colored bulbs on the Christmas tree in the other-wise dark house made for a romantic setting.

Holding my hand, something he excelled at besides kissing, he started in. "This is so nice sitting here with you basking in the glow of a nice Christmas. I look for-ward to the time we can snuggle on the couch with our kids asleep upstairs after a joyous day."

I jerked my hand away. "There you go again, plan-ning my life for me," I snapped. "I'm not going to be a lifer's wifer."

He retreated to the far end of the couch, barely get-ting out, "I didn't mean now." Tim looked like a scolded dog, fearful I was going to beat him.

I fumed silently. When I cooled off and realized this wasn't getting my itch scratched, I pulled out some mis-tletoe I'd hidden in the end table drawer and held it over his head. "You have to kiss me now. You can't refuse." He kissed me tentatively but acted afraid to go further. *Looks like he won't even try to feel me up tonight. Damn.* I went to bed that night desiring more, much more.

Tim was an infrequent visitor over the winter. The two times he came, he was distant, possibly depressed. I sliced him up verbally whenever he said anything about our future and he'd retreat into his shell. By spring 1969, he was so intimidated he didn't try to make out at the passion pit.

"Hey, you're watching the movie," I said, irritated by not being molested. It had been ages since we'd been this alone and he was ignoring me.

Star or *Thoroughly Modern Millie* was on the screen, I forget which. Tim liked musicals and thought Julie Andrews was gorgeous.

He obediently hopped into the back seat of my blue 1967 Mustang while I stowed my glasses on the dashboard. I held the hem of my loose-fitting spring mini-dress high as I dashed around the car so it'd be above my butt when I reclined on him. Not wanting to miss my first chance in ages, I dressed for sex—only panties, bra, non-interfering dress, easily-discarded slip-on shoes, AND diaphragm. Nothing else. No slip. No cursed pantyhose. I wanted to dispense with the panties and bra but Tim would be shocked. I reclined across him in a position to give him full access to my vital parts. My boobs wanted to be fondled so much they were throbbing.

"I'm not wearing anti-attack clothes tonight," I said in my sexiest voice, hoping he'd get the hint.

"I noticed." He kissed me softly on the lips and sustained his sweet kiss.

I parried tongues as encouragement to keep going, and guided his hand to my left breast. *Should've done this sooner. I've been such a fool.*

Soon, his hand was on what my skirt and panties normally cover but much too soon.

You're far from finished fondling my tatas. "Not yet!" I grabbed his wrist and guided him back to my breast, this time under my dress. He massaged me through my bra.

Aaaaah. It felt so much better than doing it myself. When he headed south again, I snapped, "Now the other one."

He obediently cosseted my other girl while I kept close watch in case his hand wandered away from where I wanted attention. Apparently intuiting I wanted my bee stings dandled without interference—by this time I'd accepted they weren't going to grow any more—he tried to slide his hand up under my bra.

"Unhook it," I said. *One thousand one...one thousand two...*

He reached around me with both hands and tussled with my bra hooks for what must've seemed like a half hour to him. I knew I was teasing him but I was going to give him everything he wanted plus a lot more. He got the top one unhooked but struggled with the others. *Don't do it for him. He'll think I'm easy. I want him inside me even more than he wants to be in me but I can't let on that I do.*

Eventually, he freed my bra and pushed it up out of the way. I pulled my dress up to my chin, leaving the thin layer of translucent tricot covering my pelvis as the only thing between my waiting naked body and him. I arched my back, bringing my left breast to his mouth. He suckled me.

Whoooo. Please don't stop. When he flicked my erect nipple with his tongue, my floodgates opened, drenching my panties. It felt even better than I imagined.

I held his head in place, keeping him from pulling away but shifting him from one bittie to the other.

Do this all night. Please. We took no intermission when the dancing hot dogs marched across the screen. *Should I suck his hot dog or let him put it inside me?* Afraid I'd put him off, the only feedback I felt I could give Tim when I liked something was to let him continue. I didn't say anything, pant, writhe, moan, bite, or kiss even more passionately. The only feedback I couldn't control was my wetness.

"We won't need lubricants," he said as he massaged my pussy through the cheap unsexy panties my mother bought me, "when we make love."

This feels so nice.

He curled his fingers around my soaked crotch and probed me through my thoroughly saturated underpants.

Whooo. Don't stop. I remained silent and motionless, saving my energy to soak in these wonderful new sensations. It felt so much better than when I do it. I just flinched a little when his hand slipped and his middle finger slide up my butt. That even felt good. I was surprised. I wiggled my butt, suggesting I wanted my pants down.

Taking the hint, Tim tentatively tugged them down to my knees. *He's the first boy to see or touch my dark red triangle. This's exciting.* I pushed them down to my ankles and spread my knees as far as I could. *I'm ready for anything.*

Tim slipped his middle finger inside me slowly, cautiously feeling his way around as if he was exploring an uncharted cave which was what he was doing.

Oooh, this feels good, really good. Keep it up.

He silently fingered me until the lights came on at the end of the second feature, taking breaks only to kiss me passionately when his hand tired.

I could show him how. No. He'll think I masturbate a lot.

The problem with two novices is that neither has useful experience.

Tim knew nothing about women's anatomy and erogenous zones. He could've gotten me off had he given my clit a tiny bit of attention, but I was too shy to tell him how. He was so unsure of himself he didn't even try to unbuckle his belt. Maybe I'd been too difficult in the past.

When headlights started shining in the windows, I broke the silence, "Didn't the Asian prostitutes teach you things?"

"Didn't go," he said, red faced like he'd been caught doing something wrong. "I wanted to be worthy of you."

Shit! I'm not getting devirginized tonight. I smell myself all over his hand but he doesn't seem to mind. I'm still really wet and want it badly. I pulled up my panties. He rubbed my snatch through them, and kissed me some more.

When I pleasured myself at home that night, I fantasized about how good it would feel when I finally had Tim inside me. I luxuriated in how nice it felt for a man to give my body his undivided attention, even if he was awkward. The night wasn't a complete bust. We'd gone way farther than ever before and I liked how it felt. A lot. *Next time I'll get him inside me—one orifice or another.*

Not seeing Tim for a couple of weeks moved me to formulate a plan to spend a weekend alone with him. I started saving money for airfare—Mom and Dad wouldn't let me drive the four hours up to his airbase—but a glitch arose in putting the plan into action.

"Mary Louise, you can't come. I've tried to find someone to put you up but failed. I'm sorry," he said in a defeated tone of voice.

"Find us a motel," I commanded. This wasn't working out the way I wanted all along.

"But your parents—"

"I'll take care of them." Never had to lie to them about anything important before but I didn't want to miss this opportunity.

My period arrived suddenly and heavily while I was

waiting for my flight in the Newark airport. I rushed to the ladies room but my undies were already bloody. I cleaned up the best I could under the circumstances and changed into the only fresh pair I had with me. During the flight, I felt some leakage but the commuter plane didn't have a restroom. I dashed into the terminal restroom on arrival to clean up again but had no more fresh underpants to change into.

Tim picked me up and took me to lunch. He was very guarded, acting like he was guilty of something.

Oh, yes. We'd lied to my parents about where we were staying. If he knew what I had in mind, he'd really feel guilty. Maybe he did but I felt horny, hornier than ever before, maybe because my clit had been throbbing since I woke up.

During a break in our conversation, I said, "A visitor arrived unexpectedly."

Tim looked around the room, puzzled. "At home?"

Damn. He didn't understand. "My monthly visitor came." Still foggy. "My period came today. It's usually very regular but this time it was late and caught me by surprise." *He understands it's safe for us to have sex now, I hope.*

Tim showed me around the area in the afternoon and we checked into the motel before dinner. All we did was to get the key and throw our bags into the room. He seemed afraid to set foot in it.

Rain poured down during dinner after which I suggested we take in *The Prime of Miss Jean Brodie*, a movie I wanted to see because it starred an emancipated redhead. Like always, anything I wanted to do was fine with Tim.

On the drive to the movie, he commented on the stinking elephant in the room. "At a ninth grade band concert, a clarinet player named Clarence blurted out,

'Some girl's having her period. I can smell it.' I couldn't smell anything and didn't have a clue what he was talking about. I think this is the first time I've ever smelled a girl's period because I've never smelled anything like this before."

Damn. I hoped this didn't put him off. Probably wouldn't. He'd wanted me for a long, long time but I smelled awful and it was getting worse. It had never happened before. All I could do was ignore it. The throbbing was the most intense it'd ever been and got worse by the hour.

After the movie, we returned to the motel. Tim aimlessly fooled around with his bag.

He's never been alone with a woman like this and doesn't know what to do. Kinda funny. Don't see any rubbers in his bag. Better take control or the trip'll be a bust.

"Take your clothes off. I want us to be naked."

Although stunned, he obeyed. Standing naked by me, he looked scared.

Maybe he doesn't understand that I'll let him do anything he wants to me tonight. "Let's get into bed." I pulled the covers and top sheet all the way down so we'd have the entire bed for our playground.

"O—okay." He laid down and held me as if he wanted to sleep in my arms.

I kissed him. He kissed me back and snapped to attention, poking me where it felt oh so nice, but he went no farther.

Annoyed and impatient, I said, "I want us to be upside down. Put your head by my feet and vice versa."

He did as I commanded.

I slid down till we were face to groin or, in my case, lips waiting for my target of interest. *Ummm. I like it.* Somehow I intuitively knew giving oral sex would be my absolute favorite from this very brief test, even before trying anything else. *Love how he throbs in my mouth. Better quit before he thinks I'm a hussy.*

"How do I taste?"

"A little salty." We lay there a good while, not moving or touching each other. *My smell might be putting him off. He's such an innocent. Damn period. He's probably guilt ridden from lying to my parents and afraid he's going to knock me up. Nothing's going to happen tonight.* "Let's get some sleep."

He got into a normal position and fell into a deep sleep, not touching me the entire night.

Smelling worse than before and disgruntled, I boarded the plane for home the next day.

❦❦❦

"I'm home" I shouted as I walked into the house one afternoon after work.

Daddy didn't respond with his usual "The Carver-Watkins spy's here" because I'd beat him home that day.

I walked into the kitchen where Mother was feeding Mike and Jake their after-school cookies. "You've got a letter from Tim," she said, handing it to me.

"Did you read it, Nosey?" *Why'd I say that? She's never opened my mail. Maybe because she always takes Tim's side.*

Mother glared at me. "Of course not. You've sure been grumpy since you visited him. Did you fight?"

Dear Mary Louise,
I've met someone. She's—

Tears streaming out of my eyes prevented me from reading farther. My legs trembled and my stomach churned.

"What's wrong?"

"T—Tim d—dumped me," I stammered through my crying.

Mother showed me no sympathy. "I'm surprised it took him so long."

"Huh?" *What on earth could she mean?*

She looked at me disapprovingly. "He needs affection."

"You think I shoulda screwed him?" I tried but he wouldn't.

"Boys! Go play outside." They dashed out, cookies in hand, while she handed me some tissues and pointed to the breakfast nook. "Sit down."

I sat down and dried my tears while she retrieved a forty-ounce Falstaff from the fridge and took a large swig.

"You need to be nice to Tim. Show him you're happy to see him, thank him for the gifts, smile at him, compliment him, show him you want him in your life. He adores you. He'll wait until you're married for sex. That's not a problem."

"What makes you think you're right?" *How could she know any of this? Things are different from when she was young.*

"I see things, lots of things, and I've lived a lot longer than you have." She unconsciously peeled part of the label off the beer bottle while she talked. "I saw him comfort you the time Daddy got in trouble over the Paregoric. He's a keeper."

"I don't want to get married and have a bunch of kids," I sobbed.

"Beth rushed out and married the first bum who came along and you're rushing to get rid of a young man who loves you deeply and would be a good husband and father." Mother was being the most serious I'd ever seen her. "You can put off having kids as long as you want these days. That's not a problem. Tim'll wait and you'll want children someday. I know you will."

"What can I do?" Only then did I realize I wanted Tim in my life. I'd always taken him for granted and never considered the possibility of losing him to another woman.

"Call him and apologize for not treating him well and promise to be nicer to him in the future. Offer to visit him immediately. I'll loan you the money."

I called him that very evening. "Tim, I'm sorry. I want to apologize for anything I may have done."

"I didn't mean to hurt you, Mary Louise, but Zelda wants me in her life."

"I want you. That's why I'm calling."

"I wanted you to want me so much. When you didn't, the air force sent me to a shrink because I was depressed."

"Is there anything I can do now?"

"It's too late. Do you realize that you've never complimented me? Not even a tiny one. I'll always have a place in my heart for you, though."

❧❧❧

Right then, I decided to explore the myriad of experiences Tim had denied me. I aroused him with the first kiss, but even when he looked like he was about to ejaculate out of every orifice, he wouldn't give me what I wanted. How boring was that? I was too shy then to take matters in hand myself. I was downright embarrassed to remain unfucked in this time of free love. Girls no prettier than me got all they wanted, and without being nagged to get married.

"You look prettier when you first wake up in the

morning than the cheerleaders do all made up," he had told me early in our relationship. Oddly, he seldom flattered others. Perhaps this was because he was smitten. *He's history now. Have to put him out of mind. I want sex, and I want it now. So far behind. So much time to make up for. Who'll give me what I want?*

CHAPTER 4

Sex and Good Grammar

With Tim out of the picture, I had to look elsewhere or never have a date. Surely, I could find other guys who aren't obsessed with big—or even average—boobs. Maybe the girls at work could help. Most of them said they were getting laid regularly.

Mornings at break, especially on Mondays, the girls in the office shared their previous nights' exploits.

"Friday night, I had this hunk in the back seat of his car outside the dance," bragged Sybil, a true Jersey girl with hair blacker than I'd ever seen before moving east, stacked in a beehive, push-up bra, skin-tight pegged pants, and three-inch spiked heels.

"Where was Bob?" I couldn't believe she was saying this.

Sybil had said he was ready to pop the question. Maybe this was her last chance to get some strange cock before she was stuck with Bob's every night.

"You didn't!" said Cynthia, the perfectly put together secretary, a decade older than most of us who'd make some lucky guy the ideal wife—provided he'd wait till she had at least an engagement ring on her finger.

Sybil straightened up in her chair and slapped the table. "Friday's my night."

"Weren't you afraid someone'd see you?" This was a surprise. Sybil has acted like she really wanted to marry Bob. Maybe she was just bragging.

Sybil lit a cigarette. "Half the cars in the lot were rockin'. He might've been in one of them for all I know."

"I overheard Henry say he got Sherry in accounting." I didn't exaggerate. That was the impression he gave the guys at the water cooler.

Sybil blew a smoke ring. "In his dreams. She was gettin' her butt bounced in a Ford next to me. What about Adam?"

"He's going with someone." I tried not to sound too interested in any of them.

Jackie smirked as if she'd had all of them. "Maybe not for long. Frank and Gary are available, Mary."

"Mary Louise. Rather have you call me Tookie if that's too hard." I felt half-naked when people said just my first name. They must think I'm not worth two more syllables.

"I've been with both of them," pretty, buttoned-up Sally chimed in. "Gary wanted me to blow him. Yuck. He settled for a hand job after I told him I was on the rag and not in the mood."

"That Frank wanted me to swallow. Eeeuuuuw." Jackie faked swallowing with a look of disgust.

She's lying.

"Aren't you worried about getting pregnant by someone other than Bob?" *Why does she want to marry him?*

"I'm on the pill," said Sybil.

"I thought you had to be married to get a prescription," I said, hoping she was telling the truth.

"Not if you have severe cramps and an irregular period," said Jackie.

"You mean…" I asked, preferring to take pills rather than fool with the diaphragm.

"That's right," Sybil said. "We all do it and our gynos write us prescriptions. They don't want us poppin' out bastards all over the place."

"Oh." *If Daddy knew I was on the pill, he'd be crushed. He can't ever find about my diaphragm.*

"Kid." Cynthia—the poised, stylishly dressed executive secretary—took me under her wing like a younger sister. "You better be ready to put out if you want to go out these days. It's a whole different world now."

"I'll keep that in mind." No problem. That was exactly what I wanted to do and do it a lot.

Knowing the guys at work all had more experience than Tim—who had none—convinced me sex'd be better with them than if I'd waited for him.

The girls' stories got repetitious, but I was still jealous and unpenetrated. Work provided several sophisticated and worldly college-educated co-workers who might do the dirty dance with me. I didn't mind that some were married because I wasn't looking for a husband, at least not one of my own. I wanted adventures and experiences. No way did I want a life like Mother's. My wonderful father loved her deeply, but he was the only man she was supposed to sleep with. Being bored in bed could explain her drinking and some other things.

Before I'd found someone interested in deflowering me, my parents broke some not totally unexpected news.

"Mary Louise, Daddy's been transferred again, this time to Massachusetts," Mother said right after I got home from work one late-May afternoon. "We'd like you to come with us. It wouldn't seem like home without you."

"Sissy, please come," Jake begged as he climbed on my lap and clung to me.

"I've got a life here, now. I like my job and don't think I'd easily find a new one to compare with it somewhere else."

"Mom, do I get Tookie's room at our new house?" Daniel prodded.

"With Beth and Mary Louise gone, we won't need as large a house."

Mike and Jake looked crestfallen, not just from not having their own bedrooms but from knowing they'd miss my mothering them. I didn't realize how much I'd miss them.

A month before my nineteenth birthday, I rented an apartment in the same building as my sister. It wasn't much but was in a safe neighborhood in easy commuting distance to work. With just two stories with four units on each floor, it offered relative privacy. The owner maintained it fairly well and kept rents low but I barely afforded the smallest unit.

Being all alone, with my parents three states away, and having little income, was scary at times, but total freedom made up for any downsides. I could do as I pleased, stay out as late as I wanted, and screw whomever I chose *whenever and wherever* I chose. I remember coming home to my little apartment the night after my family moved away. I walked in the door, flopped on the couch, and shouted, "Halleluiah, I'm free. I go on the pill tomorrow."

"I'm really on my own now," I announced at lunch the next day.

"Bob's buddy Sebastian doesn't have a girlfriend," offered Sybil.

"Is he smart," I responded. "That's important to me."

"Not really." She sighed.

"My brother's friend, Cyril, is real smart," said Jackie. "He's a math genius. We can double date Saturday, if you'd like."

"Sure." The risk of a lousy date was better than sitting home Saturday night petting the kitty. "What're we doing?"

"Goin' to a Mets game. They have season tickets."

"That's great." Always considered myself to be a working-class girl sitting in the bleachers swigging a beer enjoying a game. Only problem was I didn't like beer and didn't like to be around drunks and have a low opinion of people who use poor grammar.

Around five o'clock Saturday night, I heard a car honking loudly in my parking lot. From the window, I saw the three of them pull in in Cyril's Pontiac GTO. Jackie's boyfriend, Angelo, wearing a pin-striped Mets hat, hopped out of the passenger seat and got in the back with her. I bounced down the stairs and plunked my bottom on the passenger seat. Cyril, in a blue Mets hat and pin-striped shirt, scanned me up and down like a boy ogling the merchandise on his first visit to a whorehouse. He floored it, taking off before I had my door closed.

He must have considered me spermworthy. He looked like he would've pushed me out of the car if he didn't.

"Here," Jackie said, placing a cold beer against my neck.

"No thanks," I said, noticing the open bottle wedged between Cyril's legs. "Don't drink. Are we stopping somewhere to eat."

"No time," said Cyril. "Don't wanna miss battin' practice. We'll eat at the ballpark."

Feeling warm, I started to roll down my window.

Cyril shouted, "Don't. Roll it back up."

"Huh? Will it fall out or something?"

Jackie leaned forward and whispered into my right ear, "This isn't a real GTO. Cyril put GTO emblems on his Tempest and sprayed his windows so people will think he's got A/C."

"But I'm hot."

Cyril pointed to the dash, saying, "Open the vent then."

I did. It was only a little better.

"The *Daily News* says spitballer Perry's throwin' for the Giants," Angelo said, with a tone of inevitability.

"How're the Mets doing?" I asked, not having a clue about what was happening this or any previous season.

"Nine games behind Chicago but the Cubs'll fold. They always do." Angelo seemed confident this would happen.

"Tookie's old boyfriend's a Cubs fan," said Jackie, who was sporting a blue Mets cap.

"Too bad for him," Cyril said. "She's a Mets fan now—or she's walkin'. Giver her the hat behind you."

Jackie handed me a well-used cap from the shelf behind the back seat. I expanded the band and jerked it on. "Okay?"

The boys grunted then started a conversation about the Mets chances against the Giants that lasted until we pulled into the parking lot.

We marched double-time to the gate. Once inside, the guys headed toward the seats. Jackie grabbed my hand. "Let's pee first," she said then tugged me off in the direction of the restrooms.

"Whaddya think?"

"About what," I asked. *This may be the worst date of my life but it should get me what I want.*

"Cyril. Whaddya think I'm talkin' about?"

"He seems very knowledgeable about baseball," I said, trying to be diplomatic.

"He thinks you're hot."

"How do you know that?"

"Him and Angelo watched us walk out of work yesterday afternoon. Ange told me."

"He hardly said a word to me." *But he's already had sex with me mentally several times. He better save some desire for after the game.*

"He's never had a girlfriend before. Spends all his free time on cars and sports."

Tim hadn't had one before me but he was a great boyfriend until he got serious. "Never?"

"One-night stands but nothing regular."

A one-night stand might be exactly what the doctor ordered.

"Took, we'll sit between the guys so they havta talk to us."

"At least we can talk to each other that way."

Our seats gave us a pretty good vantage point for watching the players' wives. The instant something happened on the field, I'd pick out the ones cheering excitedly or hiding their heads and, from the reactions, figure out which players went with which wives.

"Make a note of the section they're sittin' in so we can avoid it in the future." Jackie said.

"Why?"

"Because they're gorgeous and we don't wanna be compared to them."

"Check."

Both guys focused their attention on the game during play. Between innings, they worried about their stomachs. The first time I cheered—I stood up when everyone else did unsure of why exactly—I caught Cyril gaping at my ass when I went to sit back down. *Better not look his way when I'm standing. Need to keep him interested.* Not much happened till the fourth inning, when light-hitting

Giants' second baseman Ron Hunt singled. To keep from getting bored, I'd bought a program chocked full of statistics on both teams' players and checked out each player as he came up to bat.

"Oh shit," Cyril said. "McCovey's up with a man on."

"He's been tearin' up the league," Angelo piped in.

The entire crowd watched this at bat intensely but didn't have to wait long.

"Damn," Cyril said, when the crack of Willie McCovey's bat echoed around Shea Stadium. "Gentry should've walked him."

"Kinda tough with only one out and a man on first," Angelo countered. "But maybe he should've. We're down two runs after that blast."

Both runners slowed down and trotted around the bases when they saw the ball land in the seats. When a man wearing a Giants hat waved the ball with glee, a Mets fan poured his beer on him, eliciting a loud cheer from the partisan crowd.

Awful expensive at these prices. Could've bought me a nice meal at a good restaurant for what a hot dog and a beer cost here. Cyril stood up, waving three fingers. "Need three beers here."

The hometown fans got gloomier in the bottom of the fourth when Garret and Jones made two quick outs but perked up a bit when Kranepool singled and Swoboda walked.

"Don't let him foolya," Cyril yelled when the light-hitting Mets third baseman came up to bat.

"Take one for the team, Charles," Angelo shouted. "You probably can't hit his fastball. Forget the spitter."

"Holy shit," they shouted in unison when he launched a three-run homer putting the Mets ahead.

The home fans erupted in applause while the players

circled the bases. In the bottom of the eight, Charles came up to bat with two men on base.

"Just like last time," Angelo cheered. He'd become much more positive about the game's outcome.

"Don't jinx him," Cyril said. "A little bingo's good for a run."

This time, Charles singled to center driving in the fourth and last run.

With the game apparently in hand, Cyril shifted his attention to his score. "You don't look an' dress like no Jersey girl I ever saw."

"I haven't lived here two years yet and I'm not Italian." *If you haven't noticed, my red hair didn't come from a bottle.*

"You don't talk like no Jersey girl, either."

"I'm working on it."

He chuckled. "Don't work too hard on that. Jersey girls have smart mouths."

"Watch it," Jackie snarled, overhearing the conversation. "Better to be smart than stupid."

"Better to be nice than a wise ass."

Jackie turned toward Angelo and Cyril watched Tug McGraw finish his warm up.

McGraw held the Giants in check the last two innings and a jubilant crowd filed out.

Angelo and Cyril argued about which would be the best route to take home and picked what must've been the worst one. It took forever to get back to Jersey. Once there, on more familiar turf, Cyril's eyes shifted to my crotch as much as the road.

Will it discourage him if I say to watch the road? Don't want to die a virgin in a fake GTO. We stopped at Jackie's place where she and Angelo got out. Angelo gestured to Cyril with both hands but I didn't have a clear view of what he was doing. Based on their guilty laughs,

I assumed it had to do with gaining carnal knowledge of me.

Jackie yelled to me, "Don't do anything I wouldn't do," laughed, and waved goodnight.

Have they set me up to get screwed by someone who has trouble constructing a proper sentence? Can't I have sex and good grammar?

As we headed for my place, I pondered my immediate future. *I've never had a boy in my apartment before. Do I ask him to come up for a night cap when I don't have any booze? Do I tell him I want to have sex? He's gotta wash his hands before touching me after being in the ballpark all night. If I asked Tim to come up, he'd follow me like a puppy dog.*

"Do you have a roommate?"

Wants to know if we can use my apartment. Don't look too eager. "Are you looking for somebody to date?"

"Depends."

"Depends on what?"

"How this one turns out."

Cyril pulled into the parking space in the dark corner of the lot where the maple tree's leaves blocked out the light.

"What a great night," he said. "The Mets came back and beat Gaylord Perry, even after McCovey homered and Bobby Bonds hit a triple. And McGraw was great!"

Not knowing how to react, I affected a smile and sat quietly in my seat, not reaching for the door handle. I pondered whether it might be better to do it in the car. He reached around me with his long arms, pulling me to him for a kiss.

Not awful. Not good either. One thing Tim was, was a good kisser.

I kissed back to encourage him to continue. Expecting his tongue next, he caught me off guard—not that I would've tried to stop him if I knew what he was up to. He felt me up through my blouse. I pressed my chest into his hand to encourage him but he pulled it away. The next thing I felt was his hand sliding up my bare thigh.

"Slow down, Cyril. You're moving way too fast."

"Can't wait any longer. You got me hot and bothered." He grabbed my skirt, pulled it up, and tugged on my panties.

I pushed him away. "Slow down. You need to warm me up to the idea."

Nostrils flared, he grabbed me in a bear hug.

I squirmed loose. "Don't be an ape."

"Prickteaser. You lead men on and don't follow through."

"I'm no pricktease." *Not anymore.* "Drop your pants. You better be ready for action, bub."

He sheepishly unbuckled his jeans and slid them down.

"Drawers, too. I've got to see if you're ready to step up to the plate or not. If not, you're out of the game."

He unsnapped his boxers and pushed them clear, revealing an erection ready enough for me to start work.

"Relax and enjoy this." *Hope his tastes as good as Tim's. I'll suck it in as far as I can to start.* When I leaned toward him to get into position, he grabbed my hair and forced my head down.

Thwack. I slapped him across the face. "Why don't you just rape me and get it over with?"

"I'm sorry. I just want you so much."

"You'll get what I want to give you. Don't expect anything more."

Chastened, he leaned back in his seat.

No blow job for you now. Don't deserve one, especially my first. I should get something out of this. I've haven't even held one in my hand yet.

I grabbed his penis and held it. Ooooh. I liked how it felt, especially the throbbing. *Better start doing something or he'll think I don't know how.* I jerked it a few strokes.

He froze. "Whoa. Not so hard. You tryin' to rip it off?"

I loosened my grip and pumped it slowly.

It feels even nicer than I expected. Sucking on it'd be fun but he doesn't deserve it. He's squirming like it doesn't feel good. Maybe I'm squeezing too hard. See how he reacts when I tickle the underside. The book was right.

It's fun having complete control over him. My wrist's getting tired. Better make him come. Try faster, looser strokes. He's breathing harder. I'm getting close. He's about to erupt.

I aimed his Roman candle away from me and toward his beloved Mets jersey just in time.

He thrust his hips up, banging the bottom of the steering wheel. "Aaaahhh!"

That's a lot more than I expected. Oooh, he's still squirting.

He pushed my hand away. "Stop. I can't stand it anymore."

I'd never felt such power. What a rush.

"There," I said, wiping my hand on his sleeve. "You can't say I'm a tease now." I opened my door and got out.

"Hey, don't go. You're pretty good at this. We're just gettin' started."

"You're finished. Go home." I slammed his door and turned my back to him.

He banged on his door to get my attention. "But I don't have your phone number."

"Call Dial-a-Prayer," I said over my shoulder. "Try getting in touch with me, I'll report you as a stalker." I raced up the stairs to my apartment, locking the door behind me.

Leave the lights off so he won't know which apartment's mine. Better keep them off till I'm sure he's gone. I loved my tiny apartment. I'd decorated it how I liked—to the extent my microscopic budget allowed—and kept it immaculately clean.

Mother was a pretty good housekeeper, but with three boys and a husband constantly messing it, her house was always junked up. Having few possessions other than books, I kept an orderly home from the beginning. I can't stand clutter.

These guys were too immature and not smart enough. At least Tim was smart, probably Mensa eligible. That should be a good place to meet intelligent men.

CHAPTER 5

Third Base

The girls ambushed me Monday morning at break. "Tookie, you must be sore from all your screwin' this weekend," Jackie gushed.

The other girls oohed, aahed, and snickered.

"Huh?" *What's she talking about?*

"Cyril said you fucked his soul right out of him. You wanted it so often he ran out of rubbers in the middle of the night." Jackie looked so proud of herself for having something on me.

"Do I look like I could have that kind of power over a man?" *How gullible are they?*

"He said you screamed incessantly for more and he drove all over town frantically looking for a place that was open that had a rubber machine."

They must have thought I was so stupid not to be on the pill and didn't use a diaphragm. "Do you all rely on guys to provide the protection?"

Jackie wasn't giving up on the story for anything. "The gas station by the Turnpike had a machine but it only took quarters and he had no change, so he got five dollars' worth, including a French Tickler."

"Do you think I'd be able to walk after a night like that?"

"If it wasn't your first night like this or if you're a nympho," Diane said. She was the sluttiest one of the lot who had probably done much worse than I'd been accused of doing.

She was usually quiet, not wanting people talking about her escapades. "How much practice did you have before taking in a guy like this, Diane?"

"He says you went wild over the French Tickler," Jackie continued. "I guess it is true: the quiet ones get the most sex, especially the redheads."

"A lady doesn't tell," I said, stalling and unable to think of something better.

Might be to my advantage for people to think I'm easy and adventurous.

The girls' mouths dropped open at my tacit admission to a weekend of debauchery.

"You got that backward," Sybil piped in. "A gentleman doesn't tell and Cyril just proved he isn't one. I bet he didn't get past first base, if he got that far."

"He didn't even think about slowing down there." If kissing is first base.

"Break's over. Time to get back to work," said Jackie, the one who usually lingered the longest.

I'd hardly gotten back to my cubicle when Sybil scooted in. "Is any part of it true? Did you really tear his shirt off him?"

No use trying to lie to her. She'd see through it. "He did try to feel me up. That's getting past first base, isn't it? And he tried to get in my panties."

Surprised at what she was hearing, she raised her eyebrows and her lower jaw dropped, leaving her mouth wide open. "He didn't hit a home run, did he?" she said, after composing herself.

"I don't think so. Is a hand job second or third base?" The baseball analogy confused me, especially because it was oriented toward the male being the aggressor. If I got some guy to fuck me, did I hit a home run, or did he, or did we both?

"You choked his chicken?" She clearly couldn't believe her ears.

"I liked it, especially considering the options. I want somebody to tag all my bases but not an ape like him." It felt great, having control like that over a man.

"For a shy girl, you're brave. Third base next time?"

"Depends on who steps up to the plate. Cyril ejected himself from the game. I didn't tear off his shirt, by the way."

"Jackie says he bought an expensive new one to replace it."

"Don't doubt that. I aimed his fire hose at his front and cleaned my hand on the sleeve."

Sybil smiled broadly and chuckled. "Gonna let Tim touch all your bases?" She locked onto my eyes and wouldn't turn loose.

"I would, but he dumped me."

"A little more experience, and you'll be ready to go bar hoppin' with me." Sybil winked and went about her work.

I took the Mensa exam and came close—only one point short of acceptance—but not good enough to get me into their gatherings to meet those brainiacs.

As rumors about me flowed around the office, some men flirted with me, but were generally awkward about it. Most were intelligent and had college degrees, but many were on the dorky side. I saw their wives and girlfriends at the Christmas party and, flat-chested or not, I could compete with them. I didn't know how to attract men so I asked Sybil for advice.

"Lots of eligible men work here but none ever ask me out."

She rubbed her forehead for a few seconds before responding. "Many single men don't consider dating women they work with because a nasty break up could create unpleasant situations they'd want to avoid."

"But the only single men I come into contact with are at work."

"I didn't say none of them would date you."

"How do I identify the ones who would?"

"Here's an idea. Make yourself more attractive to men and see which ones respond."

"Tim liked me just the way I am."

"Does Tim work here?"

"No."

"Stand up and turn around—all the way around—slowly."

I did but it felt strange.

"Step one. Don't wear anything that shows your knees."

"That eliminates almost all my skirts and dresses that aren't out of style."

"Get some slacks that fit better but not tight. Black and navy blue are probably the best colors for you."

"I don't wear button-front blouses anymore because they make me look flat."

"Good. And get yourself some shoes that girls wear."

"I can't wear heels."

"Flats're okay. Loafers, low-heeled pumps, something like that."

Forget about falsies. No way was I going to disappoint a guy when he saw me naked. No false advertising from me. No lipstick or makeup or sexy clothing. No, siree. I didn't want to fool anybody. I wanted them to be pleasantly surprised when I took my clothes off. No guy was going to feel compelled to give me a charity fuck. Anyone I bedded was going to enjoy it. I'd make sure they did.

༺໑༻

I delivered punched card decks, paper tapes, and reports to people when I finished my work on them, exploiting the opportunity to evaluate my new way of dressing while I meandered through the building. Aiming a compact mirror behind me on my walk about when near anyone I found remotely interesting, I wiggled my butt and noted which guys ogled me, which ones peered cautiously, and wrote off men who ignored me.

Women who put out for promotions or raises were sluts. I'd screw men for the pleasure I got from it and for the pleasure I gave them, not for personal gain. But first, I needed someone to pop my cherry.

CHAPTER 6

Adam

One quiet afternoon, when few others were in the office, I walked into Adam's cubicle to show him some figures I'd run for his project. Several years older than me and not overly handsome, Adam was blond, a bit gawky—after all, he was a statistician—tall enough at just under six-feet, athletic, but not overly so, and had very large hands and feet. Could the old wives' tales be accurate?

I decided to give Adam the honor if he accepted. I took a deep breath and set my shyness aside, knowing this wouldn't take more than a minute. I could abort if he wasn't receptive.

He looked up, surprised it was me standing in front of him. "Yes?"

He scanned me up and down, as if he was more interested in my vital statistics than those on the report. Good. Adam looked like a guy who'd been getting laid regularly, but had been cut off. Not drooling exactly, but not far from it. He must've heard the rumors about me.

I circled around his desk to get behind him. "Here are the numbers you wanted on the spermicidal jelly tests," I vamped in my sexiest, inexperienced, nineteen-year-old virgin voice as I wisped the ends of my hair across the side of his face and blew ever so lightly across his neck while I placed the listing in front of him.

If he reacted negatively, I'd stumble and bail out. It wasn't Brut, that was Beth's husband. Not Aqua Velva, Dad used that. And Tim wore Old Spice. I liked that better, but Adam smelled okay. Kinda sexy.

He looked confused, as much by my come on as why I ran the report. "I thought Jim was running these, Toots."

"It's Tookie to *you.*"

"Okay, Tooks. Did Jim run these?"

"He's off this afternoon so I banged them out. It work for you?" I delighted in throwing men off balance, even back when I was afraid to initiate contact. Tim was too easy. Adam was my first real test. *They say he's experienced but he hasn't come on to anyone in the office. He might be too shy for that.*

"Don't know. Haven't read them yet, Tooks." His tone reflected irritation.

"Not them. *It.*" This was fun. He didn't have a clue.

"Oh, I've used SAS lots of times." He looked annoyed.

I'd set him up perfectly. "Not SAS, silly, the jelly."

"Not really." Finally getting my joke, he grinned as his face turned pink.

Now to flirt when he knew I was flirting. "What do you use?"

"That's personal, don't you think?" he parried back with ease.

"Just wondering about our products." *Hah!*

"Doing anything Saturday, Tookie?" His voice was calm but his eyes showed lust.

Success. He thought he was going to pork me. "Aren't you going with someone?" The rumor about him was true.

He looked cocksure of his way with women. "I am. To dinner with you."

"Depends. What do you have in mind?" I wasn't letting him off too easy.

"Pizza Villa's the best around."

He's not getting away with that. "Emile's has a great prime rib. I'll make reservations."

The man paid for everything in those days. I hardly made anything, while living in a high-cost area, and every penny not spent helped. So, I made dinner part of my dates to cut down on my food bills. Also, I didn't want word to get around that I was cheap, even though I was because I didn't drink.

He looked better up close than I expected. A different barber and better-fitting slacks would do the trick. I liked his thick hair, but not the style. Didn't need any help in the ego department.

"What's your address, Tooks?"

"Have to run errands in the city. I'll meet you at your place." No way did I want him in my bed a second longer than necessary. If I didn't like it, I could get up and leave whenever I wanted if we did it at his place.

I spent my lunch hours and evenings leading up to our date studying the new sex manuals that had just come out, paying particular attention to the acts I thought I'd enjoy the most. My one miscue was not noticing that Carol, the blabby executive secretary, was on the prowl when I practiced on the longest, fattest banana I could find. She saw me tilt my head back as I licked the underside of the curved end from bottom to top and started a new rumor about me.

Sybil followed me back to my cubicle at the end of afternoon break. "You've got to be more careful, Tookie. Carol's spreading a rumor that you practice giving blow jobs on bananas."

"Do you think the men'll hear it?"

"You're gettin' a bad reputation here."

"Being a goody two shoes didn't get me anywhere, did it?"

"It did get you a marriage proposal, didn't it?"

"One I didn't want."

❧❧❧

As I pulled into his parking lot, I compared it with mine. Nice. New. Clean. No litter. A definite positive, but I wasn't going inside just yet. Adam answered the door, dressed better than at work, but without a tie. He wore navy-blue Sansabelt slacks, striped shirt, and gray glen-plaid sport coat. He furtively looked me up and down but, more than his eyes and smile, his undisciplined tongue gave away what was on his dirty mind.

I wore black slacks with a white silky blouse over the armor-plated bra I wore to keep my nipples from drawing attention to what I didn't have.

"Come in." *Sounds innocent but don't want to risk missing out on dinner.*

I feigned a look at my watch. "Better not. We'll miss our reservation." *Need to know more about you before we swap fluids.*

"Maybe later?" His not-so-sly grin gave away his intentions.

Better not let him feel so confident. "Have to get up early for volunteer work."

Adam conversed easily at the restaurant, a more up-scale one than I could afford, but within my comfort zone. I ignored his bragging. Self-centered like Jersey high school boys, he took a half hour before getting around to asking me about myself. Had to overlook East Coast ignorance or I wouldn't find anyone to date.

"Don't Arkansas girls marry young, Tooks?" he asked, deadly serious.

"I don't talk about it." That was a rude, bigoted question and he didn't deserve a decent answer. Besides that, I was only born in Arkansas. I never lived there.

"Divorced?"

"Annulled." Tough keeping a straight face. He was so gullible. Couldn't let him assume rolling in my hay was a sure thing.

Adam's confidence showed he'd been around the block a few times. My attraction to him wasn't only physical. He was smart, too.

Desire covered his face, turning me on.

"Dessert? I hear their—"

"No thanks." I love chocolate, but don't eat dessert when I want some action. It dulls my senses.

"Check!"

He must've read my thoughts.

He raced his Chevy II back to his apartment, not fast enough to attract police attention but faster than anyone else on the road that night, and roared up to his apartment, just missing a Ford's fender by inches. His engine—make that his car's engine—hadn't quite stopped turning when he shifted into high gear. His frenzied octopus arms groped me as if they were looking for buttons or zippers they couldn't find.

"Slow down. Don't like being pawed," I scolded, pushing him away. Didn't expect him to be this aggressive.

He backed off. Way off. And sulked.

"Don't pout." Why are men such babies?

"I bought you a nice dinner, Toots, and now you won't—"

"Stop right there," I said, looking him square in the eyes. "I enjoyed the evening with you very much—until now. I'll give you a second chance if you behave yourself." Some choice. Don't get laid before I'm eighty or be treated like a piece of meat.

"Huh?" His befuddled look told me he was clueless.

I kissed his lips softly to model what I wanted then. "No tongue. I'll bite it off."

I attributed his behavior to his being overly horny and too sure of himself, but after I warned him, he complied readily.

Not as good a kisser as Tim, but we could work on that. I kissed him more passionately and embraced him firmly as a signal for him to continue. I gave him my tongue when I was ready for his. After a few minutes of kissing, he tried to unbutton my slacks.

He's trying to do it right here. Damn ass men. They ignore my tits. I grabbed his hand, pulled it onto my right breast, and held it there. He flicked my erect nipple through my blouse.

I felt myself moisten but held his hand in place so he'd continue fondling me. Too soon, he tried slipping his hand under my blouse.

"Aren't you forgetting someone?" I placed his hand on my left breast. "She wants equal time."

Most men didn't seem to understand that we small-breasted women enjoyed having our boobs played with more than other women because our nerve endings were more densely concentrated. The same number were squished into a smaller area.

"Okay."

He seemed content to just make out for a while longer. He probably figured I'd let him screw me before the night was over.

I wanted him to fondle me under my blouse but didn't want him to realize I'd removed my bra in the restaurant restroom so I'd get more pleasure when he felt me up through my blouse. It'd also allow me to strip more quickly when the time came.

And now's the time! "I'm thirsty." Why wrestle in the car when there's a couch and bed at our disposal?

Adam needed no further hint. His feet threw gravel as he tore around the car to let me out. He nearly dragged me up the flight of stairs and pulled me into his apartment. "Make yourself comfortable."

I felt odd, standing alone in his living room, as he dashed into the kitchen to fetch me a drink. It was now or never. Couldn't be passive like I was with Tim. Adam wanted me and surely wouldn't reject me if I tried. I heard the familiar sound of ice cubes clinking into a glass.

"I've got Coke, orange juice, beer—"

"Ice water's fine." His place was nicer than I expected. He must have had a cleaning lady—and she used Pinesol. Shouldn't catch any diseases getting naked here. This was no bachelor's pigsty. I could almost live here. Time for the main course.

He handed me a tall glass of water half full of ice cubes.

Seeing a photo on the mantle next to a bunch of Temple memorabilia, I pointed. "This your family?"

He turned his back to me to look at the photo.

Perfect. I silently placed the glass on an end table, slid in behind him, reached around his waist, and unbuttoned his slacks. Then, I tugged the button tab with enough force to unhook it and unzip his fly as he spun around.

Boxers? I hadn't thought much about men's drawers before. Tim's briefs hid everything except that he desired me.

Adam looked stunned, as if he'd never experienced anything like this before. "What're you—"

"Stand still. I want to play." With a flick of my wrist, his trousers fell to his ankles, allowing his throbbing member to salute me. *What a surprise! I expected you to be inside his boxers, but you're so excited to see me you escaped out the fly. Those old wives may know something after all.*

No longer able to resist temptations of this sort, I gripped him in my hand. *Feels like a hot sausage with a pulse. So much nicer when it's my choice.*

Adam flinched, "Not so hard, please, Tookie."

I loosened my grip a little and Big Adam relaxed. Little Adam pulsated and I moistened as he got larger and larger and throbbed more without me doing anything. *Oh, oh!* I hadn't pulled his underpants down.

"Now I see why men wear boxers." I could've climaxed in my pants just holding his hot, bulging rod, but I wanted to try something before he deflowered me. If that was too painful, I might not have wanted to do anything else that night.

I released him and tugged his boxers down with both hands, but Little Adam blocked their retreat.

Adam flinched again. "Don't break my boy."

I stretched his waistband out and slipped his boxers over Little Adam and let them drop to the floor. I knelt to get a closer look. I tentatively licked his head once like it was an ice cream cone. *A little salty, but okay. So far, so good. Now to put practice to work.* I sucked him into my mouth.

Adam squirmed. "Your teeth."

"Whoops." I covered them with my lips, licked his head with my tongue, then set to my task with vigor. Stroke by stroke, my confidence grew.

"Aaaahh."

Adam's whole body quivered so much I grabbed his butt with both hands to keep him still enough to stay in my mouth. "Are you a virgin?" Thought he was experienced, but he didn't act like it.

"No one like you." He didn't have enough breath to say more.

He must have been telling the truth the way he was panting and his body convulsed. My basic blowjob pleased him so much I reserved the extras I'd been practicing for future encounters. Women's magazines and the girls in the office complained that men bored quickly if you didn't vary what you did in bed. My oral repertoire should keep him happy for a good while.

"Oooooo." He jerked me to him by the hair. He wasn't large enough to gag me but he pinned my forehead to his pelvis.

I'd found my calling. "Ease up so I can continue."

He loosened his grip on my hair and I continued to suck and lick him with my lips and tongue, not neglecting his head's sensitive underside. After a minute or two more, he moaned and thrust his hips toward me. Adam's wails of ecstasy excited me. His pulsating prick titillated my tongue and put my body in extreme arousal mode. I happily pitched my tent in the swallow camp.

Adam stood in a daze as I rose to my feet.

I gave his balls a gentle tickle. "Orange juice and a few apple slices? Where's the bedroom?"

He nodded in the affirmative and pointed toward the hall.

Purse in hand, I headed off to the playroom.

His bedroom was clean enough, at least for this one time. Temple U pennant on the wall and a bobble-head Bill Cosby on his dresser. Now for his bathroom.

It was okay, too. I was surprised. I stripped quickly and folded my clothes neatly. *Where can I put them? No hamper. Next to his English Leather should do.* I grabbed a clean towel and popped in a breath mint before returning to my operating theater, his bedroom. I gave no thought to having him use a condom. I only worried about getting knocked up and the pill was supposed to take care of that.

I pulled down the covers and top sheet on the left side of his bed—he was right handed—placed the towel where I'd be lying, and slid in between his plaid sheets, covering myself with the top one. It smelled fresh. He must've done his laundry that day. Lights off. Didn't want him to see my body yet. I hoped for the night of my life, but prepared mentally for the worst.

Adam looked shocked to find me in his bed. "H-here you go."

I took the OJ and apples from him, placed them on the night stand, and patted his side of the bed. "Join me."

He ripped off his clothes and dove into bed.

I drank about a third of the OJ and ate a couple apple slices. I'd never needed OJ at night before. My body must've craved the sugar for energy to replenish what I'd expended or to stockpile more for what I was about to use.

"So?" I fished for a compliment.

"So what?"

He was clueless. The girls at work and the magazines warned me about insensitive men. "Did you enjoy it? Will you ever want it again?" How thick could a guy be?

"You're fantastic. I always liked it, but I never thought it could be half as good as yours. Yes, I'd like it again sometime. How 'bout now?"

"No, it's my turn." Supposedly, first erections are more exciting but the second ones last longer. I may have needed him to go at it for a good while to devirginize me.

"I—I don't like giving oral sex to women." His sheepish voice betrayed the guilt he felt about refusing to reciprocate.

"Why'd you ask me out if you like men?" He deserved that for not complimenting me without being asked.

"I like women. It's the ah…ah…" Even in just the moonlight coming in the window I could see his face turn bright red.

"That's not what I have in mind." *Not sure I want your mouth there, either. Fuck me and do a good job of it. Get cracking.* I pulled his head to my left breast, but he pulled back.

"A couple of minutes to catch my breath?" His breathing hadn't slowed, possibly due to fear of having to eat me.

With no lump under the sheet, I might as well let him rest a little to reload. "Okay, but you'll have to put me in the mood again." I monitored his condition with my hand while I tried to think of suggestive things to say.

"You like sports, Tookie?"

"I went to a basketball game on my very first date." Sporting events were fine. Just didn't want a steady diet of them.

"How'd that work out?" *Sounds smug. Is he insinuating something?*

"Great. It resulted in a marriage proposal." *Jerk.* He tried to make it sound like I failed with Tim or I hadn't gone out with guys of his caliber before.

"I'm a big Yankees fan."

"You don't feel so big right now." I gave his flaccid fuckstick a gentle squeeze. *I might be easy, but you're going to work a little for it.*

Apparently getting the hint, he started sucking my left breast. Didn't notice his windows before. Too high for anyone to see what we were doing even if the curtains were open, but let in just enough light to see what I was doing and not enough to for him to see my body well.

Good.

After Adam suckled my breasts, I got impatient and nudged his right hand downward. He enthusiastically fingered me, but to little avail. I underestimated Tim. He got me more than moist enough very quickly. Adam didn't get my juices flowing, but he sure was ready to hump me.

"Not yet." I clasped my hands together around his neck and pulled him down when he raised up, presumably to mount me. I guided his middle finger to where I pleasure myself. He tried valiantly, but didn't have the technique. I focused on how good Tim made me feel and how moist I got blowing Adam. It took me awhile, but I was finally ready for my maiden voyage. Adam was ready when he was on my first breast.

"I want you *now*." I pushed up against Adam's chest with both hands to help get him into the missionary position. He bounced to his knees, his smile so wide I saw the moonlight reflect off his oversized teeth.

"Ready or not, here I come."

"You better not come too soon." *Shoot your wad early and I'll kill you.* Nothing fancy for my first time, just your basic bang. Didn't want a wham-bam-thank-you-ma'am other girls complained about. Though it better to make it easy for him. I parted my legs and bent my knees to give him a clear shot. He crouched on his knees between my legs and readied himself to drive me home. As he leaned forward, I grabbed his hymen buster. Although he wasn't throbbing as much as earlier, he was plenty hard enough. I pulled him into me.

"Uuuuhh." He thrust so hard he smashed my ass into the mattress but didn't penetrate me.

"Ow." He didn't slip into me easily like Tim's finger. I adjusted my knees and hips for better alignment and easier penetration.

He pushed against my inner thighs. "Wider."

I spread my knees as far as I could. He rammed himself in and pounded me as if he was drilling all the way to China.

I bit my lip. "Ouch." The deed was done. "Please continue."

He humped me like a rabbit on speed, rattling the bedsprings and banging the headboard against the wall with each jab.

"Ow!" I winced as he jackhammered me. "I've never done this before. Ease up." I didn't expect it to hurt this much. Tim would've been gentle.

"You're a *virgin*?" He sounded genuinely surprised.

As many times as I'd intentionally said things to shock guys, I'd never surprised a man as much, before or since.

"Yes," I mumbled with more than a little embarrassment.

"No shit?"

He didn't believe me.

"No shit. Fuck me but don't bore a hole into the apartment below."

He eased up a bit, maintaining a comfortable rhythm.

He deserved a reward for deflowering me. So, I squeezed him as tightly as I could with my formerly virginal vaginal muscles and humped back as energetically as I could, under the circumstances.

"Aaahhhhh!" He mercifully came and collapsed on top of me. "You're really something, Tookie. You're not *really* a virgin?"

"Not anymore." *I better not be.* I felt blood and who knows what else dripping out between my legs and wanted to clean up. I also smelled sex for the first time, my special scent mixed with his.

"No virgin gives head like you." He still wasn't convinced.

"I practice at home a lot." Didn't he know some girls—not me—blow guys to retain their virginity and to keep from getting knocked up? "Something else you probably won't believe is you won the Daily Double. You got my first blowjob, too."

"I don't believe you. You're too good."

"I don't lie about such things." Feeling crushed under his weight and very uncomfortable with various bodily fluids trickling out of me, I pushed him away. "Get off me. I need to clean myself."

They warned me the first time wouldn't be all that great, but no one told me how much I'd enjoy going down on him. A quick shower refreshed me. Ready to curl up next to Adam for the night, but feeling vulnerable, I put on his bathrobe. I preferred sleeping in the nude, but I needed to be cuddled just then.

What the hell is this? Adam was sleeping like a satiated bachelor who finally had sex after a long drought. I nudged him, but he just turned over and snored louder. Wanting at least a little emotional support, but getting none, I dressed and left, disappointed.

The next morning, I reflected on the previous night's activities with mixed emotions while I soaked in the tub to relieve my soreness. Just thinking about how his meatsicle excited me when I sucked it made me want to play with myself. What control I felt with his joystick in my hand.

I wasn't so sure about having him inside me, but I'd try it a few more times to see if it got better—on my terms.

These pills damned well better work. Tim would've cuddled me afterward, and I would've fallen asleep in his arms. That was the problem with sensitive types. They gave you what you needed when you needed it most.

Later, while I perused the *Sunday Times* looking for

something interesting to do that afternoon, the telephone startled me.

"Where'd you go, Tookie?" Adam actually sounded peeved.

I couldn't believe it. "What the hell kind of question is that? You damn well know where I went. If you ever want to see me again, you've gotta change some things, and quick. I can't believe you're such a shithead."

"Like what?"

He doesn't understand why I'm upset. Geesh. What a moron. If he got through college, anybody can. "You don't want a girlfriend. You want a prostitute. You say I'm fantastic and don't even kiss me after fucking me."

"What do you want me to do?" Panic flowed across the phone line.

"Hint: Like being with me?" *Put another way, do you want to be she-bopping at home alone on Saturday night or do you want to be humping me? You better be quick.*

"You suck like a vacuum cleaner."

Not very good, but he was under pressure. "I'll take that as a compliment, but you better improve a lot in a hurry."

"Tookie, I've never met anyone quite like you. You gave me the most unbelievable night of my life. How's that?"

He actually sounded sincere. Nice turnaround. "A little better. What's my name?" I like it when guys say my name, even better when it's my real name.

"How 'bout we do something this afternoon, Mary Louise?"

Too sore to screw. No way was I going to reward him other ways for treating me so badly. "Tell you what. Wednesday after work, we take in a light supper and a movie." I'd be ready for action again by then but, as much as I hate to miss out, I wasn't putting anything in my mouth I couldn't chew. "But don't expect anything."

CHAPTER 7

Growing a Penis

I picked a rose blossom from one of the bushes outside my apartment and placed it in a vase on my desk on Monday morning, snapping its stem so the blossom hung down.

Several girls—most wearing miniskirts so short they showed everything they had when they sat down, bent over slightly, squatted, climbed stairs, or did anything but stand perfectly erect—bubbled into my cubicle during morning break.

"Is it true? You and Adam did the deed?" Sybil sounded like she was sincerely interested. The others were hoping to hear some new gossip.

"Why do you ask?" *I see he's great at keeping secrets. Better not tell him anything I don't want spread round the office.*

"He's strutting around like a peacock, but hasn't said anything," said Jackie.

She worked in his department and would've seen him.

"Last week I overheard him brag 'No girl ever resisted my charms.'" Cynthia never lied. She didn't look like she was pleased with me.

I said nothing, but shifted my eyes to the rose with the broken stem.

"He was your first? I thought you wore out Cyril a while back," Jackie said.

"I couldn't see any point in denying it. You wouldn't have believed me anyway."

As this news spread around the office, my attractiveness quotient improved among the men. Barbara Bush must have been right about oral sex. The other girls seemed envious. Maybe they weren't getting anywhere near the action they claimed.

After lunch, Sybil brought me some cupcakes.

"What's the occasion?" It wasn't my birthday or anything.

She stared at them, then me, and back to them like a cat with an empty food bowl. "Guess."

There were little penises in the icing. "Thanks, I guess. Cherries would've sufficed."

"It's a Carver-Watkins ritual. You get them for the next girl."

The young women at work had a bunch of rituals that usually cost me money I didn't have. Bridal showers, baby showers, divorce showers. If sex change operations had been in vogue then, they would've had sex change showers. I never had the opportunity to give another girl cupcakes.

The girls stopped gossiping and scattered when they saw Adam approach.

"Should I make dinner reservations for this weekend?" he said, almost drooling.

"Depends on how you behave Wednesday. Now make yourself scarce. You've got the whole office gossiping about us."

Stupidly thinking it'd be a good idea to tease him by unveiling my body bit by bit starting with our chaste movie date, when he wasn't allowed to touch one square inch of it, I wore my shortest miniskirt, which was at least twice as long as those other girls in the office wore. He chatted nicely at supper and took me to see *Goodbye Columbus,* a new movie several girls at work recommended. The Jewish *Graduate,* one described it.

I froze as the voice on the screen said, "By the way, sweetie, what have you been doing with yourself this summer?" The rumors about rats infesting this old theater were true. I felt something crawl across the portion of my upper thigh the miniskirt was supposed to cover. I looked down to see a rodent of a different type.

Thwack! I backhanded Adam as hard as I could, but did him no harm.

"What was that for?"

"Get your hand off my…uh…penis…if you don't want it broken," I wasn't strong enough to make good on that threat, but could give him a kick in the balls he wouldn't forget. *I should walk out now, but I want to see how it ends. Forget skirts for dates. I should kick him in the nuts the next time I see him.*

As soon as the credits started to roll, I dashed out the rear exit and raced to my car. *Is someone following me? Better hurry. Still hear footsteps behind me.* I finally reached the dark, deserted parking lot tucked in behind the café where we had eaten.

Sensing that it had been unwise to park in such a place, I quickly unlocked the Mustang's door, ready to jump in to make a quick exit.

"Why'd you run away from me?" Adam sounded hurt and confused.

"Good night." The frost in my voice froze him in place. He needed to learn to treat me with respect.

He looked pissed off and perplexed. "I thought we're going to my place."

"You screwed yourself." I'd traded a lapdog for a prick who treats me like a cunt with legs.

"After Saturday night—you wore a tiny skirt—I thought—"

"You thought wrong, bub. You need to learn the difference between a liberated woman and a whore." Training Tim took no effort at all. He was so eager to please. But this guy just wanted to schtup me. Nothing more. He had better straighten up in a hurry.

My mind drifted to a conversation I'd had with Cynthia, who was the oldest of the single women in the office at twenty-nine. Very attractive, tall, blonde, prettier than most, better shape, too, and cultured. I couldn't figure out why no one had scooped her up.

"When I started here a decade ago, you didn't have sex with a man before he put a diamond on your left hand if you ever wanted to get married," she said. "Now, they expect oral sex if they buy you a Coke. I don't even want to think about what they'd demand after a filet mignon dinner. And don't expect any consideration after you give in, either. It's a rough new world we live in today, Mary Louise." She made it clear I wouldn't likely find a hunk with Tim's sensitivity. I wanted a hunk.

Adam's voice interrupted my thoughts. "How can I make it up to you?"

He looked earnest and I didn't want to sit at home the upcoming weekend. I needed to set some ground rules or he'd treat me like a slut. I wouldn't have that. "Take me to a nice place Saturday and don't expect anything. Feel lucky if I kiss you at the door."

"O—okay."

Just then I made a big mistake. I felt sorry for Adam and kissed him goodnight. He put his right foot between mine and held me tight. Ooh, I liked how his thigh felt between mine.

When I felt his desire rub against me, what little re-solve I had left evaporated.

Okay. What can I do now? The backseat is so small and I don't want to dent the hood. I'll try one of the standing positions I read about. I stepped back and dropped his pants to the ground. As soon as I lowered his boxers, Adam pressed down on my shoulders.

I resisted. "No blow jobs for you until further no-tice." I yanked his crank to get him ready. He reached up under my skirt and pulled my dampened panties down, dropping them to my ankles. He was about ready. I'd take him against the side of my car. It'd keep me from falling over.

Adam didn't need any more cues. He grabbed my ass with both hands and set me on the fender. I wrapped my legs around his waist and pulled him to me. As I was guiding him to my glory hole, he froze. "What's that?"

I heard the sound tires make on gravel. "A car's com-ing up the alley." I swung my door wide open and dived into the back seat. Once there, I rolled onto my back for a better view of what was going on. Adam jumped in, closed the door, and pounced on me.

Little Adam was a good bit deflated but I could re-vive him. I barely grinded against him and he was back, ready for action. Adam slid him inside my now well lu-bricated love canal but I kept him still until I heard the car pass. I veed my legs, resting my right foot against the top of the driver's seat and the left against the top of the back seat. Unfortunately, my butt was on top of the hump where there's little padding. I gripped his prick with my untrained vaginal muscles and squeezed his balls to make him come as quickly as I could because my tailbone hurt more and more with each plunge.

"Sit up. I want to cuddle now." No repeats of Satur-day night were allowed.

Adam sat up and started to pull up his pants.

I grabbed his wrist. "Not yet," I said, then hopped on his lap. I pulled the back of my skirt up to get the maximum skin-on-skin quotient. "Fondle me."

Adam reached around me and flicked my nipples through my blouse and bra.

Soon, I wanted more skin-on-skin action. "Unhook me," I commanded, leaning forward so he could reach up the back of my blouse. He didn't need to be told what to do next. I soaked it in for a while before wanting more.

I'd had it twice from the missionary position so far and neither was all that great. We couldn't risk doing it standing up outside right then, so I'd have to try something else.

I squeezed Little Adam with my butt cheeks and squirmed around a little. He responded well to my flirts, maybe too well. He poked the wrong hole.

"Slide down a little." Big Adam slid down in the seat and Little Adam popped up between my legs, closer to where I wanted him to be. I pushed against the seat with my hands and against the floor with my feet, raising myself above him. "Let's go."

Adam guided himself into me and humped away.

Much better. He was in me deeper. I bounced up and down, timing my down strokes with his up strokes. "Wooooo! Keep going. Oh shit! Lay down!" Adam did but we'd already been illuminated in the spotlight. We lay on the backseat spooning to keep as low as we could.

The light swooped through the car then stopped. A deep voice coming from a loud speaker boomed, "You've got five minutes to get out of here. If you're still here when I get back or if I ever see you here again, I'm going to run you in." The gravel crunched indicating that the cop had pulled away. Adam started to get up.

"Hey. We've got five minutes. Don't waste it." I

grabbed Little Adam to push him back inside me but he'd retired for the evening. "Okay. Zip up your pants and get out." I had to wait for Adam to get out first the way we were scrunched into my tiny back seat.

Adam trotted off into the darkness saying, "Better get going. Most of the time's up. Tomorrow night?"

I hopped out of the car, flopped the driver's seat back into position, plunked my butt behind the wheel, turned the key and mashed the gas pedal, throwing gravel as I made my getaway.

My clothes were on, just majorly disheveled, but didn't want anyone to see me looking like that, especially them. I made as little noise as possible in my parking lot and stealthily climbed the stairs to my apartment. Halfway up, I met Beth's worthless, unemployed husband going down to pick her up after work. We grunted our mutual dislike for each other as we passed.

As I got to the top, I heard him say, "Lose something?"

Oh shit! My butt's bare. I turned and flipped him the bird.

"Don't like sloppy seconds," he said in the nastiest voice I'd ever heard.

"Asshole." What a complete jerk. He'd tell Beth and she'd tell Daddy. Damn.

I raced into my apartment, dropping the miniskirt on the floor as I ran to my bedroom for something to cover my naked ass and twat. I pulled on the first thing I found, a pair of shorts, and peered out the window. After the doofus pulled out of the parking lot, I crept down to my car. They weren't in the back seat or on the front seat floor or under the front seats or in the back window or on the dash. They weren't here.

I called Adam but got his machine, "Did my panties get mixed in with your clothes? They're just cheap ones but I make so little I can't afford to waste money on new ones. Please look for them. Thanks for a great evening."

I didn't see him at work the next morning. He must've been in meetings because his car was in the parking lot. When I returned to my cubicle after lunch, I found a package wrapped in brown paper on my desk. I'd seen ads for things shipped in brown paper. *Don't want anyone to see this.*

Later, when the secretaries were in the break room, I opened the package to find pairs of Saturday and Wednesday day-of-the week panties along with a note: "Dinner tonight?"

I called his desk phone. Hearing him answer and knowing to keep office romance phone calls as short as possible, I said, "No, you may take me to dinner at the nice Italian place near you Friday night. I'll be there at seven." I couldn't let him think he could treat me badly and still have me any time he wanted.

❧❧❧

I found Friday and Sunday panties along with an IOU for another Saturday pair in my purse after I slunk into my apartment late Sunday morning. He did cuddle me afterward, and he fixed me breakfast in the mornings. Adam improved a good bit, but required frequent reminding. He never treated me nearly as well as Tim had. He willingly tried new things in bed, but nothing much out of the ordinary.

For special occasions such as my birthday or when I showed him a new trick he liked, he'd give me lingerie, most of which was disgusting, like the crotchless panties, edible underwear, and sexy garter belts. I did like the black lace panty and bra set he gave me, though. I won't admit how many sets of day-of-the week panties I got but suffice it to say I had to shift my panties to a large drawer of their own and didn't need to buy underwear until several boyfriends later.

I sucked and we screwed our brains out for several months. That was fine for a while, but I wanted a man to bring me to orgasm sometimes. Adam tried, but couldn't. Out of bed, I learned that Adam wasn't as smart as I had thought. He was just older, more experienced, and better educated than I was. If anything, I had more native intelligence. I wanted a man smarter than me. I missed Tim. Even a woman not in love likes to be adored.

A decision point came for me over a long weekend.

"I love you," he said. "I really do."

Damn. Don't like how I feel hearing that. I want to be ecstatic but I'm not. Can't fool myself. I'm not ready to look for another boyfriend. Shit.

Adam only called me to arrange trysts and wasn't discrete at work. I'd finally had it with him. Not one for emotional confrontations, I avoided him as much as possible and responded curtly when he approached me at work. He even left notes on my desk saying how much he loved me. I stopped returning his calls. He grudgingly accepted defeat, but salved his bruised ego by saying I'd stolen his soul and by hanging my missing panties from his rearview mirror. He unwittingly increased my sexiness quotient for men who'd previously found my body insufficiently interesting. Guys, who'd ignored me when I walked by before, started flirting with me. It goes to show you that a great blowjob is worth more to a man than a nice pair of knockers any day.

I enjoyed working at Carver-Watkins, but barely survived on what they paid me. Whenever I could afford the gas and tolls, I drove the two hundred thirty-two miles to visit my family in Frostbite Falls, as brother Daniel called it. I didn't think I would but I really missed my time with them. We'd never been separated before. Mother had supported me daily and Daddy's good humor always picked me up. Mike and Jake begged me to stay on every visit. It was painful to leave them but there were no jobs for me there.

My boss rated my work highly at my annual review, but gave me a paltry raise. The only promotion available to me required three years' experience and special training. I looked for another job, but stopped, disheartened, when the recruiter told me Carver-Watkins paid more than any company in the area. I was stuck in a dead-end job. What could I do?

CHAPTER 8

Doing My Patriotic Duty

I chose to believe my life was half-full rather than half-empty. Adam gave me more than dechastifuckation, he increased my confidence. From him, I learned I could get sex whenever I wanted it, even if it was rather ordinary and lacked passion. My increased confidence also helped me on the work front. Bosses and co-workers noticed I was smart and assigned me tasks normally given to people in higher pay grades, and I performed them well. Sadly, they led to no increase in salary because I didn't have the formal education for a promotion.

Still too shy to come on to men at bars, I enlisted pretty girlfriends to help. Two or three—two usually worked best—of us would scope out the joint, paying closest attention to pairs or sets of guys we found attractive. Standing next to the prettiest girl in the room helped a lot until I developed my own persona.

‿◞✾◟‿

In Spring 1970, when nights were finally warm enough for outdoor escapades, Sybil, my perky, ultimate

Jersey girlfriend from work, who attracted men like the Pied Piper entranced rats, found great hunting at Snorkels, a cool rustic dance joint in an old, unpainted barn decorated with airplane parts mounted on the walls and hanging from the ceiling. Only ten miles from home near an air force training base, it was far enough away that nobody who knew us would see us there but still within an easy drive. Bouncers at the door kept underage guys out, but let almost-twenty-year-old girls they liked in, if we promised not to drink. The disproportionately male clientele coupled with soft lighting skewed the odds in our favor.

I remember well one of my first snorkeling nights.

"Whaddya think of those two at the corner of the bar?" Sybil looked down at her Seven-Up as she talked. The blond, muscular guy talked excitedly with the tall, dark, and trim guy with him. Still in training status, these airmen were almost all young, trim, and fit. Few were flabby and fewer yet fat.

Sybil made eye contact with the blond.

She could have him. "I'll take the brunet," I said.

She caught blondy's eye again and held contact through the tobacco haze. When he started toward us, she signaled him to stop. He looked puzzled. She looked at his friend.

Her guy looked back more puzzled than before. When she held up two fingers, he seemed to understand. He and his wingman hustled over to us.

The brunet filled out his tight blue jeans the way I liked and sauntered with the confidence of a man accustomed to scoring with girls he met in bars. He was definitely not looking for companionship.

As blondy approached, Sybil slid over to him, leaving me the raven-haired hunk.

"You've got the most beautiful red hair I've ever

seen," he said, exuding confidence almost to the point of being cocky.

Nice come on. He wasn't here as a favor to his buddy. He wanted to bugger me. Now to see what I wanted him for. Not good with small talk, I'd learned a few tricks that led to much success at picking up guys. For starters, I wore a hippie-slut dress that camouflaged my least attractive features and screamed, "I'm easy," increasing my nympho quotient in some quarters.

"Thanks. What brings you here?" This would be good for a couple of minutes.

Any question at all usually got guys talking about themselves. This guy chattered at length. I feigned interest, but cogitated about what, if anything, I was going to do with him.

"What do you do in the air force?" This one often generated fifteen minutes of chatter. Guys this handsome didn't usually hit on me. I got the quiet, cerebral types, something he wasn't. I had three choices: do him outside immediately, give him my number so he could ask me out on a proper date, or go fish for another. I'd already learned not to get it on with guys in the parking lot. One quickie was all I'd get, and I always wanted it to last longer than that. I chose option one, my favorite. The decision made, I waited for him to make a suggestion, any suggestion.

"Let's step outside where it's quieter," he said.

That was my cue. I winked at Sybil to tell her I was leaving with him—we always drove separately.

"Okay." I picked up my purse and headed for the door. He followed so closely he rammed my butt when I slowed down at my car. *Don't need to check if he's ready.* "I know a better place to…uh…talk."

He grabbed me when I reached into the trunk to retrieve a blanket.

"A little patience, please!" I wrenched myself free and strode toward the lake the bar overlooked. He hesitated a few seconds then scampered to catch up. We marched fifty yards along the shore to a large stone that marked the edge of my favorite summer playground, a mattress-sized soft mossy area nestled in a patch of chokeberry bushes. I often spread the blanket for my comfort and my legs for my heroes' gratification in this secluded spot.

"Ha, ha, ha, ha, ha." I laughed loudly and twitched wildly when he touched one of the large ticklish regions on my hypersensitive body that surround much smaller erogenous zones when he tried to undrawer me. I grabbed his hand and held it still. Tired of losing unmentionables in the bushes, I'd dispensed with my day-of-the-week panties—no bikinis or thongs for me, I prefer comfort to fashion and don't keep my bloomers on long enough to warrant wearing them on barhopping maneuvers—and bra before starting out on night maneuvers.

"*What?*"

He might've been confused. Sometimes men think I'm playing games when I'm just supersensitive around their strategic targets.

"Shssh. Gimme a second." I wished it wasn't so overcast. Even a partial moon reflects enough light off the lake for me to see men's reactions when I pleasure them. I would enjoy seeing his expression when he reaches under my skirt, but it's too dark. With no unmentionables to guide him, he lost his bearings and touched me in tickle-sensitive spots.

I tried to be funny. "Do you prefer men?"

"No. It's so dark I can't see anything." He sounded frustrated and embarrassed.

"Want me to guide you?" It was time to get down to business.

"Ooookay," he said with a sense of defeat.

"What're you looking for?"

"Your bra."

I guided his hand up to a breast. "Will this do?"

"Just fine," he answered while circling my nipple with his finger. "How do you like to be fondled?"

"I like new experiences the best." *See what he comes up with.*

He crawled under my dress up to his waist, tongue first, moistening the area around my nipple and it, too, without licking it.

"Whooo." I dampened myself elsewhere when I felt his warm breath blow across my moist nipple. I pulled his mouth to my other breast, and we were off to the races. A good time was had by both, but, as usual, even better for him. I gave him an experience he could share with his grandchildren. Scratch that. Make that his air force buddies.

Afterward, I gave him a phony name and number. I don't know if he called or not. I never saw him again. But he must've told the guys in his barracks about me because I noticed airmen looking expressly for my long red hair shortly after I serviced him, something I hadn't experienced before.

By the Fourth of July, Independence Day, I no longer needed Sybil as bait. I came here alone on Saturday nights when she was on dates with her boyfriend and—usually—bedded the stud of my choice. A guy'd saunter in, buy a beer at the bar, and try to look casual as he scanned the room. His head'd stop short when he saw me. I'd look away but few bothered to establish eye contact first. They just toddled up to me.

"Come here often?" Occasionally, one would come up with something original or funny but seldom.

I didn't mind their hokey pickup lines. I wanted sex.

They graciously gave it to me and me to them. By aiding and comforting our armed forces, I was doing my part in improving our troops' morale. What could be better?

I honed my skills, tried new positions, experimented with tricks I read about in books, and even learned some new mattress dancing moves from my one or—rarely—two-night-stands and, surprisingly, a little from those I turned down.

I didn't want scenes with guys I didn't want to shag, so I'd politely excuse myself for the ladies room and pick up my purse. I followed the well-worn path through the peanut shells, passed the door labeled "Pilots," and waited my turn in the line at the door marked "Targets" for one of the three stalls in the undersized lavatory. I learned much from the broadsheets posted on the backs of the stall doors and sidewalls as I sat on the toilet seat lid long enough for the guy to realize I wasn't returning. I drank very little liquid of any kind in bars because I feared every disease imaginable lurked in those gross johns. Reading the educational flyers on the walls corrected a misimpression I held.

I'd foolishly thought the owner named the place Snorkels because they had something to do with airplanes. On the contrary, a snorkel is a sex act with multiple permutations.

I learned, to perform as well as receive. Those sheets showed me how to give, or direct my lover to lavish me, with several variations. I wouldn't have known about this welcome addition to my rapidly growing bag of tricks if guys I wasn't interested in hadn't hit on me. I thank them for the gift.

⧼⧽

"Rowena, I think I'm falling in love with you," said

a shy, inexperienced, gentle one as he rode me the second weekend in a row.

"Don't be silly. You'll forget me before your plane retracts its wheels." He reminded me of Tim, so I imagined it was him—the one guy I wanted to bed me but didn't—who throbbed inside me.

Some guys insisted on doing it doggie style. At first I complied, but I didn't like doing it that way because it seemed so impersonal, as if I didn't matter to them. I learned to be more assertive and demand they look at me, at least the first few times.

As I became more self-confident, I injected humor into my love-making sessions, usually about their shortcomings. Some of them couldn't take a joke very well. I'd become a bona fide smart-ass Jersey Girl.

Sybil and I never breathed a word about our Snorkels exploits at work, although she slipped and called me Rowena a couple of times. Most girls were so blindly anti-war, they blamed our young soldiers, calling them baby-killers and worse. I knew better. The government tore Tim from me against his will. He didn't want to go. I, too, was against the war, but didn't blame the boys who were drafted and sent thousands of miles from home to fight people they'd barely heard of before in places they didn't know existed.

That might be why I so enjoyed spending those evenings at Snorkels, on and off my blanket. Those boys deserved to be rewarded for the tremendous sacrifices they were making.

I must admit I wasn't completely altruistic. I greatly enjoyed my nights spent with them and became more of the woman I wanted to be by being kind to those young men.

భాఖ

In late August, Tim shocked me with a call out of the blue.

"I'd like to see you this weekend, Mary Louise," he said with utmost sincerity and some remorse.

"Have you broken up with Zelda?" Didn't want her to have him, even though I didn't want him.

"This time it's final," he said with a note of resignation.

May have to adjust my weekend around his visit. "When will you arrive?"

"Late Saturday morning. I work Friday night. I'll get there at eleven if I leave here at seven."

Friday would be my Snorkels night that week. "I don't live at home any more. My apartment's in the same building as Beth's. Remember where it is?"

"Yah. See you Saturday."

He arrived right on time—Tim was punctual to a fault—gym bag in hand.

"You look so different," he said. "Your hair's so long now."

"You don't like it?" He fell in love with my old look, so he might have had difficulty with the new.

My Indian braids hung down to my nipples, making me look like a hippie, which I wasn't. I never tried drugs and hated alcohol. They were spoiled rich brats.

"You were beautiful just as you were. This'll take some getting used to."

"You'll sleep here." I pointed to a foam chair in the living room that opened into a cot. "Nothing's going to happen. Get it?"

"Yes," he said, slumping like a balloon with its air being let out.

Wanting to minimize the time alone in my apartment for fear of weakening, I said, "Let's do something."

"I called my old roommate. He's out now and has invited us to go out on Long Island Sound on his motor-boat."

No sooner had we pulled out of the marina into the Sound on calm water than my stomach fluttered. Never having been on a boat before, I didn't know I was susceptible to seasickness. "Long Island Fisherman," as Tim's friend identified himself on the radio, gave me a Dramamine tablet. Tim helped me below where he gave me the pill and some water. He held me till my stomach calmed. A few minutes later, I was fine and enjoyed the day's activities on the water.

That night at my apartment, I helped Tim make his bed then got into mine alone and with the door closed. *He still loves me. No doubt about that. Will he try anything tonight?*

I awoke to find him quietly reading the Sunday paper in his bed-returned-to-chair.

"Like to have a bagel for breakfast?" I asked with little food in the house.

He looked confused by my question. "Don't know. Never had one."

Shit. My sex books are right by where he slept. He'll think I'm a slut. "You'll like them. There's a good place between here and my work. I'll give you a tour after we eat."

Tim liked cinnamon-raisin bagels with cream cheese, a new treat for him. I showed him around my office: my cubicle, the keypunch machine, and teletype where I also punched paper-tapes sometimes.

"How do I look?" I asked, after I wrapped a paper-tape around my head like an Indian headband.

"Pretty, of course, but like a hippie Indian chick. What do the people in the office think?"

"They think I'm a little weird but they like me."

Tim and I were so much alike, other than him being

repressed sexually. We were both very intelligent, shy, awkward socially, came from poor families, and had alcoholic parents. I'd never realized this before.

Tim drove me back to my apartment to drop me off and pick up his bag. We just looked at each other when we said goodbye. No kiss. No squeeze of the hand. No "I'd like to see you again."

I let him leave with the impression I had no further interest in him then went into my bedroom to watch from my window as he drove away. *This's the last time I'll ever see him. Tim's out of my life forever.* Not long after that, Daniel wrote that Tim had married Zelda.

The days soon got shorter, the evenings colder, and my ass froze, even under a blanket on my moss bed. It was time to move back indoors, but where, and with whom?

CHAPTER 9

Bartholomew

No sooner had I determined to take a hiatus from Snorkels, than my work phone rang unexpectedly, interrupting me from analyzing some birth-control-product data.

"Tookie, I have some questions about the Noknockup-Nine study," said a vaguely familiar baritone voice.

People irritated me when they disrupted my concentration. Thinking his was a low priority call, I responded brusquely. "I'm tied up all day."

"We'll just have to talk about it over lunch then," he persisted.

"Okay, but you're buying." Demanding he pay should have gotten him off my back.

"I'd love to treat you. Meet me at the back door at noon sharp."

Uh, oh. He must want something. He said, "love to." Shift gears, Mary Louise. This guy must want more than an explanation of the effectiveness of a spermicide. He might want a field test.

I slipped out the back door a minute before noon, but no car was by the door. Just then, a brand new white

Buick Riviera coupe zipped up. The passenger window lowered, allowing a gust of cold air to blast me in the face.

"Get in," came from the disembodied body on the other side of the tinted glass as the automatic door latch clicked open.

"Power windows. Cool." I plopped my bottom onto the burgundy leather bucket seat as my window rose automatically in air-conditioned luxury. I couldn't consider buying a car like this on my meager salary, but riding in it sure was nice.

Behind the wheel was Bartholomew, a private-school-educated, mid-level marketing manager with a master's degree who hadn't previously paid me any attention. Although he was not conventionally handsome, I found Bartholomew sexy. Perhaps it was his quiet, confident manner. Possibly it was the smell of Boswell's Berry Cobbler tobacco emanating from his tweed sport coat—I was a sucker for pipe smokers. His nondescript body didn't send chills through my loins but his sophistication, intelligence, and witty repartee sure impressed me.

We soon arrived at Cynthia's Sin, a restaurant near the office, but well beyond my budget.

Overwhelmed by the opulent Victorian interior, I whimpered, "I can't afford this." It was two days to payday, and I didn't have enough to buy a Coke there.

"Reserv—" The maitre de looked up from the reservation list to see Bartholomew standing in front of him. "Oh, yes. I have the perfect table for you. Follow me." He led us to the most remote corner of the dimly lit back room to a table away from any windows and not visible to others in the purple damask room. "Will this do, sir?"

Bartholomew subtly winked at the maitre de. "Perfect, thank you, Romando."

I'd never seen a man tip someone just for seating us

at a good table before. I felt like the heroine in a Victorian novel who was the target of a seducer, but this was one girl who wasn't trying to avoid her "fate worse than death." Was he planning on taking my share of the cost of lunch out in trade? I wouldn't have minded that.

Apparently sensing my discomfort, he said, "My treat. Remember? What I learn from you will be well worth the cost of a lunch—even here."

He couldn't have really meant that. The Noknockup-Nine tests were about the simplest analyses we ever ran. Well, I'd been seeing that some of these people higher up the food chain weren't all that smart. I focused on our conversation and pretended I was eating at Elby's to distract myself from the lavish surroundings.

I nervously gobbled my lunch while Bart savored his. "While you're finishing your steak, I'll start going over the report I brought with me," I said. "This's the chi-squared test. It determines how well our study participants fit the distribution of people in the general population who're likely to use a spermacide along with a condom."

"So this number means that results from our sample should be representative of the people who will buy the product?"

Doesn't act like he's putting on that he didn't know this before. Wow! "Precisely." *That's what I'm trying to tell you. Otherwise we'd be hosed and would have to run the test all over again. I can't believe you didn't learn this basic stuff years ago. I didn't take stats in high school, but figured this much out by reading part of a book from the department library and asking statisticians questions.*

"This has been a most productive lunch, Tookie. Keep in mind I'm just an English Lit major who has been working in marketing ever since college."

"Do the test results make sense to you now?" *You*

can't not understand it. But if you want to trump up some phony reason to be alone with me again, I'm game.

On the way back, he lowered his voice as if he had something important to say. "I still have some questions about its use with Spartan Maximums." He maintained eye contact unusually long, especially for someone driving in traffic.

Hmm. He might want to try out the new ribbed condom on me. I'm up for that. Actually, he's the one who'll have to get it up. I'll have to snatch a box of them. Now to determine if this is business or pleasure. "Wednesday at seven?"

Bart broke into a wide smile upon hearing my suggestion. "Tavern on the Green?"

Pleasure it is! He wants to take me on a real date and spend a bunch of money on me. He must want me badly. Wait till Sybil hears this. "Too far away for a week night." *Don't want him to know I'm uncomfortable in such ritzy places.*

"Charley's Other Brother?" His raised eyebrows suggested real interest.

"Fine." *He must really like me. He's the most sophisticated man who's ever shown a tiny bit of interest in me. I could fall for him.*

"Keep this between us," he said quietly in a very serious tone. "Better not be seen going in together. I'll wait a few minutes."

"Understood," I said, getting out of his new Riviera. "Better zip your fly."

He looked down, seeing it was closed, then looked at me, puzzled. I gave him my gotcha look. He laughed. *It's nice he can laugh at himself.*

I strolled back to my desk, daydreaming about what my date with Bart would be like. Did he want to talk about opera and ballet? I didn't know anything about either of them, but I wanted to. Or did he just want a piece of my young ass?

Sybil darted into my cubicle, interrupting my reverie. "You better watch him," she said, looking concerned. She was seldom this serious and rarely warned me about anything.

"Who?" We were discrete.

She looked me straight in the eyes with an intensity I hadn't previously seen. "You know damned well who. I saw you with him."

"Just business." I always wanted to be a femme fatale and have secret rendezvous with debonair men. He was more like Ray Milland than Cary Grant.

"Monkey business, if I know you," she scowled, "and him."

"What about him?" *Better compare notes. She's been around here a lot longer than I have.*

"This isn't first hand, mind you, but Carol told me his wife's Catholic and believes sex is only for procreation—and she doesn't want children."

"So?" That was why he didn't have any kids. Everybody knew women from his generation didn't enjoy sex like we baby boomers did.

"He wants oral sex in the worst way and she won't—" Sybil grimaced. "—even if he lets her spit."

"Why should I believe this?" The girls in the office said they didn't like it, either, but most of them would blow a guy in Macy's window if he'd agree to marry them. Bart's wife probably gave him enough to get him to walk her down the aisle, then locked her jaws after the honeymoon.

Sybil looked to her left then to her right. Seeing no one approaching, she nodded. "Carol talks to all the executives' wives. She gets them to spill their guts. I don't know how she does it, but she does."

"What makes you think he's just a horny ol' billy goat hitting on me?" Bart treated me with more respect than anyone except Tim and he was willing and able to spend a ton of money on me.

"Carol caught him listening in on the girls in marketing gossip over lunch and they'd make a marine blush. He probably thinks you'll give him an Around the World."

"Can a man his age get it up four times in a row?" *Three orifices, four ejaculations. Where to start?*

"He's only thirty-five, but you're too much of a hygiene freak for that," she said, waving her hand like she was swatting away a pest.

"I like washing men." *Could arouse him that way, too. He'd love getting it on with me four times in a row. Bang, bang, bang, bang. That'd be more than he gets in a year now, I bet.*

Sybil rolled her eyes. "Be sensible, Tookie. He's married."

"I've got to make a change. Nights're too cold now for Snorkels." Didn't enjoy getting my bones cracked against cold, hard ground with my teeth chattering. I had never done it on leather seats, but thought it would feel nice. He surely had a good heater.

The nights until our date dragged on slowly, and I thought of nothing but Bart. Days weren't too bad. Work kept me occupied most of the time.

Butterflies fluttered inside me and I felt a warm rush when I finally saw Bartholomew's Riviera pull up from my bedroom window. I'd tried on and rejected every outfit in my limited wardrobe before deciding on the first one.

Already dressed and ready to go, I raced out the door and down the stairs to greet him, not wanting him to see my apartment until he was ready to get naked with me. It could have turned him off because he might have been uncomfortable with my threadbare surroundings.

"You look especially lovely tonight, Tookie." He pecked me on the lips so unexpectedly and pulled away so quickly, I had no time to react one way or the other. He opened the car door for me, and closed it after I climbed in. I sat there dazed, not wanting him to know how excited I was about going out with him. The last time I'd felt anything like this was on my first date with Tim. I barely spoke in the restaurant because I had to pee so badly. My parents gave me plenty of dating advice, but they neglected to say anything about urinary etiquette.

"I haven't been here before." Bart looked the place over while we waited to be seated in the recently opened trendy restaurant which was packed, especially for a Wednesday night. "I overheard my secretary talking about it and thought you might like it."

"I used to like TGI Friday's best, but now this's my favorite." Several people at work frequented Friday's and I didn't want to be seen by people who knew me when I was on dates.

As soon as we got a table, a waiter pressed us for a drink order.

"I'll have a whiskey sour and the lady will have a…"

"Cranberry juice." Although I hadn't found an "adult beverage" I liked, I momentarily considered ordering something to make me look older and more sophisticated. But the waiter might have carded me, and I didn't want Bart to know I wasn't twenty-one. Besides that, as sexually active as I was I needed to ward off bladder infections.

"About the report—"

"I forgot it." He lifted his palms up and smiled.

We both knew his interest in the report was just a ruse to spend time with me.

He chuckled. "Good. I want to hear all about you."

"And I thought all you wanted was for me to be a test subject for Noknockup-Nine and/or the Spartan Maximus." *Let's see how he reacts to that flirt.*

He blushed a light pink, but quickly flirted right back. "Oh, a lot more than that. You might be the ideal subject for a longitudinal study, say three times a week for decades."

"How many times each night? Four, five, six?" I could play this game, too.

Bart involuntarily spit out the water he was drinking.

The waiter brought the flirting to an end by bringing our drinks. Bart raised his glass to me. "To us."

"To us." Clink. *Nice and simple, easy to remember. Use that toast on dates unless something better comes along.*

"What do you recommend?" Bart asked when the waiter impatiently tapped his pen against his order pad.

The harried waiter acted as if he expected us to already know what we wanted. "Women like the salads, but men usually prefer our burgers, which are quite good and unusual."

"The lady will have the Southwest Chicken Salad with—" He looked at me. "—honey mustard dressing."

I nodded. He instinctively knew what I wanted. This was nice.

"And I'll have the bleu-cheese burger with steak fries, medium well. And a Heineken. I like a beer with a burger. And another cranberry juice for the lady."

No guy ever ordered for me before. Bartholomew was really a gentleman. I wanted to throw him down on the table and have my way with him.

I wolfed down my salad to get him back to my apartment as soon as possible. "I have dessert at home, if you'd like some."

"I'd love it." He tossed several bills on the table and trotted me out of the restaurant.

Back at my place, I handed him my door key. He unlocked it and pushed it half open. Before he could pull the key out of the door, I leaned into him. Welcoming the invitation, he pressed his already hot lips against mine, kissing me passionately as his body pinned mine to the door jamb. I hadn't come up for air yet when I felt him fiddling with my buttons.

"I can get them off quicker than you can." I didn't want him to see me naked until he was, too. He wouldn't back out then. I bumped the front door closed with my butt and pulled him through the living room into my bedroom.

"It's not how efficiently they're removed, Tookie, it's the pleasure one gets from the removal. Relax. You'll enjoy this. I know I will."

"Okay." He was smooth. *Ooohh.* I liked how he slowly unbuttoned each item, folded, and placed it carefully on the chair. I liked how he kissed each part of me as he unwrapped it. Either his wife's body wasn't much, or he saw so little of it, mine looked good to him. Maybe my willingness to share it turned him on.

"See, that didn't hurt a bit and I get the joy of seeing your magnificent body in its unobstructed glory."

Maybe my black bra and lace panties made me look sexier.

"My turn." Impatient, I undressed him quickly without the regard for his expensive tweed sport coat and slacks he gave my discount store duds. During our first fully naked kiss, he lifted me up and placed me gently on my back in the middle of my bed. He was confident, but gentle. He definitely knew his way around a woman's body. Rather than taking the lead as I usually do, I surrendered myself to him.

"Oh, ooh, oooh. This feels good. Don't stop." Bartholomew touched me as gently and to please me much as Tim did, but much more skillfully. I hoped he'd be as patient with me.

"Relax. I know what I'm doing." He continued, varying speed, intensity, location, and technique with no apparent hurry. He acted as if he had all night—and he did if he wanted it. It didn't take that long. It took quite a while, but I savored every second of it. Being the center of attention the first time since Tim, I was in no hurry. No siree. I just laid back and enjoyed what he was doing until I could hold back no longer.

"Oh. Oh God. Oh God. Yes. Yes. Keep going!" *I'll kill you if you stop now. You're so close.* "Yes. Ooooh. I'm coming. I'm coming. Yes, Yes, Yes!" *Just keep doing what you're doing. I've never felt anything within miles of this before.* "Bart, Oh Bartholomew, Oh Bart, OmiGod, God, Bart, Bart, Bart."

I collapsed in rapture, panting to catch my breath. Had I not been so out of breath, I would've told Bart how deeply I felt about him. But it was much too soon for that. I lay still for a full two minutes savoring what I'd just felt.

I kissed him all over his face, head, and hands. "Thank you. Thank you. What would you like me to do for you? Just name it." Every page in my playbook—and some that weren't—was open to him. I wanted to give Bart a night he'd remember always.

He just soaked in my kisses. "Surprise me."

I started his Around the World by having my favorite organ for dessert.

He'd popped my other cherry, so to speak, by being the first man to bring me to orgasm. But not with his penis, as I eventually learned, that doesn't usually work for me. Bart helped me discover that I'm a moaner, with my volume exponentially relative to the pleasure I'm experiencing.

He stayed over that night and the next—with neither of us getting much sleep—but couldn't Friday because his wife was returning from her West Coast business trip. We made the most of the few hours we had to ourselves in my bedroom after work. I enjoyed watching Bart put on his clothes and especially how he tied a perfect Windsor on the first try.

"Tookie, these have been the best three days of my life. I thought I'd loved before, but I was just practicing until you came into my life."

"Ditto." I couldn't believe I said that. It's better keep quiet and not sound stupid. Bart didn't seem to mind and kissed me good bye so passionately he sucked the oxygen out of my lungs.

Neighbors gave me odd looks when I went out for a late supper after he left, possibly because I was so loud the last three nights.

The single guys flirted, but I wasn't about to get involved with anybody who lived that close. Getting rid of them when the affair ended could be messy. I wanted to avoid drama.

Young and inexperienced, I believed Bart's complaints about his wife and his professions of love for me. I also relished the intrigue, danger, and adventure that came with this illicit relationship. I denied it then, even to myself, but besting a competitor fed my ego. I planned my liaisons meticulously, something else I enjoyed doing. I became a great logistician by organizing our trysts around our schedules, planning getaway weekends when his wife was—frequently, but not frequently enough—out of town, keeping feelings and plans under wraps in the office, avoiding places where we shouldn't be seen together, and not leaving tell-tale evidence on Bartholomew or in his car.

I got a lot of different things from my time with Bart. He took me to several Broadway shows I couldn't have afforded at the time, introduced me to luxury hotels and secluded New England resorts, explained museum exhibits to me, and took me to my first *Swan Lake* performance, something for which I'll be forever grateful. More importantly, he raised my satisfaction quotient an order of magnitude. Wanting to please him as much as I possibly could, I upped my game and broadened my repertoire.

One thing about Bart nagged at me. He wasn't circumcised. I didn't know dicks came any other way until I got my hands, and other body parts, on his. As much as I enjoyed the considerable amount of time I spent with numerous joysticks in my extremities and orifices over the years, I do have some hang-ups, foreskins being one. I find them gross. I fear they weren't properly cleaned since their previous usage. I tried to overlook Bart's cutis because he gave me so much else, but I couldn't completely.

Bartholomew gave me something besides sex and adventure: valuable career advice.

"Do you know where you are on the org chart, Tookie?" He leaned back in his seat at the far end of my couch and fiddled with his pipe.

"In the box at the bottom?" I'd never given my place on the org chart any thought. I wasn't even sure what purpose it served.

He took the pipe out of his mouth and blew out a puff of smoke. "You're in a pool box. *You're* not really on the org chart since *your* name doesn't appear anywhere on it."

"Does it matter?" He irritated me. I took academic classes in high school and this sounded like business school mumbo jumbo. The only thing I appreciated from this "little talk" was his pipe's aroma.

"Only if you want to make a living wage." Looking oh so smug, he put his pipe back in his mouth and took another puff of it.

"How do you get on the chart?" No one had ever discussed anything like this with me. Daddy and the men he worked with did the same job all the time, just on different blast furnaces at different sites. If they had org charts, they didn't move up them.

"Get a college degree. Otherwise, you'll stay where you are." He looked very serious saying this.

What crap. I valued my free time and didn't want to spend my prime sitting in a stuffy classroom or doing homework when I could be getting naked with a man. But I needed a raise and wouldn't get one without college.

Carver-Watkins and its competitors employed numerous statisticians and, fortunately for me, the local state university offered programs in that field. Taking Bart's advice, I enrolled as a stats major taking night and weekend classes.

I'd always liked school—the classroom part where I excelled and felt special—and enjoyed college, even though working my way through was a grind. The biggest downside was greatly reduced weeknight trysts and weekends with Bart. We drifted apart, seeing each other only when it was mutually convenient.

One day out of the blue, Cynthia invited me to lunch at Rocky's, a popular place near the office where coworkers often lunched.

"I want to catch up with what you've been doing the six months you've been assigned to the New York City office," I said to open the conversation.

She sat with her back to the corner where she could

see whoever happened to walk in. "We've got to talk—seriously."

"Okay. About what?" I hadn't a clue. I'd kept my affair with Bart a secret from everyone but Sybil and hadn't been with another guy for months.

Cynthia leaned over to me and whispered, "You've got to end your affair with Bartholomew."

I was stunned and took several seconds to compose myself. "What affair?" Maybe she was bluffing. She shouldn't have known anything about it.

She straightened up in her chair and addressed me as if I was her kid sister. "Don't BS me, Mary Louise. I know all about it. I know all of Bart's tricks and you're a fresh kid who needs to be warned."

"I—I—" We'd been too discreet for her to know anything.

"When I was your age, I was just as sure of myself as you are, but I learned a valuable lesson the hard way from Bartholomew."

"I hadn't heard anything about you and Bart." Where was she going with this?

"Has he taken you to my place yet?" She stared me down until I answered.

"Your place?" Why would he take me to her apartment? I wasn't following her at all.

"Cynthia's Sin. It's named after my youthful indiscretion with Bartholomew. The owner's a friend of his who renamed it when he took it over several years ago. Has he taken *you* to the private niche in the far back corner yet?"

"Yes." There was no point in lying about it.

"That's where it took place. Bartholomew acted the perfect gentleman on our first date, but after he had me hooked, he seduced me in full view of hidden cameras.

He surprised me with the photos a week later. I threw up all over him. He thought it was a big joke."

"And you were serious about him?" *Bastard. Some gentleman he is. No wonder Cynthia's so wounded.*

"I was. I even believed all that bunk he spread about his wife and thought he'd leave her for me. Fool."

He was despicable. I did him any way he liked and I didn't mind people gossiping about me, but I don't want any pictures taken. Period. I believed Cynthia. Better to end this before I got hurt. Besides, there was a guy in calculus class I wanted to get to know better, in the biblical sense. Be that as it may, I'd give my affair with Bart the ending it deserved.

❧❦

On a non-school night, I noticed Bart working late on a rush project. I occupied myself with homework until everyone else had cleared out. When we had the place to ourselves, I changed into the hippie dress I wore at Snorkels and used for office sex. If someone interrupted us, I could flip the skirt back down to quickly appear fully clothed. I stuffed my panties into my purse, and slunk in silently behind him where he stood at a filing cabinet intently looking for a folder, not hearing me enter.

Bang. I plopped him flat on his back on his oversize-executive desk using the element of surprise to make up for our size difference.

"What're—"

"Be still. You're going to enjoy this." I aimed to make sure he did this one last time.

Craaack. His suspender buttons popped off when I jerked his pants, boxers, and all down to his knees.

I stroked his stalk a few times and he reported in ready for action, even more quickly than usual. "Here I come. Lie still." My unsexy desert boots got me up on top of his desk in short order—I choose comfort and practicality over fashion.

Almost dripping in anticipation of the fun I was about to have, I eased myself onto his throbbing thumper. *Should I let my skirt engulf him completely or not? Let him watch my pleasure palace work its magic one last time or do I have him look me in the face? I want to drink in his shocked expression as I give him the last he'll ever get from me.* So, I pulled my skirt back from his face. It didn't take many thrusts to launch his payload.

Perhaps poking my lubricated finger into a place I'd never before explored helped. I spied a rush letter his secretary had typed for his signature. When I rose, I watermarked it with his dripping pollen. What fun!

Unable to keep a straight face any longer, I hopped down and left. "Thanks for everything. Next time your friend opens a new restaurant, tell him not to name it 'Tookie's Nookie.'"

He lay on his desk, stunned.

"Ciao. It's been great." I waved back at him as I flipped my skirt down and exited, feeling I'd regained some self-esteem by kissing him off in style.

Now, how would I get Calculus Guy's attention?

CHAPTER 10

Exhibitionist

I learned something about myself that day I hadn't realized before. Exhilarated after leaving Bart's office and braver than ever before, I pranced out the door to drive home. When I lifted my skirt so I wouldn't trip over it when climbing the concrete steps leading to the parking lot, a cool breeze reminded my naked heinie that my drawers were in my purse.

"Yes!" Here was my chance at last. I was parked in full view of a security camera—and it was far enough away they wouldn't know who it was.

Rather than hopping into my car and dashing off, I positioned myself to give the camera a full frontal view. I leaned back against the piece-of-shit Vega, that I bought when my Mustang gave out, as if I was a model at a car show and stood still long enough to get at least one security guard's attention. I then flipped the skirt of my office-sex dress over my head and spread my legs wide to give the guards the best possible view. I paused a few seconds, then slowly pulled the panties out of my purse and shook them with a flourish before stepping into them as deliberately as I could, first the left foot, then the right. Dressing one-handed proved so difficult, I stuffed my skirt into my mouth and bit on it to free up my other hand. I slowly wriggled them up into place then massaged my love basket for effect.

Holding the skirt in front of my face was essential for anonymity and to keep it from giving me unwanted modesty. They could see everything they wanted, but they couldn't see who was flashing them. Thinking I was anonymous made my first serious attempt at exposing myself to strangers easier and more fun. I was so far from the camera, they surely couldn't make out whose muff was flashing them.

When I tried to pull out of my parking spot, the hem of the ankle-length skirt got tangled in my feet. I pulled it safely out of the way, then thought, "What the hell?" and hiked it high enough above my nearly transparent thin white tricot panties for anyone close enough to easily confirm I'm a natural redhead, another feature that made me special.

I drove as slowly as possible past the gatehouse to give the guard at the open window a close-up view. I barely heard him say, "Damn it, why don't we have color monitors?" as I idled by.

I laughed all the way home. I didn't need applause to recognize my Oscar-worthy performance.

୧৽୧৽

After work one bitterly cold evening the following winter, that crappy Vega wouldn't start. Apparently remembering me from my performance months earlier, every guard not required to remain at one of the gates scurried out to assist me. I was too naïve to realize they knew exactly who I was.

"Can we help you, miss?" the first guard to arrive asked.

"This damn Vega won't start. It barely cranks at all." *Better clean up my language from what I really think about this worthless car.*

"May I have the keys?" he asked, after looking under the hood. He had no better luck than I'd had.

Seeing nothing good happening, the oldest guard approached me. "I'm afraid this may take a while, miss. You better wait in the shack." He gave me hot chocolate to drink while I warmed myself next to the heater. When they finally got it running, one of them drove it over to me while two others piled in as passengers in case it stalled.

As they all climbed out at the guard shack, I rushed out to meet them.

"You all have been so kind. What can I do to thank you?" I was so grateful I would've done *anything* to thank them.

One of the guards winked. "You thanked us in advance, miss."

I recognized him as the one whom I flashed my beaver on the way out in the summer. I winked back. Although I'd envied girls adventurous enough to strip off their clothes or boink in public, I'd never previously considered exposing myself before. I didn't know I wanted to be an exhibitionist. The closest I had come came before wasn't close at all.

Well aware of how construction workers in the City whistled and hooted at women who happened by, I prepared myself mentally should this ever happen to me. When it did, I chose to interpret their wolf whistles as flattery—I don't get many compliments, so I take them any way I get them—and turned to face them.

Rather than complain, shriek, or swear at them like a lot of girls did, I curtsied low as if bowing to the queen.

On rising, I said, "Thank you. Thank you. Thank

you!" while throwing them kisses Dinah Shore-like, then turned and swished my ass as I walked away. They responded with a standing ovation.

I love being adored!

CHAPTER 11

Calculus Guy & Mensa Man

Pssst."

Evelyn, the dowdy new friend I'd met at the beginning of the semester, looked away from the hunk working a difficult calculus problem on the blackboard to see what I wanted.

I raised my eyebrows high then shifted my gaze to the guy.

Evelyn scrunched her nose and squinted her eyes, distorting her face to look like the witch from Hansel and Gretel.

Good. I didn't want to break up a possible friendship over a guy. I mouthed "okay" to her and returned my attention to the front of the room.

"Pssst."

I turned to see Evelyn warning me off by violently shaking her dishpan blonde hair "No."

I fantasized about integrating Calculus Guy's root until break when I marked time in the hall outside the classroom with Evelyn, all the while plotting a strategy to accidentally run into him.

She and I had recognized each other in the student union the second night of class and introduced ourselves.

We made a ritual of going over our homework, which we continued through the remainder of the term, and for other classes we found ourselves taking together the rest of our undergraduate careers.

Like me, Evelyn was the first in her blue-collar family to attend college. She chose to pursue a career in the new computer field. Super-short, bland, and with a plain face makeup would've helped, she wasn't unattractive to men, she was invisible.

She frowned. "Get those thoughts out of your mind. He's poison. He's already had half the girls in class. You'd just be another notch on his, uh, bedpost."

"He hasn't had me yet. When he has, he'll want encores. They always do."

"You don't really sleep with guys on the first date?" asked my repressed friend.

"Not if it'd make turning down a second date awkward."

I had to act cool because I'd never been with a player like him before. With two minutes to go, I said, "Got to go to the john."

As I turned the corner, I ran right into him, getting bounced off the wall by his solid six-foot frame.

"Watch where you're going." He looked annoyed at first but, after ogling me up and down, he smiled.

"Sorry. I was going to ask you to explain how you did that problem after class, but I can see you have no pity for a girl in distress."

"I'm always glad to help a pretty girl."

"Cut the bull. You know I'm not pretty." I'd never seen eyes as black as his.

"You're the prettiest girl in the class."

"Keep saying things like that and I might think you're trying to get into my pants."

"You'd like that, wouldn't you?"

He was the most confident man I'd encountered.

"Too soon to say." *Black wavy hair. Eastern Europe? Spanish?*

"Want me to help you after class?"

"Wait in the room for me. I have to walk Evelyn to her car."

He smirked. "She afraid of the dark?"

"Give me ten minutes and I'll be back. And she's not to know."

He nodded and left. He also ignored me during and after class as instructed.

I fantasized about my tryst as Evelyn and I walked down the hall.

"Go on without me," I said, turning to go into the ladies room. "I'll be a while."

She waved as I pushed the door open. "See you Thursday in the Union."

I popped in a breath mint and ran a brush through my hair before returning to the classroom.

Calculus Guy's normally straight mouth turned into a shit-eating grin when he saw me standing in the doorway. He stood up, filling his already tight jeans even tighter with his enthusiasm.

Alone, I flipped off the light switch but left the door open so as not to arouse suspicion. "Give me a second for my eyes to adjust."

He didn't.

He led me by the hand until we bumped into something large, probably the professor's big desk. Simultaneously, I felt what I wanted in my mouth probing my backside and his hands fondling my front.

Ooooohhh. Just relax and enjoy this.

I sucked in my gut to make it easier to unbutton me. That didn't take him long. I arched my back to press my pubis against his probing hands.

Aaaahhh. I've wet myself already. Hope he doesn't mind. Apparently not. Never let a man bend me over something like this before. Hmmm. He's having trouble putting it in.

"Want me to remove my Tampon?"

He chuckled and started exploring my backside. "So that's why you're so horny?"

"Normal for me."

"I've been lusting after your can since you first walked into class the beginning of the semester."

He squirted something on my other hole before sliding what felt like a finger in. I flinched.

"Relax. You'll be surprised how good it feels."

It felt better than I expected and wasn't too painful.

He pulled it out already? Oh. Now I know why. The bigger one wasn't his finger.

"Never done this before. It might not go in easy."

Bam. He pounded me hard against the desk.

"Ease up. This hurts."

Bang, Bang, Bang, the desk rattled as he humped me not quite as hard.

"Quieter," I whispered. "Somebody might hear us."

"You'd like someone to walk in and see us, wouldn't you Tooks?"

"Don't want that kind of reputation here, too."

Whoooo. He just hit the spot. I didn't know it'd feel so good there. I needed to grab onto the desk to hold still so he didn't fall out. He just came! I felt warmth in there. I couldn't usually feel it the regular way. No O but it felt good.

What'll we do next? In me's not a good idea? Blow him? Too gross. It's my turn.

Before I could make up my mind, he said, "Bring a blanket Thursday. I'm going to show you the best place on campus to do it."

"What?" *What the hell's going on here?*

I heard his boot heels clack against the terrazzo floor as he left. I pulled up my pants and ran after him but I was too late. He was nowhere to be seen.

I left my blanket in my trunk on Thursday and didn't see Calculus Guy until he walked in while the professor was going over the first homework problem. I tried not to look in his direction and he didn't look in mine. I ran after him at break, catching up with him outside the men's room.

"Where'd you go Tuesday?"

"You were great. Meet me at the stairwell with your blanket after class." He disappeared into the men's room leaving me standing in the hall.

I felt like a fool but, after depositing Evelyn at her car—I wasn't about to share a word of this with her—I ran to the stairwell, blanket in hand, to find him impatiently waiting tapping his fingers on the hand rail.

"What took you so long?"

"Had to walk Evelyn to her car and retrieve the blanket from mine."

"Bring it to class with you next time. Come on." He led me up the stairs, not stopping at the top floor. He kept going until we got to the top of the building. He opened a door and we stepped out onto the roof.

He looked at me confident I'd be dazzled with the tremendous view from up there. "What do you think?"

"It's a great place for a picnic. Help me spread out the blanket."

He seemed genuinely confused. "But we didn't bring any food."

"Pull down your pants and lie down."

Getting the message finally, he had them down before I could blink.

Hmm. Should I start him off with my basic blowjob

for beginning boyfriends or should I step it up a little? He's been with lots of women, but a bunch of them could rightly be considered charity fucks. Hmm. Better give him a hair drag and see how he responds.

Apparently, he'd had his way with lots of plain girls with little experience who appreciated the attention, however brief. Let's just say he didn't rush off after round one that night. Barely able to walk after our last round, he stumbled toward the door.

"Don't you want my phone number? We can have lots of fun this weekend."

"Don't need it. We can try out Passion Pond Tuesday. Don't forget your blanket."

"How about Saturday night?" I hated being treated like a bimbo he didn't want to be seen with.

"Have to work." He looked downright sincere saying that.

"After work."

"Too tired," he said over his shoulder as he walked away.

He expanded my repertoire but I wanted somebody who could be mistaken for a boyfriend. Until I found a real lover, I'd have fun with him.

And I did. I dated a lot of guys in my early twenties during and after (mostly) Calculus Guy, almost all of whom I balled, few of whom I saw more than a couple of times, and even fewer I remember at all. One in particular was unforgettable.

"Tookie, I'm finally doin' it and I wantcha to be with me." Sybil bubbled like I'd never seen her bubble before.

"You're not getting that tattoo?" I despised tattoos.

Sybil vacillated between a butterfly on her shoulder and "Lucky you" where her lovers would see it just before hitting pay dirt. I strongly advised her against "I taste better than I look."

She probably chattered about tattoos just to get a rise out of me.

"Nooo. I'm gettin' married! And I want *you* to be my bridesmaid."

"Of course, I'll do it." I was losing a partner in crime and I'd waste a lot of money on an ugly dress I couldn't wear again. "Tell me everything."

"My clock's tickin'. I'll be thirty soon." The expression on her face looked more like a tycooness making a business decision than a woman looking forward to her honeymoon.

"So you're jumping on the first bus to Babyland." I'd seen this before. A girl turns thirty, panics, and throws her freedom out the window when a guy with a pulse willing to marry her happens by.

She fiddled with the strap on her shoe. "I don't wanna end up like Cynthia."

"She's smart, beautiful, talented, and knowledgeable about many things." Cynthia was so many things I wished I could be, except the sex part. She was far too picky.

"And alone," she said, looking me straight in the eye.

Sybil spent a half hour giving me all the details: how he asked her, when she was getting married, in what church, where she was going on her honeymoon, and on and on.

"I need photos, full length if possible." I wanted to choose who I'd be spending rehearsal night, her wedding day and, maybe, night with.

"Here." She handed me photos of the four groomsmen and the best man for good measure. "I knew you'd ask. I've been a bridesmaid with you before, remember?"

"What about him?" I held up the picture of a tall, dark, and good looking man a few years older than me.

"Charlie. He's just your type."

"And what type's that?" I didn't think I had a type. I couldn't be limited to a single type if I was going to tally a hundred, fifty even.

"Besides the physical aspects, he's very smart. He's in Mensa."

"Sign me up for Mensa Man."

The night of the wedding around two in the morning, after the groomsmen had passed out from drinking too much at the reception, we girls compared notes. The others had dated Charlie or had friends who had, but didn't know we'd just started thumping thighs the night before after the rehearsal dinner. Drink freed what few inhibitions the others had. I was cold sober.

"And he said, 'I don't like how you smell.' She told him she'd douche when she had her period. He said, 'That's the only time you smell good.'"

"Charlie told Sally, 'My dick's committed to you, but my heart isn't.'"

"He told me, 'You're not Miss Right, you're Miss Right Now.'"

"He can't be that bad," I said. "I think he's cute."

"Eeeeeeuuww," they said in unison.

They continued bashing my Mensa Man for several more minutes while I sat back and quietly took mental notes. Charlie had tickled half the women in North Jersey's kitties, and even those he hadn't hated him. Forewarned, I didn't let myself fall in love with him.

He did have some good qualities, as he was completely uninhibited and taught me things I wouldn't have learned with anyone else. He also took me to some Mensa gatherings—enough to learn that a significant minority of the active members bordered on sociopathic. I didn't want to be around them and neither did the inactive members, I'm told. That was why the majority were inactive. From those unpleasant experiences I gained a confidence boost. I learned I was smarter than many of the un-der/unemployed so-called top two per cent.

As I said earlier, I'm an exhibitionist wannabe, meaning I wanted to shock people with overt sexual be-havior, but don't usually have enough nerve to follow through. Charlie didn't mind. In fact, he encouraged it. The first incident happened when we were driving across Kansas in my less-than-worthless-even-though-it-was-still-pretty-new Vega.

"Want to drive?" I pulled off onto the wide shoulder on a flat, quiet stretch of I-70 and hopped out. Charlie and I switched seats Chinese-fire-drill style. While he pulled onto the highway and accelerated down the road, I settled into the passenger seat to rest.

"Yaaaawnnn." I breathed deeply twice, but couldn't sleep. I realized I wasn't tired, I was bored. I was also hot. It was summer on the Great Plains and the Vega's A/C didn't work above eighty degrees. Twisting like a contortionist, I reached under my blouse, unhooked my bra, wriggled it off one shoulder, and pulled it out the op-posite sleeve. That helped a little.

Charlie grabbed my bra, twirled it around, whistled, and challenged, "Take it off, baby. Take it all off."

"You asked for it." I untied my shoelaces. Off came my sneakers and socks. I wriggled out of my pedal push-ers, then pulled my blouse off over my head.

He grabbed a handful of my pubes through my draw-ers. "I wanna see your flaming cunt."

"Owww! That hurts." *Smack!* I slapped his arm.

"I'll let go if you promise to get them off."

"I promise. You're not getting shit tonight." I lifted my butt off the seat and slid my undies down past my knees.

"C'mon. Finish the job. Show me your soul-stealin' snatch. Now."

I jerked off my sky-blue panties and lifted my ass as high as I could, revealing my fiery fur box, if only to Charlie. He snatched my not-so-briefs out of my hand, covered his face with them, and sniffed.

"Not now!" I grabbed them away from him. "You can snort them if you want at the motel. Keep your eyes on the road and your hands on the wheel. It's okay for your mind to be in the gutter, where it usually is, but not your hands and eyes."

Just then a semi pulled alongside on the left. The driver, alone in the rig, wouldn't have been able to see anything. The yellowed rear window blocked his view so badly he couldn't have told if I was naked or wearing a parka when he was behind us.

"Let him pass. He can't see anything from where he's sitting." *Oh well.*

Charlie took his foot off the gas long enough for the truck to surge ahead and ease into the lane in front of us. The Vega objected when he stomped on the gas pedal. It eventually pulled alongside the semi, synchronizing speeds with the truck until I was even with the driver.

Beep. Beep. Charlie got the driver's attention by honking the horn. The steamed passenger door window didn't give him much of a view. "Roll down your window," Charlie chided. "Give him a thrill."

I cranked it down halfway at most.

He laughed. "Bawk…bawk, bawk, bawk…bawk. Chicken."

"Okay." I lowered it the rest of the way, arched my back, and shot the trucker the briefest beaver on record, then punched down on Charlie's right foot with my left, causing the underpowered Vega to labor forward and slowly pull away from the truck.

The truck driver applauded my performance with his air horn. *Hooonk, hooonk.*

I threw him a kiss out my window but gave him no encore. When we were far away, I let up on the gas and covered myself. Thus ended my only up-close-and-personal flash. I feel awkward sharing it because it shows how conservative and inhibited I really am.

My other exhibitionist incident took place coming back from the city on the bus late at night after seeing *Oh! Calcutta!* Charlie'd had a little too much to drink and tried to kiss me.

"Behave yourself." I didn't like booze-fueled sex, especially when I was sober, which was always.

"C'mon. Afraid to get naked and do somethin' ex-citin'?"

Seldom able to resist such a dare and still titillated by what I saw on stage, I decided to play. "You're on. Pull down your pants."

I rolled down my pantyhose—it was panties or pan-tyhose for me in those days, never both, often none. With a little help from my spittle-wetted fingers, I got his kiel-basa sizzling in short order. *Better take control. He's not very agile in this condition.* I lifted my skirt and settled myself gingerly onto his waiting lap post.

"Whoooo Hoooo!" I had the bus ride of my life. No orgasm, but did I moan every time we hit a bump. Being the only passengers that pitch-dark night, no one saw us, not even the bus driver. My groans of pleasure might've gotten his attention if he hadn't been playing his radio so loudly.

So, my exhibitionist attempts after the conquest of the security guards fell pretty low on the exposure scale.

Charlie's boorish behavior eventually became too bothersome, and he tired of my complaining about it. After our last dust up, neither called the other to patch things up or to break up. With Charlie out of the picture, I needed a new diversion.

CHAPTER 12

Brief Encounters of the Middling Kind

Was that done by Caravaggio or Tintoretto?" I whispered to Doug, the intelligent, witty, ruggedly handsome guy sitting next to me in art appreciation.

"Tintoretto," he responded with a lascivious tone and look.

Much more than fuck buddies, we pioneered "friends with benefits" decades before the term was coined. We shared a number of interests, but I wasn't ready to settle down and he wanted a family. Doug's problem was that his wife only lifted her skirt when she was ovulating. The rest of the time, he was mine—mostly when I was between relationships.

My easy-come-easy-go attitude toward men protected me from getting hurt, and the ease with which I replaced them boosted my self-esteem. Whenever I needed a new boyfriend, one soon appeared.

One beautiful fall Saturday when I didn't have the rent, I found hiding in the library all day too confining. So, I set my homework aside and meandered down the block to the deserted playground behind the old red-brick school where the empty swings beckoned. I'd always loved swinging as a girl. Flying up to the bar and going fast and high exhilarated me.

I recalled a time in fifth or sixth grade about the time boys first noticed girls—other girls. I swung on the swings because I liked the freedom of flying off the ground more than wasting my time hoping a boy would notice me. One boy—Billy Kessler, I think—trotted over to see something forbidden. I soared above the bar and, when I descended, my dress flew up.

"I see London. I see France. I see Tookie's underpants," Billy chanted while gazing fixedly at my ruffled panties.

I instinctively spread my legs wider to give him a better view. Billy was the first boy to look at me in a sexual way. It was nice. Boys often gave the pretty girls attention, but this time I got a little. I pumped the swing to soar higher and exposed myself longer on the way down.

Not amused, the teacher on playground duty interceded. "Billy," she scolded, "get away from here right now," and swatted him with her hand. "Tookie," she called, "keep your dress down. It's not ladylike to let it fly up like that."

After that, I daydreamed I was the temptress in the book my friend Franny found in the public library. She was way ahead of the rest of us regarding all things sexual and liked to share what she knew. None of us read the whole book because we didn't have the courage to check it out or risk being caught with it at home. Franny turned down the corners of the pages with the good parts so we could find them quickly.

I imagined the heroine to be like Greta Garbo, and pictured her vamping around the way she did in old movies I saw on TV. I imagined myself in her place and, from that day forward, felt very womanly when swinging, even wearing jeans and a sweatshirt like I was when a quiet blonde nine-year-old girl with pigtails wandered up and hung on one of the supports.

She looked shy, as if she could use a friend. I pointed at the free swings. "Like to join me?"

"Wouldn't I be bothering you?" Her little voice could barely be heard above the birds chirping.

"Course not." *Why's this thoughtful little girl here by herself. Haven't seen her around the neighborhood before.* "You live around here?"

"No, I'm with my dad this weekend." She hid her face behind the post while she spoke.

Her parents are probably divorced and her dad doesn't know how to play with a girl her age. "Have any friends here?"

She shifted to the other side of the pole. "No, Dad moved here after the divorce."

"Like to have one?"

I knew how it felt not to have any friends. I was lonely for most of my childhood. Tim gave me a sense of belonging until they took him away. It was the worst ever when we moved east. I was a senior. The others had their friends already and most were heading off for college.

Now, Amy and I swung happily, chatting about nothing of importance while establishing a bond. A not very attractive, smallish, olive-skinned man with bad teeth approached. "She bothering you, miss?"

"Not in the least. She's good company. You her father?"

He looked like he was drowning. Her needs were probably a mystery to him. His name was Edward. I let him take me to coffee after we tired of swinging, only because I wanted to avoid my landlord and homework for a while longer. We went on our first date two weeks later. Because I didn't enjoy being with depressed men, but really liked being around Amy, I arranged my availability to coincide with her visitations. We were like a little family those days but, without Amy, I didn't want to see him. I tried maintaining a relationship with her after breaking up with him, but he lurked about whenever I visited her, creating uncomfortable situations. My inability to deal with him kept me from seeing Amy anymore.

Missing Amy's friendship prompted me to volunteer for Big Brothers, Big Sisters. I spent time with another girl her age who needed the emotional support she lacked at home. Her mother was too busy working and taking care of her younger siblings to give her the attention a young lady needed.

We lost touch later, but I found the experience extremely rewarding. I helped her catch up with her schoolwork and took her to museums and parks where I played games with her, as if we were both nine. I also read to her and had her read to me to improve her reading skills. I picked books I hadn't read as a girl, but would've liked to. We both looked forward to hearing what happened next each week, as if we were waiting to see the next installment of a serial at the movies. I swore I'd have a daughter of my own someday.

❦

Frank, Gary, and Henry drifted in and faded out of my life quickly—as boyfriends, that is—but, unfortunately, persisted as coworkers. Gary took me to a decent restaurant, where we conversed pleasantly. Nothing special but, even as much pleasure as I gave myself masturbating, I often needed to get my hands on a live man. So, I accepted his offer to come into his apartment for drinks.

"I've got *something* for you. Make yourself comfortable while I get it." He disappeared down the hall.

Shit. What kind of place is this? Nymphs and satyrs

everywhere I look. Drapes are closed. What's he up to?

"Close your eyes and hold out your hands," he called from the hallway.

This is soooo weird. Hell, I'll just see where he's headed. I heard something being rolled in and stop next to me. Something rustled, then I felt something heavy on my hands. It felt like leather.

"Open your eyes." He excitedly danced from foot to foot.

It was leather—a black leather skirt—the cart was loaded with black leather shit.

"Put it on. It's your size. I checked."

This wimp was a masochist. I'd have fun with him as I'd always wondered what it would be like to be a dominatrix.

"You put this on but get naked first," I said in my most commanding voice as I handed him a dog collar from the cart.

He must've been wearing breakaway clothing, he stripped so quickly.

"Now turn around." I clamped handcuffs on his wrists, clipped a leash onto the dog collar, and led him to the fireplace where I tied the leash to a heavy andiron. "Stay." I pointed to his feet like you'd command a dog. "Do you like how I look?"

"Very much." His eyes told me he was telling the truth.

"Want me to get naked?"

His breathing sped up. "Oh yes."

"Turn around."

"But I want to look at you," he begged.

I picked up a riding crop from the cart and threatened him with it. He complied instantly.

I took off my shoes and slacks, tossing them where he could see them with his peripheral vision. "No peeking." I tapped him across the butt, hard enough to sting but light enough not to leave a welt. I undressed bottom first in front of men. It seemed to excite them quicker than when I went top down. I wriggled my panties to the floor. "Bad boy! You peeked." I strode over to him. He didn't peek, but I wanted him to see my nether regions.

He turned to address me and got an eyeful.

"Peeking's not allowed." I threatened him with the riding crop.

"I didn't peek." He made himself as small as possible.

I lifted his balls with the business end of the riding crop.

He shuddered.

"Drop to your knees and stick out your tongue." I menacingly pressed down on his shoulder with the crop. "Farther. You can do better than that. How can you eat me if you can't get it out farther than that?" I stood directly in front of him with his nose touching my belly. "Get lower. You're not lined up." I thwacked his bare ass. "That's what you get if you don't mind."

This was great fun and I didn't even have the leather get up on yet.

"You're going to like this. I unexpectedly started my period on the way over and don't have tampons with me."

I loved seeing the sick look on his face. Sometimes guys didn't appreciate my jokes.

Being a dominatrix came easily to me. I amused myself and titillated Gary by spanking him like a little boy, making him wear diapers, and punishing him for minor infractions. Yes, that was Gary.

Frank was the one who was so intimidated by me. The girls in the office said Frank had had little experience with women, and he put the money other guys spent on dating into his car.

"Tooks, thought I'd warn you that Frank's excited to shine his flashlight into your twinkle cave." Sybil's silly grin gave away her disgust for him.

"*Thanks,* I thought you said he didn't like girls."

She rolled her eyes. "I said he doesn't know what to do with us."

I thought I'd like a ride in his new Corvette but didn't want to waste a Saturday on him.

Not unsurprisingly, he called that night.

"Yeah, I know who you are, Frank. What do you want?" This had Sybil's fingerprints all over it.

"Well—uh—uh—uh—would you—uh—uh like to—uh—uh go—"

Let's get this over with. "I'd like to go for a drive in the country Sunday afternoon—if the weather's nice." That gave me time to clean up and change after my Saturday night "date."

"That's great."

"I'll meet you at two in the parking lot of the mall at Exit 8A." Nobody would see us there, and it was close to a place I wanted to go for a top-down drive.

With a head scarf covering my hair and sunglasses hiding my eyes, I positioned myself in his passenger seat. "Drive out through the horse country around Mendham."

He smiled like a cat who caught a chipmunk. "Okay."

I enjoyed feeling the wind blow through my hair and seeing the looks on guy's faces as we rolled past, but Frank was a terrible conversationalist and his flabby body didn't excite me. As the sun lowered and traffic thinned, I spied a small deserted park on the right.

"Pull in here," I commanded, pointing to the park driveway.

He complied with a gleam in his eye and crept slowly along the gravel driveway and into the parking lot to avoid chipping the paint on his precious fiberglass chick magnet.

I pointed to the most remote corner of the lot. "Park under the tree over there."

As soon as we stopped, he made an awkward move. I pushed him back in his seat.

"I—I—I'm sorry." He sulked against the driver's door as far away from me as he could get in a Corvette.

"Have a little patience." I pressed his chest firmly enough with my left hand to keep him still. After a minute, I unbuckled his belt, causing him to squirm. "Don't do anything. You'll enjoy this." The cramped quarters under the steering wheel inhibited my movement greatly, making it impossible to give him anything approaching my best but I soldiered on. He came as quickly as he was aroused.

"You're the best by a mile," he said, when his breathing slowed down enough to speak. "I never imagined it could feel this good. I've never experienced anything like this before."

"Neither have I." Except it was on the opposite end of the scale.

"Really?" He looked shocked and his eyes were as big as headlights. "I heard you're the best and have done everything possible."

"Never in a Corvette. This was my first." *And last in this one.*

"Like to get something to eat?" he asked with eyes radiating lust.

"Just drop me at my car." *Can't decide what to have for supper.*

"Next weekend?"

"You need to clean your upholstery now, Frank."

I must have been doing something wrong. I wasn't meeting anybody worthwhile. College students couldn't afford to take me out, and I'd gone through the younger guys at work. The profs who flirt with me were dorks. I had to try something different. But what?

CHAPTER 13

Sugar Baby 1973

S ee you all next Saturday," my professor said, closing the Sunday afternoon session of my weekend class.

Wanting to avoid an unexpected arrival by my rent-collecting landlord, I stopped off for a burger at my favorite off-campus joint. *Shit. I've worked at Carver-Watkins five years and have two years of college credit but nothing to show for it. I could use a man about now. That should get my mind off my troubles. The Plumtree ought to be a safe place to get picked up.*

I drove to a high-end business hotel near the airport and made my way to the lounge, where I sat alone at a table along the wall. I spotted a nicely-dressed businessman who'd ogled me from the bar and circled my lips with the tip of my tongue, as if I was licking my favorite fluid from my favorite organ, for his benefit.

"Rowena?" A baritone voice I didn't recognize, calling my stage name, broke my concentration as it drifted into my left ear.

Don't turn. Could lose both of them and have to go home unfucked. Can't do that. It's been ten days already, and I really need it. Stay focused.

He threw down his drink and backed away from the bar.

Here he comes. What should I say? Shit! He's leaving. Need a Plan B. What about this guy next to me. Don't look at him. Get a glimpse of him out of the corner of your eye. Still there. Oooh, very expensive suit. I turned to my left and made eye contact with a well-groomed, well put together, reasonably attractive man a decade older than me. He'd do. You bet, he'd do.

"I hear you're pretty good, Rowena," he said, opening.

"Better than that." Who told him about me? I didn't see anybody there I knew. The bartender was new. He couldn't know me. It was late, this guy wanted to score, and I was the best bet in the place. It might just be his turn to get lucky.

Instead of trying a better pickup line, he pulled a crisp hundred dollar bill out of his wallet. "Let's go," he said, waving the bill.

Thinking the money was to pay his bar tab, I followed him. When he didn't slow down at the cashier, I figured he had something else in mind.

What the hell. Try anything once. Although I hadn't actually been offered money before—I didn't count all-expenses-paid trips to the islands with guys I'd previously met—several pick-ups had told me I was better than most pros they'd been with. I knew I wouldn't disappoint him, I but felt a bit odd about taking money for what I would've gladly given him for the fun of it. A week's salary, tax-free? Rent was due, I was short and I liked being appreciated.

"Wait in the ladies across from the elevators," he said as we walked toward the lobby. "Count to fifty, then come up to room seven twenty-three." When the elevator dinged announcing its arrival, he grinned. "Go."

He left his door ajar for me, so I walked right in.

"Pull out all the stops and I'll double it."

Whatever they were. I don't think I pulled out all the stops, but I did treat him to a new trick I'd been itching to test. He apparently enjoyed it. Slipping out of his bathroom from cleaning up afterward, I spied two crisp hundred dollar bills on the dresser. As I picked them up, he asked if I had a card. I slinked toward the door.

He jumped off the bed, blocking my exit.

Oh shit. Evelyn said I was taking too many risks. "Please," I begged. "I've given you what you want."

"And I'm quite pleased, so pleased I want to make you an offer." He pointed at the easy chair in the corner of his plush room. "Hear me out before you make a decision." Apparently sensing my unease, he said, "Put the money in your purse. It's yours."

It was very late and he was being creepy. "What do you want?"

"It's simple. I'll be coming to town every Sunday evening and leaving forty-eight hours later for a long time, several years, most likely."

"So?" *Guess I was so good he wants me to service him on every trip. Never been with a guy with such a square jaw before.*

"I hate staying in hotels, even nice one like this, and will pay well to avoid it." He seemed earnest.

"Where do I fit in?" *I don't run a motel and my place is a dump compared to this.*

"I want you to pick me up at the airport Sunday evenings at six thirty, drive me to your place, feed me dinner, drive me to work at seven Monday mornings, pick me up from work at five thirty, repeat for Tuesdays, and drop me at the airport after work. It's that simple."

"You left something out. What do we do between dinner and work?" As if I had any doubts.

"Sleep, of course."

"I only have one bed." Not that I would have minded sharing it with him.

"I'll let you share it with me," he said, as if he was negotiating an order of automobile parts from a supplier.

"What's in it for me?" Diamond Jim Brady was expecting an awful lot for his two hundred.

"I forgot to mention you'd be my dinner companion Sunday and Monday evenings at nice restaurants, sometimes with clients. You might have to be my cousin or some such."

"What's in it for me?" I repeated. *You're irritating me.*

"Sorry. I got distracted. I'll pay you four hundred a month. Cash. Up front."

He wanted to hose me moneywise, too. "I can get a hundred, sometimes two, a trick and you're only offering four hundred for an entire month."

"If you were a pro, you could get a hundred a trick but you're not a pro. That's why I want you. You're a smart girl who's trying to better herself but are having a hard time without a degree. I want you to have the money to get that degree and I enjoy being with you."

How the hell does he know that? "I still don't think that's enough."

"Rowena—that's your real name, is it—lots of guys'll screw you for free, and maybe give you untreatable diseases, but guys who pay want something different and you're not it."

Insulted, I jumped to my feet. "I don't have to take this from you or anybody."

"You misunderstand. I wouldn't want you so much if you were a pro."

"You have an odd way of complimenting a girl."

He took my hand and kissed it. "You're *exactly* what I want, green eyes."

"And that is?" I could only imagine what he was going to say next.

"I want a companion I'll be proud of being seen with. Someone who could be the girl next door or my niece or an old friend. Someone with a face I want to see when I go to sleep at night and wake up to in the morning. That's all."

"And who'll screw you all night long?" He wanted an American Geisha.

He looked into my eyes seductively. "That's the Hollandaise on the asparagus."

Any misgivings I had about taking money for screwing him evaporated when he complimented me. He had a strange way of convincing me to do him whenever he was in town. "What makes you think you're right about me?"

"I'll bet you all the money in your purse this was your first time," he said, sounding even more confident.

It was scary he knew so much about me. "Can I have a few minutes to think this over?" I couldn't bullshit him.

"Take as much time as you want. I'm not going anywhere," he said, opening a newspaper.

This would double my pay, more after taxes. Bank three hundred of it to build up a cushion for tuition, car repairs, any other things that pop up. I didn't want to take money from his wife and kids. "Hold out your hands. Both of them." No rings or suntan lines. "Turn them over." Nothing there either. "Thanks."

I wouldn't be able to take Monday night classes but I'd have enough cash to register for more than one a term and be able to finish sooner, especially if I was celibate and didn't waste time on dates. Good way to get rid of my Sunday-night horns. I'd be extra ready when I picked him up.

"Will carry out be okay? I don't cook." *This might be a deal breaker.*

"If it's good. We start next Sunday. You'll need clothes for dinner out next week. Meet me at Talbots at six thirty tomorrow."

"I have clothes." I wasn't about to blow what he just gave me on dresses just to please him.

"Not the kind you'll need."

"Talbots! They'll burn through all I've got and more."

He smiled for the first time. "I'm paying. You'll be wearing them for me."

"I guess I'll see you at Talbots then." Things like this didn't happen to ordinary girls like me.

"One other thing. You've got to be exclusive. I don't want any diseases or ugly scenes with boyfriends."

"Understood." I was between boyfriends anyway.

"I assume you live alone."

"I do."

"Roommates are unacceptable. Don't breathe a word of this to anyone, and don't do anything to raise suspicions."

"Like wearing the Talbots outfits and flashing the money around?"

"I don't worry about you flashing the money around. You need it for bills. You won't want to wear the Talbots outfits except when you're with me because you don't dress to call attention to yourself. Over time, you'll need new ones. When we replace the ones you get tomorrow, you can start wearing the old ones on a limited basis and say you got them at a thrift shop. Over time you'll build up a nice wardrobe"

"Sounds reasonable." Everything he said sounded

reasonable. Why did I feel so funny about this whole thing?

He reached out to me with both arms. "Come here and seal the deal with a kiss."

I cautiously went over to him and kissed him tentatively. He hugged me and kissed me tenderly. It felt like I was with Tim again. This was strange, very strange.

❦❦

It was raining when I arrived at Talbots, so I parked as close as I could and raced through the front door, expecting to find him there. But he wasn't. I looked around but didn't see him anywhere. When I turned around to leave, I saw him walking in the front door, soaking wet.

"Where were you?"

He shook off some of the water. "Outside, waiting for you."

It had been a long, long time since a guy waited in the rain for me, like never. "The restrooms probably have those electric hand drier blower things. If you sit under it, you can dry your hair and the nozzle swivels around so you can dry off most of yourself. You just have to keep pressing the button. Try it. It works. I'll go to the ladies and wait there for you. Go on." I pushed him in the direction of the restrooms.

I was reading the detective novel I kept in my purse to kill time when waiting for doctors and oil changes when he came out considerably drier.

He smiled. "Which way is the ladies department?"

"Follow me." Disliking shopping, I took the most direct routes through stores, which meant squeezing between clothing racks intentionally placed close to each other to discourage shoppers from doing what I did. He followed in my wake without knocking too many things off the racks. I passed lingerie and stopped, not knowing exactly what he had in mind.

He looked around until he spotted a nicely dressed middle-aged sales clerk. "We could use some assistance, miss. My…uh…niece needs some things to wear for her new job. She'll be entertaining conservative clients, so nothing too flashy."

"What sorts of events will she be attending, sir?" She looked even more suspicious when he said I was his niece.

He thought a second. "Dinners, plays, concerts—oh, and cocktail parties this season."

"She's come to the right place. What size are you?"

"Seven?" I hadn't figured out all these different sizes.

"Maybe. Take off your coat."

He helped me off with my coat and held it while she measured me all over my body. I felt funny being touched by a woman like that. She stepped back to look me over, taking mental notes about my figure, I suppose.

"Let's start with suits. They're quite versatile. Do you have a favorite color?"

"Green."

"Hmmm. Not a lot in green this year." She walked to a rack a couple of aisles away and returned with something on a hanger. "How's this?" She handed me a green glen plaid suit. "Try it on."

When I came out of the dressing room, she guided me to a three-way mirror. "Stand here." She looked me up and down and tucked and pinched the material around my butt and bust. "How do you like it?" she asked, looking at him.

"I think it would look great on her if it fit better."

"Exactly."

I felt her press me here and there, particularly around

the boobs and rear, marking the suit with chalk. "A little tailoring, and it'll look marvelous."

"I—We'll take it," he said. "Now, how about something for the theater?"

We drifted over to what I consider the ugly-bridesmaid-dress area.

"Try this on to see how this looks on you," she said, handing me a short chiffon dress.

Trying to put some humor in what was otherwise a painful experience for me, I twirled like a ballerina in the dress.

"Above the knee doesn't work for her," said the clerk. "Low cut either. Hmmm. I think we have something that'll be perfect for her build." She retrieved a beaded dress from a distant rack and handed it to me. "Put this on."

He nodded and I trudged off to the dressing room again.

Something about this dress made me feel sexy. Maybe it was the fringe at my knees. I dutifully positioned myself in front of the three-way mirror. I looked like someone else, someone pretty. My dark red hair contrasted so beautifully against the ivory dress.

His eyes looked like Rolls Royce headlights, they opened so wide. "Wow!"

"It'll look even better when it's altered." The clerk grabbed a handful of the material in the back, tightening up the front. She then chalked my hips. "I'll let it out a little here to let it move more freely when she walks. Do you want it?"

"I'll say. Do you have it in other colors?" He almost drooled.

"As a matter of fact we do. Want to see them?" She left without waiting for an answer and returned with similar dresses in several different colors. "Here," she said handing a red dress to me. "Hold this against yourself so we can see how it looks. By the way, these are all on sale. Frankly, the flapper look hasn't done well for us. So many of our patrons are too busty."

"No," he said. "Try the blue one. Red's too flashy."

I held the blue dress up to my chin as directed. I felt like a mannequin.

He shook his head. "How about the black one?"

I exchanged dresses with the clerk and held the black one up against me.

"We'll take it, too. She can wear these for a range of social events."

"The right accessories can make them more formal or more fun, depending on the look you want at the time. The headbands and garters are thrown in. Madam will need shoes and purses?"

"I guess I'd look funny wearing these," I said, looking down at my desert boots.

"Let's not break the bank," he said. "A pair of black high heels and a small handbag should be all she needs.

"We have a couple of black beaded models that would work nicely. Come with me." She turned to me, pointing, "Sit over there and take off your shoes and socks."

Seeing myself in a mirror across the shoe area was disconcerting.

I looked like a whole different person in this dress, unsure if I was comfortable. Maybe I'd have to be someone else when I wore it. Someone demure and sophisticated. Didn't know if I could pull it off.

"Hold this one against the dress," she said, handing me a beaded bag. "Now the other."

"We'll take the first one," he said.

"Put on these footies and we'll try some shoes," she said, handing me nylon hairnets for your feet.

"Shoes are no problem. I have perfect arches."

"Let's try two-inch Mary Janes first." She slipped a nice-looking pair of black patent leather shoes on my feet. "See how they feel walking."

I wobbled across the room. "This isn't as easy as it looks."

"Haven't you worn heels before at a prom or wedding or something?"

"Never. Always wore floor-length dresses. Didn't want to buy shoes." Heels stressed my ankles.

He chuckled. "Flats'll be fine."

"Will this be all, madam? Do you need undergarments or nylons? Jewelry?" She looked hopeful of an even larger sale.

"Throw in a half dozen pairs of pantyhose. I've never know a woman who didn't need them."

"Matching slips?"

He nodded.

"How soon will you need the dresses?"

"Have them ready on Thursday. She'll try them on again to make sure they're right."

"That's my day off."

"Wednesday then."

"Wednesday, it is. How would you like to pay?"

He turned to me. "Change back into your clothes while we settle up." He remained silent until I was out of earshot. When I returned, he handed me a stub. "Give them this on Wednesday and make sure everything fits correctly." He looked at the sales clerk. "You will be here then to make sure the alterations are done correctly?"

She smiled, probably mentally computing her present and future commissions. "Of course."

We walked silently to the exit to find rain still pouring down.

"Have you eaten?" He didn't wait for me to answer.

"Might as well get something to eat in the mall instead of getting soaked again."

"Am I on the clock now?" Was he expecting something?

"Nooo. I'd like to get to know you better over a shared meal." He sounded hurt. "I have work to do tonight and you're free to do whatever you want—provided it doesn't involve another man. In that regard, you've been on the clock since last night. Okay?"

"Fine. I'll give you no reason to doubt me. I don't have a boyfriend or anybody I'm interested in seeing." I wasn't going to screw up this deal.

He looked over a list of food places in the mall and picked an Italian place. During the meal, we distracted ourselves by talking about food. When we finished, it was time to leave.

"I don't know your name. What should I call you?" What had I done? I'd agreed to be a man's mistress, a kept woman, and I didn't even know his name—not even a fake one.

"What would you like to call me?"

"I don't know. Daddy Warbucks?" He was going to be my sugar daddy after all.

"Call me Daddy in private, DW in public, David Ward if someone presses you for a name."

"That isn't your real name, is it?"

He tilted his head, looking into my eyes. "I haven't asked for yours have I, Rowena?"

"I like my own better and will tell you when I'm more comfortable."

"I won't press. I want you to be comfortable. I want our relationship to work."

We walked silently to the exit and departed in separate directions. I shouted, "Six-thirty Sunday?"

"Six-thirty Sunday. Every Sunday." He smiled and waved goodbye.

Chapter 14

Daddy Warbucks

Daddy smiled when he saw me pull over to the curb at Arriving Passengers at six-thirty sharp. "Sorry I'm late." I would've been early if I hadn't decided to change out of my Sunday scanties.

"You're right on time. My flight was early." He kissed me and handed me a thick envelope. "Count it. I would."

"If it's short, I'll take it out in trade." We both laughed. *Should I pull over somewhere and attack him?* I should've diddled the skittle after class, I was so horny. "You drive."

He froze as if in a stop-action photograph. "Why?"

"It's hard to give you oral sex while *I'm* driving."

He grinned as he climbed into the passenger seat. "I better take a rain check."

"You're no fun. Sorry, the offer just expired."

I pulled my crappy Vega up to a Chinese restaurant and parked. "Be right back. I took the liberty of ordering take out. They have the best Chinese in Jersey, north or south. Don't know what you like, so I ordered several things." I hoped I hadn't screwed up.

He smiled. "I'm sure it'll be fine."

I showed Daddy around my tiny apartment and felt funny when I took him to my bedroom. I didn't know what to do. I'd contracted to be his sex slave. *Do I initiate things or does he control everything?* "Will you need closet space?"

"Only while I'm here. I usually bring three suits and shirts that need to be on hangers."

"Do you want me to do your laundry while you're away? I can easily toss three pairs of socks and underwear in with my wash."

He kissed me square on the lips and rubbed my ass. "I want you to focus your energies on other things."

I pushed some of my hangers aside in the bedroom closet, making room for his. "You may hang your suits and shirts here."

"Thanks. Please fix dinner while I hang up my clothes. I'm famished."

I spread out the various dishes on the kitchen table I'd set before leaving for the airport. "What would you like to drink with dinner?"

"Water's fine. Do you have a lemon?"

No wine. That was nice. "No. Should I stock them?"

"If it isn't too much trouble."

"Not in the least."

"Where should I sit? Where do you usually sit? I'll sit at the other place. This's your home, not mine."

He sure tried to make me feel comfortable. I pulled out the chair I used when I was alone, which was most nights. We both tried most of the dishes, me more than him. I made mental notes of which dishes he ate the most of. When I'd had enough, I opened the conversation.

"I'm not sure what I'm supposed to do. Do I take my clothes off and wait on the bed until you want me? I don't want to screw this up. I want it to work."

Daddy chuckled. "Have you ever lived with a man?"

"Not longer than a vacation. Many weekends, though."

"We're going to be somewhere in between. We won't get bored with each other because we're always together but we won't spend all our time in bed like you do on weekend getaways with new boyfriends."

"Is it okay for me to initiate things?"

"Sometimes."

"I have a confession to make: five days without sex is a lot for me. Friends have noticed I get irritable twenty-four hours later and downright cranky after a week without."

"You'll never go sixteen hours without when I'm around. I promise. Your longest dry period will be from Tuesday morning to Sunday evening. Tuesday evening if I can fit it in. Just because I haven't attacked you, don't think it's not on my mind. We have to take care of a few things first. Come naked next Sunday and take me directly to the far corner of the long-term parking lot." He took a long drink of water while waiting for my response.

"Parking between two big trucks'll give us more privacy. You can strip while I'm driving."

He snorted. Water came out his nose when he laughed. "I like your sense of humor. If you're finished eating, we can take a look at your wardrobe. We can play after that. Put on the black dress while I clean up the dishes."

"I'll take care of them." I wasn't used to having men do kitchen work.

"I'd rather have you spending your time taking care of me. I'll hurry so I can catch you in a state of undress."

I quickly stripped down to my sexiest underwear, the black lacy bra and panties I'd put on after showering for the night's date.

Maybe I should dawdle. He might like what he sees

and forget about those stupid dresses. I'm ready, too ready.

Daddy stepped into the room and retreated immediately. "Get dressed. You're not playing fair."

"All right. If you insist." I pulled on the black slip and slipped into the black dress. "I need you to zip me up."

He spun me around and zipped me up as if he'd done it before. "Walk around the room. I want to get the full effect. Oh. Put your shoes on first and forget the pantyhose. Don't want to ruin them before you've worn them at least once."

I clomped around the room the way I normally walk.

"Imagine you're horny as hell and there are some guys in the room you'd like to bang."

I swung my hips a bit, causing the dress to slide freely against the slip and for the fringe to tickle my knees. *Oooh.* I couldn't help but feel sexy in this dress. "Now I know why you picked this one."

"Exactly. Put on the ivory one now."

"Aren't you going to watch."

"I want to see you in the dresses. If I watch you undress, that won't happen."

He made me feel more feminine than anyone had before. "You can zip me up now."

"Only wear white under this one. Black shows through. You're to be demure in public—beautiful but not too sexy. Save that for me."

"Do I have to model the suit, too?" Time was wasting.

"Quick like a bunny." He left the room again. I hoped this pattern didn't continue. I wanted him to enjoy seeing me undressed. "Ready."

"Turn around slowly, please. That blouse doesn't work. Try a different one."

I pulled out the only other dress blouse I owned.

"Doesn't work either." He shook his head.

"Don't have any more." *Geesh, he's hard to please.*

"What blouse size do you wear?"

"Medium usually."

"Take off the jacket."

He looked at the label behind my neck then backed away, looking me up and down, shaking his head.

"Do you want me to get another blouse?"

"I'll take care of it. Put everything away now." He left the room while I carefully folded and hung up my new wardrobe.

Finished, I called to him, "Daddy, I could use a little help in here."

He trotted in looking like he was as ready as I was.

I turned my back to him, saying, "Unhook my bra."

He quickly had it off and was fondling my long neglected breasts. His readiness poked my rear. "Kiss me now."

He spun me around and kissed me passionately while I unbuckled his belt. I got him on my bed as fast as I could with him fully dressed other than his pants down. It had been far too long since I'd tasted one. I forced myself not to rush. Wanted to get full enjoyment from this.

We christened my bed several ways that night and again the next morning. It was the most fun night of sex I'd had in quite a while. He was thoughtful and open to new things. The only negative was that we got little sleep. "I shower in the morning," he said, while we were catching our breath sometime after midnight. "I noticed from the state of the bathroom you showered before picking me up. So, I'll shower before we leave in the morning."

"And I go to work reeking of sex and drip all day?" I got gossiped about enough as it was.

"Okay, I'll get up early and shower first. You can do it at your regular time."

I kissed him for being considerate. "My regular time is actually a half hour later but I'm changing my schedule to get you to work on time."

"When's your lease up?"

"It expired long ago. I've been month to month for years." Where was he going with this?

I checked out his luggage while he showered. No nametags on his briefcase or carryon. No old stickers. Nothing. The briefcase was locked. Nothing in the carryon except clothes, a sewing kit, and shoe horn. No identifying marks at all. I ate and put out some juice and cereal for him to eat while I showered.

"Where to?" I asked as we pulled out of my parking lot.

"The industrial park just off Exit 8."

Good. That was the exit after mine. "Hi ho hi ho, it's off to work we go."

"Would it be too much trouble to get me grapefruit, bran flakes, and raisins for breakfast?"

"No problem at all. I might share them with you."

"When grapefruit's out of season, bananas'll have to do. I like the large, fat raisins, not the regular ones."

Fatigued from playing nonstop all night, I became giddy and warbled off key, "Nothin' could be finer than your tongue in my vagina in the mooroorning."

Daddy gave me a most lascivious smile. Without missing a beat, he responded, "Nothin' would be sweeter than my sweetie when I eat her in the mooroorning."

"Biology just isn't fair," I said. "I can blow your brains out while you're driving a car but my anatomy makes it impossible for you to munch my carpet while I'm at the wheel."

"Haven't dated any midgets, have you?"

I wanted to wipe the shit-eating grin off his face. "Should I try one later this week?"

"*No!*" His tongue ravaged my unsuspecting mouth and throat.

I pushed his head away and pulled his hand to my crotch. "You can show me you care by fingering me. I don't want to crash."

He slipped his hand under the elastic waistband of my slacks but didn't move lower. Instead, he slowly brought his hand up my front to fondle my breasts through my bra.

"That's not where I put your hand."

"Don't you like foreplay?"

"No time. You won't be able to get me off before we get to your work. I'll be horny all day."

"There's a wooded area in the industrial park that hasn't been developed yet—"

I pulled his hand away. "We'll pick up right here after work." I kissed it and planted it on my breast. After paying the toll, I asked, "Where should I drop you?"

"I'll tell you when we get there."

I drove him a couple of blocks into the sizeable industrial park, passing several large buildings along the way. "Stop here," he said when we got to an intersection with offices on all four corners.

As he got out, I asked, "Where do I pick you up?"

"Right here."

"Walk around the car. I've got something to tell you." I rolled down my window and pulled him to me by his necktie. "Thank you for a wonderful night."

His eyes twinkled. "And thank you for a wonderful morning." He tried to pull away.

"Haven't you forgotten something?"

He patted his pockets with a blank look.

"Kiss me. A benefit of being a mistress is getting kissed goodbye. I demand my pay."

He kissed me nicely. "You'll get a lot more of that this evening." He continued waving goodbye until I couldn't see him in my rearview mirror anymore.

It was the same scene every time I dropped him off. I never knew where he worked, but I became intimately familiar with the wood patch. Tuesday afternoon delights when Daddy had an early flight were my absolute favorite. Because my parked car wasn't visible from the street, cheating couples who worked in the industrial park often pulled in alongside mine. Daddy insisted we remain out of view but he did allow me to moan as loudly as I liked. It fed his ego and I like to moan—a lot.

CHAPTER 15

The Morning After

You must've had one helluva weekend," said the always-observant Sybil when I dragged my weary body past her desk on the way to my cubicle after dropping off Daddy that first Monday morning. "Was it worth it?"

I just smiled and waddled on. I'd be all right when the newness wore off. We wouldn't always want each other this much. I enjoyed it while I could.

My lunch-time nap revived me a bit but I was still bushed when I picked him up after work. I found him waiting patiently, standing exactly where I'd left him. *Wonder which building he works in?* "You look like I feel."

Even in his tired state, he radiated lust. "And you look a lot better than I feel."

"Thanks. What's up tonight? Not much I hope." A couple of quickies and off to sleep would fit the ticket just fine.

"Dinner with clients. Shouldn't run late. We've got to do something before that. Get off at Exit 8A and head toward Jamesburg." He looked at a paper he took out of the inside pocket of his suit coat.

"But I'm not dressed for dinner." *What's he up to?*

After I exited, he looked closely at street signs. I passed a few side streets before he pointed. "Turn left here." Two blocks later, he pointed again. "Pull in here." He slipped the paper into his pocket.

It was an apartment rental office. Huh?

"There he is. Let's get out. Let me do the talking." Daddy strode up to a man wearing a baby blue leisure suit. I toddled behind him.

"It's good of you to show us a unit on such short notice, Mr. Lanzone. My niece just landed a job near here and needs a place to live. No need for her to waste more money on a hotel."

It was best to keep my mouth shut and look young and innocent.

"Glad to be able to help, Mr. Ward. I'll have some smaller units next month but right now all I've got available is this two-bedroom, two-bath unit."

Oh, God. Get a load of that medal and bush of chest hair exploding out of his open collar.

"It's more than she needs, but we'll take a look at it so we'll know what your units are like when a smaller one comes free." He turned toward me and gestured downward, indicating I should keep cool and go along with whatever he did.

"Take it tonight and I'll give you a great deal. Let's go."

Two baths? I didn't know anybody who had two baths. I got it. He wanted to sleep later in the morning. *What'll I use the second bedroom for? Hmmm.*

"As you can see, it's freshly painted, the carpet's like new, the appliances are great. It's in perfect condition."

I explored the rooms on my own while they chatted. Returning to them, I said, "It is beautiful but it's got to be a lot more than I can afford. I don't make much." It was a major chunk of my allowance.

"Two fifty's a lot for her to pay when she's just starting out," my "uncle" said.

"She could get a roommate and split the rent. They'd each have their own bathroom. Women like that," countered the salesman.

I hope this sleaze wouldn't be around nights and weekends.

"Rowena, check out the closet space while Mr. Lanzone and I talk in his office. You need to make sure there's enough for two girls." Behind his back, he waved at me to disappear for a while.

I played along to see where this led.

The salesman handed me the keys. "Lock it up when you're finished checking it out."

They disappeared.

The closets were enormous compared to any I'd ever had. I killed a few minutes pretending to explore the unit while they dickered. Something told me this was my new pad. Never had a "pad" before. It felt like I was moving up. The bathrooms were wonderful with showers that weren't jerry-rigged. I imagined lavishing in the tub, playing with myself until I dozed off. Earth to Mary Louise: get those thoughts out of your head. YOU CAN'T AFFORD THIS PLACE.

I locked up and joined them. Daddy and Lanzone were the only people in the office with photos of Dimaggio, Sinatra, and other famous Italians covering a wall. They sat across from each other at Lanzone's desk, grinning ear to ear.

"And the farmer had three daughters—oh. Is there enough closet space?" Lanzone asked.

"Plenty." I tried to hand him the keys but he refused them.

"They're yours now, tenant."

Did he wink at me or Daddy?

"We're running late, Rowena. I'll explain it to you in the car," Daddy said, nudging me in the back to leave.

"Where to now?" I asked after we pulled out of the parking lot.

"How do you like your new digs," he asked, looking very pleased with himself.

"Can't afford it without a roommate—unless you're the roommate." I raised my eyebrows after realizing what he had done.

"I negotiated a good deal for you—two twenty-five a month in cash, directly to Lanzone, only to him," he said in a voice lower than normal, emphasizing that I must do exactly as he says.

He spent my money without asking me. "It's a nice place, but it's a lot for me to swing. You should've discussed it with me first."

His eyes sparkled. "Oh. Did I forget to tell you I've increased your allowance to five hundred a month? That should cover the difference, shouldn't it, roomie?"

I kissed him on the cheek, the best I could manage while driving in traffic. I couldn't thank him properly while driving. I needed my right hand to shift gears and he wouldn't want me messing up his suit. I'd have to do something special for him that night even though I was exhausted.

"Have two phone lines installed. Have one billed to me and don't give anyone the number. I'll have an answering machine attached to it. Call the number and leave a message for me on it only in emergencies. Got it?" He was even more serious than ever before.

"Got it. Where to?" He was a real wheeler-dealer. He must have a lotta money.

"Your place. Need to dress for dinner, and we're running late. Step on it."

I mashed down the gas pedal. "Hah. This crapmobile won't go any faster."

―

A Talbots bag hung on my door knob. "What's this?" I said, picking it up so I could unlock my door. I thought I had picked up everything last week.

"You needed a blouse to wear with your suit, so I had them send a couple over."

I pulled the bag off the blouses and hung them in my closet.

"Make sure they fit." He plopped himself on my bed, resting on an elbow, looking at me even more lasciviously than ever before.

I took the one with a green cast out of the closet and put it on. He motioned to me to come to him. He buttoned up the back, taking intermissions to feel me up. I stood as still as I could, soaking in his fondling. "Try on the jacket to see how they look together," he said, apparently sensing me heat up prematurely.

I did.

"Now try on the other one."

I went over to him so he could unbutton me.

"Better do this one yourself or we'll never get there. Got to hurry now." He undressed while I changed blouses. Sadly, it was to put on a different suit and shirt for dinner.

"This one fits, too. Keep it on."

We dressed more or less in silence and rushed out the door when finished.

"Who or what am I tonight?" I asked while driving to a restaurant I couldn't afford. I liked the intrigue.

"You're my brother's daughter who came to New York to seek fame and fortune and is working her way through college to become a...uh—"

"Statistician?" It'd be easier to make up lies that sounded true.

"Yes. That'll do. You live in East Brunswick where you work for the Lanzone Corporation doing clerical work. Think you can manage that if they ask any questions?"

"I'll create a persona for myself on the way." I enjoyed this part. Maybe I could join the CIA.

Dinner came off without a hitch. His client's wife asked me some questions I easily fabricated answers for, then the conversation shifted to business. During their boring talk, I fantasized about what I'd be doing later.

At home, I hung up the suit and turned to Daddy. "Please help me with the buttons. Do it from behind me." That was a good position for massaging my breasts.

When the blouse was finally off, I held his hands to my bra cups. He fondled me gently, flicking my nipples just how I liked.

I melted when he blew in my ear. "Are you hungry?" he asked. "You didn't eat a lot for dinner."

I pulled down his boxers to feast on my favorite meal. "It's bratwurst time."

❧❧

Relaxing after the main course, I asked him, "How'd you know I wasn't a pro? How am I not a pro?" So many guys said I was better than a pro. Did they lie to get more from me?

"To begin with, you're a sweet girl who tries to put on a tough front. Pros tend to be hard. Most are on booze or drugs or both. You don't use either. You didn't demand to be paid in advance. That was a dead giveaway. And pros don't wear day-of-the-week panties." He kissed me tenderly. "You're a talented amateur, very talented."

"I don't know if I can move in by Sunday. I have to give a week's notice."

He rushed me. It wasn't easy letting go of the first home of my own.

"Get the new place set up for us to use, even if you don't have everything moved in. Be very discrete."

"Eventually, my friends'll find out. I'll tell them I have a roommate who's with her boyfriend most of the time. I'll put the clothes you buy me in her room. They'll never think those are mine." I was brilliant. She would be Georgette Kaplan, sort of like in *North by Northwest.*

"Don't ask them to help you move. Hire somebody who doesn't know you."

"I'm ahead of you on that one. A couple guys who have a truck and work cheap have plastered their signs all over the place. I'll get them to do it. I don't have much stuff so it won't cost much."

"I always thought you were a smart girl, good enough to eat," he said, pulling down my Monday panties.

∽∾∽

I was even more beat Tuesday morning. Daddy had me drop him off at the airport immediately after work. I did manage to let my hand slip off the gear shift a few times to shift his gears.

"Hey, what're you doing?"

"Want me to pull over somewhere?" O asked. It sure didn't take much to get him ready this time.

"No time, dammit." He sounded frustrated, being aroused with someone who'd do anything he asked, but unable to take advantage of his opportunity.

"Think of me while you're away." I made sure of that, at least for a while.

I was barely stopped when he hopped out of the car. "Sunday?"

"Every Sunday." I zoomed away as he had instructed.

On the way home, I stocked up on cranberry juice to ward off a bladder infection I sometimes got when I was highly active sexually. I wanted to be domestic for the first time in my life. I spent much of the week setting up our love nest, enjoying every minute of it. As expected, I wasn't completely moved in but enough to get us by for two days.

I even picked up some things from yard sales on my way to class Saturday morning, including inexpensive pink items to use in decorating Georgette's bedroom. She was much more feminine than I was.

After class on Sunday, I raced home to shower and primp for my date. Not brave enough to drive nude to the airport as promised, I threw on a yard-sale caftan I'd cut up and installed snaps on the shoulders. Other than my sandals, I was stark naked underneath.

"Hi," he said, looking at me funny. "Why are you wearing that?"

"I'm too shy to drive here naked as promised."

He chuckled. When I didn't take the turn to exit the airport, he frowned. "Where're you going?"

"You'll see." When we were away from the lights around the terminal, I unsnapped the caftan, exposing myself to him.

"Ha, ha, ha, ha."

"Here, I try to be sexy and you laugh at me. Jerk." I tried to cover myself with the caftan but he pulled it away.

"I was enjoying your inventiveness. You're a very

smart girl whose body I adore, especially when you push your limits to please me."

"Take *your* clothes off. I'm not going to be the only one arrested for public indecency if we get stopped."

He started slowly with his shoes and socks but sped up once we passed the long-term parking lot ticket machine. I drove down the aisles in which I'd seen large trucks parked when I scouted the lot a couple of times after school. My searching was hampered a bit by Daddy molesting me while I drove. On the third aisle, I found an empty spot screened on both sides by trucks and by a minivan in front. I pulled in so deeply my bumper touched it. Maneuvering inside the Vega was challenging but, when it came to things sexual, I was up to the task. Daddy introduced me to a new position that wasn't all that exciting in itself but the risk of being caught thrilled me.

"Oh, Daddy. Oh, God. Daddy. Daddy. I'm com—" Just then I slipped out of his grip, landing on the gear shift knob. "Ooooh ,God. Oh, God." I'd forgotten how good getting it in the butt felt. I was glad it was only a three speed without a reverse lock out.

Hungry, we put on enough clothing to keep from being arrested and headed for home. I stopped at the first phone booth we passed to call in a carry-out pizza order from a place near my new apartment. We didn't want to waste any of the few precious minutes we had together that night in a restaurant. Instead, we reenacted the *Tom Jones* eating scene on Georgette's bed, using pizza as an imaginative substitute for more suggestive food.

Not only did having our own bathrooms give us more sleep, we could have breakfast together. That night, when Daddy told me I was going to my first cocktail party, I was fearful.

"What do I do if someone talks to me? Do I say I'm

your mistress and give great blow jobs? I've nothing to talk about."

"Don't worry. Nobody says anything interesting at those things, not out in the open, at least. Skim today's paper at lunch so you can comment on the news. Make sure you know how the Yankees, Mets, Jets, and Giants are doing. Don't worry about basketball or hockey. Just say you don't follow them. Know which plays are doing well and which are turkeys. You don't have to know anything about them. Say you're dying to see whatever they're talking about most. It's easy."

"You want me to be a phony?" I had thought they were smart and sophisticated.

"Exactly. That's how to fit in perfectly. They're all phonies. We'll go to one soon and you'll be the prettiest girl there. You always are."

I kissed him, for the compliment and his support.

"Wear the beaded black dress tonight, complete with garter and feather headband."

"Who am I tonight? A niece wouldn't dress like this."

"You're my niece who's studying drama at NYU."

"That kind of niece would."

I managed to get through the cocktail party by looking aloof so people wouldn't approach me and find out how much a bumpkin I was. Fortunately, they didn't pick up on how out of place I was because they didn't hear a thing I said. Their interests lay not in sports or the theater but in the boudoir, getting into my boudoir. One lech was particularly bothersome.

"I've got an apartment near here I think you'd like to see. It's got a spectacular view," said a guy who'd had too much to drink and who had worked his way around the room from woman to woman, finally hitting on me.

"You're not my type, buddy. You're annoying me."

"What is your type?" Not bad looking, he seemed offended by my rudeness.

"Over there." I looked at a butch woman across the room.

"Her? One night with me and you'll forget all about her."

He grabbed my ass with both hands grinding my pussy back and forth against his undesired desire. I didn't let on how good those beads felt rolling across my clit.

Thwack. I slapped him hard enough that it echoed across the room. All conversation stopped and everyone looked at me. No sooner had he sulked away did a beautiful, fortyish woman, who looked vaguely familiar, approach me.

Oh no. I thought I'd made an absolute fool of myself.

"Good for you, dearie. He's deserved that for the longest time but none of us had the guts to do it. You'll never work in New York again. Better try Hollywood."

I quickly worked my way to Daddy and pulled him aside. "We've got to leave now. I've made a fool of myself."

"To the contrary. You'll be a folk hero in these parts for slapping the producer of several hit plays who preys on actresses, young and old—but mostly young. This is your night. Enjoy it."

⌘

I emerged from the bathroom, prepared for bed, cradling my arm, acting as if I was in another world. "The calla lilies are in bloom."

Daddy burst out laughing. "She's another beautiful redhead. Not as beautiful as you, my dear, but high on the list."

"Does she have green eyes like mine. Very few do."

"No. Blue. All I care about are yours."

"You be Charlie Allnut tonight and despoil this virgin spinster."

"You're far too young to be a spinster but I'll love ravaging you."

This was a night to remember but Tuesday morning came too soon.

Brrring!

"Damned alarm." I had to hurry with little time for one last round before he abandoned me for five days. I put my hands to work.

His response caused us to need our showers even more than before. We ran late that morning, but it was worth it because it gave me one more experience to hold onto for the five long days until he returned.

Besides money, I had more time and energy for studies. No longer going on blind dates, surfing singles bars, and responding to personal ads, allowed me to excel at college. I no longer worried about being able to pay my bills. I lived off my cash allowance and deposited my paychecks in the bank. I even saved my tuition reimbursement checks because I'd paid the tuition out of my allowance. I was the most content I'd ever been. Release from financial pressures pushed any second thoughts I might've had about our arrangement out of my mind. I'd think about that some other time. I didn't want to make a habit of taking cash from men, but it was nice to have the security of knowing I needn't have money worries again.

I felt superior to my girlfriends. I was appreciated for what I did, and Daddy treated me with more courtesy than any of my friends' boyfriends treated them. These girls too often got stuck paying for their dates because their loser boyfriends were broke. To top it off, their so-called lovers expected them to put out after paying to see stupid movies they didn't like and games they didn't give a hoot about. Not Mary Louise. No way. If there was one thing I wouldn't do, it was support a man. When the time came, I wanted a husband who supported me and our children, not the other way around.

Once the stability of our relationship was established, our fears of never seeing the other again vanished, reducing the urgency to fuck like minks. We still had lots of passionate sex but ended early enough to get some sleep. We were generous to each other out of bed, as well as in, and rarely argued. We each tried our hardest to please the other. In short, life was wonderful.

The one thorny area was dealing with friends and family. We decided at the outset to keep our relationship secret from everyone. People who knew me were well aware that my heavy school schedule greatly reduced my socializing time. My family wasn't as understanding after having me always available—at least over the phone—and planning for visitors was tricky. I couldn't tell relatives not to come. I explained to Mother that I had a conference or something out of town from Sunday evening to Tuesday afternoon and she'd have to come on the days in between. When the older of my younger brothers, Daniel the chess master, came to visit with her, he noticed my more confident demeanor and that I no longer struggled financially.

"Have you gotten a raise, Tookie?"

"No." I shouldn't have offered to pay. He wouldn't have noticed I had more money than before.

"Do you gamble or sell drugs?"

"No." I wanted him to stop interrogating me. I wasn't about to tell him where my money came from.

After hesitating a few seconds, he arrived at what must've been the only other option that came into his dirty little mind. "Selling your body is all that's left. I recall that you've had a lot of practice."

I didn't answer. I just looked down—silence was how I handled uncomfortable questions.

Daniel inquired no further, but concluded he was right and told his friends, the few he had, that I was turning tricks in Times Square.

CHAPTER 16

Graduation

I was still very content with Daddy two years into our relationship, by far the longest I'd had at this time—except for Tim, but he was overseas for most of it—but there were occasional bumps in the road, such as when friends called when he was with me. He wasn't possessive in that he didn't want me to have friends. He actually encouraged me to do things with the girls—just not when he was around and not in my apartment. My phone ringing triggered the first such incident.

"Homework. I've got a lot this year," I said into the phone, carrying it into the adjoining room so as not to disturb Daddy.

He followed me. "Who is it?" he asked in a loud whisper and gestured frantically for an answer.

"Sybil from work," I whispered back, cupping the mouthpiece with my hand. "She wants me to go out with her but I've begged off." I went back to my phone conversation. "Maybe Jackie can. I'll be fucked if I don't finish my homework." I hung up and turned to Daddy. "I haven't finished my homework for Wednesday. Are you going to discipline me?" I pushed down my slacks as we both laughed, me more than him.

He didn't take me up on my offer—a first. Instead he grilled me. "How'd she get your number?"

"I brought my old number with me so people wouldn't know I moved. They eventually found out but it took months longer."

"Oh." He looked concerned. "Have many of them been here?"

"Only Evelyn, so far. And my family. I've convinced them I have a roommate and have taken a sabbatical from dating to finish my degree."

He accepted my explanation and things returned to normal. I wasn't about to risk what I had for the rush of seducing a strange man. Daddy trusted me and I him. Things were great between us.

⋐⋑⋐⋑

When I was close to finishing my junior year, I had a major surprise when I answered the door right after coming home from work on a late-winter Friday.

Tim stood outside in the cold, waiting. "Aren't you going to invite me in?" he asked, eventually.

Saying nothing, I led him to my living room and pointed to the couch. "You can sit here just long enough to warm up a little. Don't take off your coat. Then you must leave. It's not my problem your heater doesn't work."

I hoped Daddy's spies didn't see me let him in and looked out the window to see if anyone was watching my apartment. I probably couldn't see them if they were there.

Tim broke a long silence. "I'm getting divorced."

"So?" I knew what was coming next and I was ready for him.

"I'd like to see you again," he said sheepishly without making eye contact.

"You're warm enough now. Be on your way. Get a car with a better heater." I couldn't risk him being there any longer.

I watched him walk to his car with his shoulders slumped from my harsh rejection.

I finished my homework for the weekend and got to bed early that night and the next to be ready for Sunday evening.

Daddy made no mention of Tim, so I thought he was behind me. However, Tim called me a weeknight in October out of the blue.

"My company's sending me to Bell Labs on a two-week business trip. I'd like to see you."

I knew what it was like to be lonely and alone. "I'll have dinner with you one night but that's it. Nothing more." If I'd known at the time that he'd agreed to do a month-long stint in northernmost North Dakota in the winter, just for the opportunity to see me, I wouldn't have agreed to see him at all.

There he is. Better not let him in. It'll be cold when we return from the restaurant, better take my winter coat. I raced to get out the door but he was standing outside waiting for me. He walked me to his rental car—a Volare, I think—and opened the door for me like always. I tossed my bulky coat into the back seat.

"It's nice of you to go out to dinner with me," he said with fear in his voice, fidgeting in his seat.

"I felt obliged because you're all alone." *Why the hell did I agree to do this?*

"Where to?"

"Charley's Other Brother. You'll probably like it. I made reservations."

"Reservations? Why do you need them on a week-night?"

"We need them everywhere every night unless the place is a dump." He was still a hick.

I didn't speak to Tim again until we were seated at a table.

"My divorce is moving forward, but it's not easy. Zelda has an infinite capacity to fight."

He looked beaten. "Ever consider suicide?" I asked.

"Only briefly. Why do you ask?"

"Some people do," I said nonchalantly, stirring my cranberry juice to give him a hint I was bored.

"What do you do outside work?"

"College classes, nights and weekends."

"Is there someone special in your life?"

I needed to dodge this question. "I loved spending time with my boyfriend's daughter."

"Why do you see him?"

"Time to go." I stood up, ending the conversation.

He drove me directly to my apartment. The instant the Volare stopped moving, I flew out of it and dashed to my door, locking it behind me. I was safe. Safe from myself. He was the only man who ever turned down my offer of sex. I wanted to improve my record to a hundred percent but I didn't dare.

Seconds later, I heard a rapping, a gentle tapping at my chamber door. I looked out my window to see my former beau holding my coat, nothing more.

"Here, you forgot this."

I jerked my coat out of his hand and closed my door, shutting him out of my life forever more.

Discouraged but not giving up, Tim called me every couple of months just to check in on me. He thought I needed to be looked after but he was dead wrong. He also had poor timing.

The next year—I forget exactly when— my phone rang on a Monday night right after Daddy and I had returned home from some soiree, a time when I dreaded receiving calls from anyone.

"Hello," I said, hoping it was only Mother or Evelyn.

"Just checking in to see if you're okay," Tim's unmistakable voice said.

"Can't talk now. Pile of homework to do. I'm fine. Bye."

Daddy emerged from the bedroom half undressed, apparently sensing something. "Are you always that curt with friends?"

"Just Tim. I hate it when people call during playtime. Can you unhook me?" I said, trying to divert his attention.

"Tim? You've never mentioned him before." He cupped my breasts with his hands more to keep me from moving away than to excite me.

"He's ancient history but doesn't want to accept it." I squeezed his hands as a hint to fondle me but he wasn't easily distracted.

"Was he your first?" He blew his hot breath along the side of my neck and down my front.

"I went out with him because nobody else asked me." I pulled his hands down to my groin. "Unzip me."

He held my zipper at the top but didn't slide it down. "But was he your *first*?"

"No! I wanted him to be, but he wouldn't. Time's awasting. Let's get naked."

"What was wrong with him?" He slowly unzipped me waiting for my answer, making it clear he wasn't going to have sex until I came clean.

I hated talking about him but thought it better get it over and done with. "He was a naïve young boy who fell madly in love with me and wanted to marry me."

"And he wasn't able to seduce you?"

"The other way around. I wasn't able to seduce him. I even got naked and he wouldn't."

"Was he gay or something?"

"Oh, no. He wanted me in the worst way but he wanted my love more and I wouldn't give it to him."

"And he still loves you?"

"He always will, and I'll never love him."

"Ever think you should've married him?"

"No." *That better satisfy your curiosity.* I wriggled my shoulders as a hint I wanted him to undress me. He took the hint and, very shortly, I took him on the living room couch with the drapes wide open this one time, hoping a neighbor might "accidentally" see me perform.

⌘

After working full-time and going to school nights and weekends for six years, I completed my BS degree with high honors. I found college coursework easier than my classmates because my grueling senior year of high school forced me to learn how to study effectively. I learned self-discipline, working hard to catch up with my new classmates. Most of my college classmates were either smart enough to get through high school without study skills or not smart enough to compete with me, with or without them. Many were younger and immature. College was a grind. Work all day, grab a quick bite on the way to class, spend three hours sitting in the classroom, drive home, study for the next day, then crash. My weekly forty-eight hours with Daddy made the routine bearable.

With my magna cum laude came a promotion to associate statistician. I finally brought home decent money and bought a used MGB sports car. As a member of the professional staff, my Carver-Watkins coworkers, the male ones, treated me more respectfully, at least to my face, but never fully accepted me as one of them. Some of the clerical girls found my new status awkward and avoided me.

My parents had moved to Ohio by this time. My brothers remained in New England, and my older sister was still in Richmond. Dad's company was computerizing and Dad wasn't taking to it well. The pressure of adapting to this new technology triggered a nervous breakdown, for which he was hospitalized. I think he worried constantly about his heart giving out and being unable to support his family. I've never admitted this before, but I worried about his mental issues being hereditary so I didn't tell people about Dad's problems.

Dad wasn't able to adjust to computers after he returned to his job. This limited his opportunities for assignments within the company. He and Mom retired a couple of years later to a tiny house in Arkansas near Mom's parents, Gom and Pop. It was all they could afford. My brother Daniel looked after them and Gom and Pop in their old age.

I flew out to visit as often as I could afford. Because I never lived in my birth state, I didn't get the opportunity to spend nearly as much time with Gom and Pop, the only extended family members I knew growing up, as I would've liked. The only time I lived within two states of them was the two years we spent in Milltown. Gom and Pop visited us much more often there than at any other time, simply because the shorter distance made their visits more practical. The only vacations my parents took were on the moves from one project assignment to the next. Pressures to meet deadlines and lack of extra cash prevented us from taking normal vacations like other families.

I was no longer living from paycheck to paycheck as they had done. My promotion and pay raises supplemented by my allowance gave me enough disposable income to buy whatever I needed and to splurge on some luxuries.

The world was truly my oyster now. I had my degree, a decent income, a nice apartment, a fun car, and a lover. My life was perfect—until the beautiful Sunday evening Daddy wasn't sitting on his suitcase by the curb.

What went wrong? I didn't even know what flight he was on or where he came from. He might've just been late.

I couldn't sit in front of the airport and look conspicuous. It was better to leave and return in fifteen minutes. If he wasn't not here in an hour, I'd leave a message on his answering machine.

After three hours and three messages, I returned home. He didn't call. No airline crashes were reported. I couldn't sleep. When my alarm went off, I didn't know what to do. What would Daddy want me to do in this situation? He'd say to go to work and don't let on that anything out of the ordinary has happened. I didn't want to create problems for when he finally arrived.

After work, the doorbell jolted me out of my reverie.

"I'm from the phone company, miss," said the man in a blue work uniform. "I've got a work order to remove a phone from this apartment."

This was strange. Daddy would have to explain it on Sunday. "Which phone do you want?"

He gave me the number and I led him to my roommate's bedroom. He quickly disconnected the phone and wrapped it up.

"What about the answering machine? That's his, too."

"It's not on my work order and isn't phone company

equipment anyway. It stays. I'll disconnect the line at the pole. I'm done in here. Any questions, miss?"

"Could I see the work order, please?"

He handed it to me. "Sure."

I read it carefully as the repairman rocked back and forth waiting. "Who is this originator?" I asked.

"That's the person in sales who took the disconnect order."

I then noticed the customer's name, David Ward, and returned the paper to him. "Thank you."

Only then did it hit me. I'd been dumped. No phone call, no letter, no telegram, no nothing. I'd had strange breakups before but this was the strangest. No fighting, no recriminations, no nothing. I needed to talk. Didn't dare tell Evelyn I'd been a kept woman. She'd never understand. Sybil would. I called her.

"Syb, got a minute?"

"Don't I always?"

That was the truth. She always had time for me, even now that I'd just about cut her out of my life for three years.

"Please don't tell me I've been a fool again. My boyfriend of three years just broke up with me and I never knew his name or where he lives." She was going to scream at me for not telling her about him.

"Sounds like the remarkable Mr. Pennypacker, the sausage maker who had families in Harrisburg and Philadelphia, and they didn't know about each other."

"That was a movie. This's real life and he *can't* have another family." No way could she be right. He was always a perfect gentleman with me.

"For three long years, you've said you didn't have a boyfriend and weren't interested in looking for one. You don't trust me much." Her voice carried hurt. "Don't think you fooled anyone in the office. The guys even rated you on how you looked after your all-night rumpy-pumpy sessions on a scale from one to ten. One for grumpy due to getting a bladder infection to ten for too bowlegged to walk after taking on the entire Rutgers squad. I stood up for you. Told them you don't like sports.'"

"Thanks," I said, trying to placate her. "It wasn't like that. He demanded absolute secrecy."

"Why'd you go along with it? No man's that good in bed."

"He was wonderful to me, in and out of bed. He might have died but I'll never know for sure since I have no idea what his real name was."

"Start at the beginning. How'd you meet him?"

"He picked me up at the bar in the Plumtree where he was staying. After we went to his room, he—" *How do I say this delicately?* "He offered to be my roommate."

Sybil glared, hurt and anger on her face. "Who was he? You must've been ashamed of what you were doing. You never told anyone anything."

"I don't know. We gave each other false names."

Incredulous, her eyes blazed at my response. "You never asked?"

"We agreed not to ask questions. He didn't, so I didn't."

"And you thought this guy was serious about you?"

"We were so good together." *Get off my case.*

"So he's why you moved. Your old apartment wasn't big enough for two people. And your female roommate never existed?"

"I made her up."

"No man'd live in that room. He didn't, did he? He shared your room—and bed—with you, his mistress." She looked smug for figuring it all out.

"Sometimes. Didn't you share your bed with Bob before you got married?"

"You couldn't afford the rent on that apartment. He had to be kicking in a lot. Was he payin' for more'n the rent?"

"Er…ah…yes. A little more."

"How much more?"

"A five hundred a month allowance. More than C-W paid me back when we met."

"He wasn't chipping in, he was your sugar daddy." She had a knack for getting to the core of things.

"In a manner of speaking."

"Not in a manner of speaking. He kept you. Those fancy clothes weren't your roommate's, were they? You'd never buy anything like that for yourself."

She knew me all too well. "He bought them for me because he needed me to accompany him to social events related to his business. He's the only man, other than Tim, to tell me I'm beautiful other than when they wanted me to do something for them."

"The picture's gettin' clearer. How often did he come, and how long did he stay?"

"I'd pick him up at the airport on Sunday evenings, drive him to and from work at the industrial park just off Exit 8A on Mondays and Tuesdays, and drop him at the airport Tuesday evenings."

"Every week?"

"Except one or two a year." Those were very lonely weeks but we made up for it when he returned.

"You've been had. The one good thing out of this is that you didn't prostitute yourself. He didn't pay you for poundin' your pussy several times a night, a hundred nights a year for three years. That's at least a thousand free fucks and who knows how many times The Blow Job

Queen, as the guys call you, serviced him other ways for nothin'. Nada."

"You're crazy. He didn't take advantage of me. He respected me and treated me very well."

"Two nights a week equates to a hundred very expensive hotel rooms, a hundred breakfasts, and fifty rental cars for two days each. At thirty-five dollars a night for a room at the Plumtree plus three dollars for breakfast, we're talking thirty-eight hundred a year it would've cost him for lodging. Add to that twenty-five hundred for rental cars at fifty a week and fifty Sunday dinners at ten bucks a pop. Those items alone would've cost him sixty-eight hundred a year and he only gave you six thousand."

"Huh?" I didn't get her.

"If he was an executive for some corporation, he was on expense account. If he was self-employed, his travel expenses came out of his own pocket. Either way, he got friendlier accommodations at a bargain basement price with tons of sucky-fucky thrown in free for a bonus. And *he* probably pocketed some cash in the deal."

I was in her bailiwick now. She arranged travel for her department. I shook my head. "It wasn't like that at all. He was very nice to me, took me to nice places, and taught me many things."

"And in return, you gave him chandelier-rattlin' sex. Remember, I saw you drag into the office lookin' like he'd ridden you hard and put you up wet all those Monday and Tuesday mornings."

"I don't believe you. It can't be true." He did everything right, said all the right things."

"Wake up and smell the nookie, Tookie. Let's say all you gave him for the six thousand a year was sex, estimated conservatively at six dickings and a blow job each week."

"Very conservatively." That was only twice at night

and once in the morning each weekday and didn't include kinky stuff. He slipped it to me a helluva lot more often than that. I spread my legs whenever he gave me the faintest hint he wanted it and sucked him off whenever I thought he was losing interest or I didn't look my best.

Sybil rolled her eyes. "Six schtups a week, times fifty weeks, gives you three hundred a year. You only got twenty bucks a trick, even less if you gave him more, count air starts, and don't consider the food, lodging, and transportation you gave him. Streetwalkers do better than that. Either way, you got screwed big time for his weekly fuckathons, honey. Don't ever ask me to partner with you. You've got no business sense."

If he didn't feel anything for me, I really was a fool. But he really did care for me. Nobody could prove otherwise. "Please don't tell the girls in the office—or, heaven forbid, Evelyn—they'll never let me live this down."

I cried myself to sleep and slept through till my alarm went off. The next few weeks were awful, but I eventually accepted the fact Daddy was never coming back.

I was just an unkept woman, a failed mistress, and too gullible to turn pro. I'd have to change all that.

CHAPTER 17

Isaac

I felt naked. It was Isaac. He was undressing me with his eyes. I couldn't believe it. He'd always ignored me, as much as I'd wished he hadn't.

I made eye contact with him.

"New glasses?" he said, looking up from his work.

"Sorry?" *Something's going on with him.*

"Are those new glasses?"

"No." *When did I switch to tortoiseshell frames? Fifth or sixth grade?*

"They look good on you." He actually smiled at me when he said this.

I was wearing an outfit I'd worn hundreds of times before. My hair hadn't changed for years. Still wore no makeup. Hadn't had my boobs enhanced. Quit wiggling my ass for his benefit years ago. Nothing about me had changed, other than my new exalted—hardly—position upon my promotion to professional staff, so he must've changed. Perhaps his wife bored him after untold years of a dull marriage.

We'd worked near each other for years and he snubbed me when I would've welcomed his attention. He upset me then, but I'd moved on. I still found him quite attractive: tall, athletic, dark hair graying at the temples, and left handed—*lefties are more creative and intelligent.* A low-level manager when I started with the company, Isaac had moved upward in the intervening years. According to rumors, the big boss had been grooming him for a major promotion to be announced soon.

The next week, I had to analyze the results of some studies for him because his regular statistician had gone on maternity leave. One morning, as I promenaded by his office, he poked his head out the door.

"Tookie, have a minute?" He stood up straight and adjusted his tie.

"I've got a meeting in ten minutes." *Phweew.* At least I had a legitimate excuse. I turned and took a step toward my cubicle.

"I'll need more time than that. After lunch?" His arrogance had dissipated. He was pleading with me.

"I'm tied up with mandatory training then," I said truthfully, but not unhappily.

"I'll just have to buy you lunch." He smiled broadly, knowing he had me cornered.

"Sure you can afford it?" *Maybe that'll put him off my scent.*

His eyes burned through my clothing like lasers.

I went because I'm a sucker for free lunches and had to talk to him about the studies sometime. I rarely got the pleasure of watching a man I have no intention of letting pork me drool. Having to get back by one protected me from myself. *Quit it, nipples!*

He focused on work. In spite of not making a pass, not even an innuendo, he radiated desire. I found him pleasant enough and wondered why he hadn't asked me out years before. Of all the men at work I desired for affairs, only Isaac had resisted my charms and, possibly because of his reluctance, was the one I lusted for most.

However, something had changed recently, and he became interested, quite interested. But he'd hurt my feelings by ignoring me all those years and I didn't suffer insults graciously.

Every time Isaac approached me after that lunch, I maneuvered things to avoid any opportunity for him to ask me out again, generally by having others present. The type of pill I took then may've affected my temperament. After being on it for over seven years, I was experiencing some side-effects. I switched to an IUD and the side effects, including grouchiness I hadn't realized I had, disappeared.

Apparently noticing my improved temperament, or on blind luck, Isaac ventured an invitation to dinner. I accepted, not expecting much to happen.

"I've never known anyone who has red hair and green eyes before," he said over his salad, never taking his eyes off me.

"I'm special. We're less than one per cent of the population." He was going to work hard for anything he gets from me.

"I'll say you are."

If he wasn't so sophisticated, I'd say he's fawning over me. "Tell me more." I craved compliments about something other than how well I perform a sex act.

"You did a great job on that analysis, especially considering you're a new grad."

That crack annoys me. "I've worked here since high school, you know."

"But not as a statistician," he said with an authoritative air.

"Want to bet?" *Little of what I know came from college.*

"It's rare to see someone so smart and beautiful, too."

"I work hard." I blushed. No man had complimented me like that since Tim eons ago. I felt something odd. Could it be? Being aroused isn't out of the ordinary for me, but something was different this time. I was falling for this guy and wanted to see lots more of him.

"Many people work hard, but you bring out subtle points even experienced people often miss."

"Tell me about yourself." I needed to get the topic off me. I wasn't comfortable.

He told me his life story, beginning with prep school and ending with his wife not understanding him or appreciating his needs. He told me everything I needed to know about him, and more, in fifteen minutes. I shoveled in my dinner so I wouldn't have to talk. I thought I'd made a good impression and didn't want to spoil it by saying the wrong thing.

"Dessert?" *He must think I'm famished the way I ate.*

I nodded as I took a sip of water.

"Waiter! Could you bring me a des—"

I put down my water and said as sexily as my voice could muster, "Dessert's on me—at my apartment."

"Check!" He pulled out his wallet and put some bills in the waiter's hand and bolted for the door, dragging me behind him. *Maybe I should give him what I'd saved for Daddy out of spite.*

I was having the best time I'd had in the months since Daddy dumped me and wanted the night to continue. Lowering my guard a little, I invited him in when we got to my place.

"Please excuse me a second." I slipped into the bathroom briefly to take off my bra and pantyhose to prepare for what I had in mind. Hoping he'd stay the night, I pulled my basket of male toiletries out of my roomie's linen closet and set it on the counter.

His eyes twinkled. "What's for dessert?"

"It's in here." I led Isaac to my bed/work room. As soon as he passed the threshold, I pushed him backward onto my bed and jumped on him crossways to both hold him down and give him a sneak preview of what awaited him under my skirt.

"Let's slow things down a bit. I'm not looking for a one-night stand. I want to savor every second with you."

Oh shit! I think I blew it. "What do you want to do?"

He patted the bed next to him. "Lie down next to me so we can cuddle a bit."

"I'd like that." I gently nudged him to move to the left side of my bed and I lay down next to him. He kissed me gently then hugged me.

"I like how you've decorated your apartment. Lived here long?"

"Three years. Couldn't afford it before then." *And I'm not telling you how I could before my promotion.*

I kissed him all over his face for showing interest in me. We progressed at the deliberate pace he set. His willingness to wait made me appreciate him all the more. No one since Tim had shown such interest in me or patience. *Should I blow him or save that treat for our next date and just let him fuck me now?*

Isaac made the decision for me by mounting me in missionary style. I followed his lead and gave him the best I could in such a boring position. Afterward, he kissed me long and sweetly. "I better get going. It's getting late." He sat on the edge of the bed and started putting on his clothes.

"No need to go. Check out the guest bathroom." *Please stay. I want you to cuddle me all night.*

He pulled up his trousers and padded into the bathroom. "Okay?"

"What do you see?" *Are you blind?*

"A basket of toiletries."

No shit, Sherlock. "Check." I loved the smell of Old Spice and stocked it for my men to wear.

"I need more than this," he whined.

Don't be so thick. "Like what?"

"A change of clothes." He rambled into the hall as if preparing to leave.

"Go into the guest bedroom and open the closet."

He looked in the closet, flipping through the white shirts until he found one his size.

"Socks and underwear are in the top drawer."

"Pajamas?"

"They just get in the way when I wake up hungry in the middle of the night. Brush your teeth and come to bed."

"I always thought you were sexy, but never dreamed you'd be this good."

"Stop lying." *He's smooth but maybe he's not lying completely.*

"I'm serious. I was afraid to ask you out before because I thought you'd think I'm too old."

"I'm the least sexy girl in the office. I always dress modestly and don't draw attention to myself." *That's the truth.*

"You've succeeded in camouflaging yourself. The wives don't consider you a threat. They worry about Marie in accounting."

"That's a good one." I laughed. "Marie's a lesbian. Keep quiet about that."

We slept little, but enough to function at reduced efficiency. I woke up first.

"Time to get up." I kissed him good morning after I finished showering. "I'll set breakfast out for you. I shouldn't be late. Nothing should look odd."

Isaac emerged from the bathroom while I was washing my glass and bowl.

"I need to leave now. Just pull the door shut behind you. It'll lock automatically."

"Kiss me goodbye first?"

I picked up the Princeton school tie that I kept around for such occasions and draped it around his neck. Holding an end of the tie in each hand, I pulled his head forward to kiss him goodbye. "Do you like it?"

"Wrong school." He grinned, rubbed it against my cheek, and sniffed it. "But it'll remind me of you."

"I'll get you a different one today. Any preference?"

"Your school colors. Leave your car at the airport after work. We can spend the evening together before her flight comes in at nine."

"Okay." I gave his dick a little squeeze. "Think of me today."

"Don't worry. I couldn't avoid it if I wanted to, which I don't."

He looked right in place in my apartment.

My next challenge was to not let on at work about what was happening between us. Being busy made it easier to keep my mind off Isaac. Late in the afternoon, he took off his glasses, signaling to me that he was ready to leave.

I meandered casually to my car but raced straight to the airport lot. I'd barely gotten out when Isaac roared up.

"You sure got here quick." *Whoa. Don't run over me.*

"Don't want to waste a second I could be with you."

I melted. "Want to go to my place?"

"Let's eat first. Have you tried Chez Nous yet?"

My stomach sank. *New boyfriends don't pass up sex. I want to be close to home in case he dumps me.* "Too ritzy for me. Let's just go to Mother's Other Place. Not far from here."

"I'll drive. Get in." He looked at me like a birthday boy looks at chocolate cake.

He wouldn't want me in his car if he's dumping me. He'd have me drive and flag down a cab after he ended it. I rode quietly as Isaac chattered on about what happened in the office that day. I braced myself for the worst when he asked for the booth in the far corner of the room. *Maybe he's afraid I'll make a scene.*

He leaned toward me and talked quietly. "I couldn't even imagine ever having a night as incredible as the one we shared last night."

"Thanks." *Is this a lead in to he's feeling all guilty and must end it?*

"I've been running on limerence all day."

"Huh?" *Is that some new kind of drug like Speed?*

"New love energy. You know, how you feel when you're newly in love."

"Is this your way of saying you love me?" *I need to hear him say it again to believe it.*

"I guess. Couldn't you tell?" His downcast expression told me he was disappointed I didn't feel his love for me.

I stopped kissing him only when the waiter interrupted me. After a simple dinner filled with more flirting than food, I felt a lot more secure.

"Let's not waste time driving all the way to my place." I wanted to give him an exciting time and show him how much I'd risk for him.

"What do you have in mind?" I could see the wheels turning as his expression changed to confused then to optimistic and finally to uncertain.

He wasn't so sure of himself when he wasn't calling the shots.

"Head back to the airport. I'll tell you on the way." I slid over and kissed him on the cheek. He looked perplexed but did as I asked and parked next to my car. "We'll take my car. Want no evidence in yours."

He thought a second, nodded, got out and wedged himself into my MG. "Where are we going?" He fidgeted nervously as we drove off the airport grounds.

"See the defunct car wash just past the corner?" This was going to be fun. I hoped it would thrill him.

"Are you sure about this?" He looked uncomfortable, probably because he hadn't gone parking in decades.

"Take off your pants. I want you ready for me when I stop." My confidence grew enough over dinner to initiate a surreptitious shag session in plain view.

I drove around back and pulled into the second stall all the way to the front. The stained concrete walls and weeds disappeared when I turned off the lights. Headlights of passing cars swam across our stall as cars made the turn toward the terminal.

"Get rid of the rest. I like you naked," I commanded as I stripped.

He looked unsure of what I was about to do. "Do police patrol this place?"

"Not usually." I'd only been caught here in a compromising position once and that was in the Vega so I didn't have to put the top up. I drove whoever I was with out of here buck naked, but the cops didn't get a good look at us.

"That's comforting." His head swiveled, taking in the cramped cockpit of my tiny MGB. "There's not enough room."

"Get out and pop the snaps around your window."

He had his free in a wink. "We're putting the top down, are we?"

"No. Just making more room. Push the top back and leave your door open when you get back in."

His skeptical look changed to euphoria when I put my face in his lap, but he still flinched each time headlights washed through the windshield. The possibility of getting caught excited me, Isaac not so much. I rewarded him by stepping up my game a notch for being a good sport. I focused on his pleasure. The thrills I got from doing it in public and knowing he wanted me got me off with less effort than usual on his part. Not wanting him to throw out his back in the cramped space, I sat on his lap for the second round. He seemed more relaxed, probably because passersby couldn't see him. He recoiled, though, whenever a northbound car hit the pothole at the edge of the road and bounced its headlights all over us, and when an engine was extra loud or if a car sounded like it was slowing down to turn into here. I got a rush from all of it.

"Time for one more." I checked my watch, the Seiko Tim had brought back for me, to make sure. I didn't want her to suspect a thing. He collapsed in his seat after the third round, limp, as if he'd had a full-body massage. I dropped him at his car with minutes to spare.

He kissed me goodbye, started to drive away then stopped, rolled down his window, and reached out to me. I grasped his hand and he pulled me to him, uttering, "Love you," and sped off.

I basked in the infatuation of a new relationship. And although I made no long-term plans for my life, I planned my love affairs to the minutest detail. I even planned out exactly what I'd do with my pick-ups before giving the guys the first indication I might be interested.

And it was always guys. Even though I dreamt about ménage a trois, I decided against them. With two men at once, I had concerns about my safety and, although very confident about my technique, my AA bust wouldn't stack up well against a woman with just A-cups if the two of us competed for a randy breast-man's attention.

To get down to basics, I saw no point in sharing a man's sausage. In this regard, I don't play well with others, although I'm exceedingly playful in bed. Already tired of time-sharing his popsicle, I plotted how to make Isaac's all my own, really my own, while he was still young enough to start a family.

Isaac assured me repeatedly that his wife no longer wanted relations with him, but all the men said that, or their wives didn't understand them, or they'd moved on from their old girlfriends. Of course, I didn't believe them anymore. However, Isaac spoke so sincerely from his heart, he had to be telling me the truth. My faintly ticking biological clock likely affected my thinking and convinced me to suspend disbelief this one time.

Although I accepted what he said as true, I knew wives held the higher ground on this battlefield. I just had to figure out how to offset wives' inherent advantages, and quick.

CHAPTER 18

Shanghaied

Going to jog by my place tonight?" I asked Isaac on the Friday of a week he hadn't been able to break away to see me.

"Last night she reminded me we're having guests for dinner and cards tonight," he said, looking down at his shoes.

"What about tomorrow?"

He fidgeted with his fancy pen. "She's been funny since you called on Wednesday. She arranged for us to spend the weekend with her sister's family in the Poconos."

My stomach sank. *"Great!" She's playing hardball.*

"Don't worry. Nothing can happen. Their cabin's set up for communal living with no privacy."

"Better not." *Why do I attract weak men?*

All alone with nothing to do all weekend, I felt him slipping away. What could I do? What have other women who had weak men done? Wallis Simpson? Yes. She was the one. Her first husband—or was it her second?—introduced her to the "Shanghai Squeeze" in a Shanghai brothel. But I didn't have an expert prostitute to tutor me. Drat.

I pulled my copy of the encyclopedia of sex techniques from where I keep it hidden in my bottom desk drawer and flipped through it. I quickly found what I wanted, but needed a prop to get started.

The office was unusually quiet due to many people taking off because they'd finished a major multi-year project on Wednesday. Bored, I took lunch early at eleven-thirty instead of my usual time and raced to the nearest sex shop to make my purchase. Overwhelmed with their assortment of aids, I waved at a salesperson.

She helped me sort through their selection of marble eggs to choose one that should be just right for me. In a stall in the office ladies' room, I popped the egg into my untoned vagina to start training immediately.

That it felt strange is an understatement, even for someone used to having all manner of foreign objects animal, vegetable, and mineral inside her on a semi-regular basis. Cigars, cucumbers, and the occasional carrot slid easily into me, but never a Coke bottle. I wasn't about to risk that one. After inserting my first cucumber directly from the crisper drawer, I learned that temperature matters—a lot. The egg didn't need to reach the Fahrenheit of a piping hot cock but, for comfort, had to surpass the ambient temperature of a heavily air-conditioned office. Fortunately, the hot sun shining on the dashboard of my car more than sufficiently incubated my new muscle builder.

Keeping the egg in place while toddling to my desk challenged my ability to keep a straight face while masking my strange waddle and fear of the egg dropping. I didn't quite make it from the restroom across the aisle to my cubicle. Feeling it slipping out, I held it half in place by shoving my right hand between my legs and staggering bowlegged the few remaining steps. No one saw me because the building was almost deserted. I pulled out my chair with my left hand, repositioned the egg with the right, popping it back into place as I flopped down. I made a mental note, *To self: Don't try this again at work until my muscles are stronger. Practice at home wearing just a dress or skirt until I can hold it in place for an hour.*

Being a natural at all things sexual, over the weekend I practiced Kegel exercises until I learned to control my vaginal muscles well enough to begin serious Squeeze training. Sure, the egg fell out of me and rolled across the floor a few times. But by Sunday evening, I felt it coming loose soon enough to squeeze with my vagina muscles to halt its fall and then tap it back up in place with my hand.

Being prudent at work the next week, I only put it in over lunch on days Isaac and I weren't grabbing quickies. He wasn't able to break free in the evening often and almost never on the weekends. I looked forward to a conference in Las Vegas we and several others from the office would be attending in a month. In the meantime, I exercised my muscles.

Every chance I got at home, I doffed my panties and popped in the egg. Soon, I ventured out on errands with it inside me. Stop lights provided opportunities to squeeze my muscles. Pretty soon I slowed up for lights just to get more practice time. After a couple of weeks, I held it inside me all day without a problem. Then it was time for the next step.

Carrying a marble egg in my love canal all day wasn't the objective. Giving Isaac an unforgettable experience was. I worked tirelessly at gaining control of my vaginal muscles until I could waltz around my apartment holding a pencil in place daydreaming about how great it was going to be. I loved telling the girls about the time I practiced while wearing a miniskirt too short to wear in public—brother Daniel called it a wide belt. It provided convenient access to reinsert a dropped pencil while barely covering the essentials or covering my bare essentials, whichever way you choose to look at it, in the unlikely case someone should drop by or look in the window of my ground-floor apartment, providing I didn't sit down.

When the doorbell rang, my attention shifted to a shower gift I'd ordered and rushed to see if it'd arrived. The deliveryman's jaw dropped when I snatched my Ticonderoga number two to sign for the package.

Using my squeeze box as a pencil holder wasn't my aim. Giving Isaac the experience of a lifetime just by tightening and loosening my muscles top to bottom or bottom to top was what I had in mind. Kegel exercises didn't require the egg and could be done anywhere at any time because no visible parts moved. Staff meetings became more interesting when I imagined Isaac inside me as I secretly did my exercises in plain sight. One evening at home, I popped a long skinny practice balloon. I smiled with satisfaction knowing I'd mastered the "Shanghai Squeeze."

Other than semi-frequent nooners—lunchies might be more apt because of my preferences—and the rare before work meet up, Isaac's time with me was limited. Getting so little action didn't make me happy at all. I appreciated the notes he mysteriously left on my desk and the clandestine phone calls he made when I least expected to hear from him.

He carved out time for me each Wednesday night while his wife was at choir practice and Saturday mornings when he "jogged a few miles," but I needed more—a lot more. I wanted to share seeing movies with him. I even thought a daughter with my red hair and his curls might be nice.

Because I was going with Isaac, I didn't hook up with Doug to relieve my tension and pleasuring myself wasn't enough. I needed Isaac.

"Hey, I can get away this afternoon." *I won't take no for an answer today. I'm so horny I might take you right here if you resist.*

"I don't have anything important scheduled, but—"

"No buts. Tell them you've got a dental exam and take a late lunch. There's going to be some fancy fucking in that motel room you won't want to miss out on it."

"We might be seen."

"Your love is a lie."

My knight sighed. "Okay. Meet me at the Maple Grove at one thirty."

"Tie a handkerchief on the doorknob."

I instinctively drove to the back of the motel where I saw Isaac's car parked. I parked several spaces down from him to not make it too obvious and skipped to his room. He not only marked it with his handkerchief, he left the door ajar.

"Please latch the door, Tooks, and join me," he patted the bed next to him when I came in.

I turned out the lights so I couldn't see the less than romantic surroundings, stripped quickly, flopped onto the bed next to him, and we were off to the races.

"Tookie, I've missed you so much the past few weeks."

"Me too." *Convince me.*

"It's not just the fabulous sex. I miss being with you, talking with you, even about ordinary everyday things."

"I've missed you a lot, too. What are you going to do about it?"

"I'm working on something. Don't ask what yet."

With that encouragement, I wore him out. The last time he came, he was almost dry and so sore I used lotion on him to reduce friction and help relieve the tenderness. Unfortunately, the lotion included an anesthetic to reduce his pain. It so desensitized his dagger, I couldn't get him hard no matter how much I sucked, stroked, or licked him. Ever resourceful, I tickled his balls lightly and, eureka, it rose. But when I pulled him inside me, the anesthetic put my pleasure giver to sleep, so to speak. We were done for the day and, more importantly, he was done for the night, too.

I rested well that night, secure in the knowledge Isaac wouldn't be fooling around on me. I also felt content for the first time in my adult life because I'd found true love and nothing could tear us apart. He was probably working on a divorce. I hoped. Life was good. Isaac salved my fears the next morning at work.

"Nothing out of the ordinary happened last night. I did some yard work and ate my favorite meal for dinner. Beat, I went to bed early and crashed into a deep sleep."

Deep sleep. Favorite meal. I bet she was pissed.

She—I refused to say her undeserving name—made scheduling rendezvous harder and harder by filling their social calendar with events requiring his attendance. Needing to avoid suspicion added an extra level of difficulty, but with a little daring, we arranged a tryst—one of my favorite words—or two each week under the guise of running errands.

"When's her next business trip?" *If she doesn't go somewhere, anywhere, soon, I'm going to drag you into a stall in the john at work and have my way with you.*

"None scheduled right now."

"Bummer. We'll just have to take one of our own."

"The ASA convention in Las Vegas is coming up."

Bingo!

Chapter 19

What Happens in Vegas

A weeklong tryst in Las Vegas was a great idea. Two time zones away made it all the better. But could I cope two more months with so little time with him? "Let me handle the arrangements. I'll get us adjoining rooms."

"We can't be seen together," Isaac whispered so his secretary wouldn't hear.

"We won't." I'd make sure no one suspected anything.

I used much of the free time I wished had been filled with rendezvous planning the trip to Vegas. I was used to having my weeknights free because I usually saw boyfriends only on weekends but I wanted to be with Isaac all the time. If I arranged for adjoining rooms on the concierge floor early, the rest would probably be taken before anyone else in the office made their reservations. Adjoining rooms would eliminate the possibility of anyone knowing we slept together.

I laid out my plan during a midweek lunchie intermission. "Pick an elevator tower. It doesn't matter which. I'll use the other." I showed him the building layout.

"North?" He looked like he didn't understand why I did this.

"*Always* use the north tower. I'll use the south. No one'll ever see us go up or come down together."

"What about meals," he asked, a little less confused.

"We'll eat with the largest group and sit as far apart as possible. We'll also schedule activities with others. You with the guys. Me with the girls."

"Do we talk at meals?"

I shook my head. "Just pass the butter."

"What about sessions?"

It was nice he craved being with me.

"I'm working on that. We're in different tracks so won't be in the same session more than once or twice. I'll schedule some holes where we're both not in sessions, but everyone else is."

I planned our days down to the minutest detail to maximize our fucking time. Isaac and I would return innocently enough to our own rooms, ostensibly to make phone calls back to the office, use the bathroom, get some papers, take naps, change into swimming suits, or get to bed early.

Once in our rooms, we'd open the adjoining doors and make full use of our love nest.

For my order of play, I left my new "Squeeze" for the grand finale. I wanted Isaac to dream about me on the red-eye home. It might just encourage him to work harder at arranging dates with me.

I just knew this was going be the most wonderful week of my life.

The majority of our group arrived at Newark airport on time the morning the convention started and huddled in a group talking about plans for the week.

"Sarah, where are you seated?" None of my close friends were making the trip. I knew Sarah from a project a couple of years earlier. She was pleasant enough and would make a good beard.

She looked at her ticket. "Fourteen C. You?"

"Thirty D." I'd just accepted the seat assignment the airline assigned me.

"I'm in Thirty E," Isaac piped in.

Shit! I can't sit next to him. I'm not that good an actor. We're screwed.

Isaac bailed us out. "I'll switch if you two want to sit together."

Sarah beamed. "Would you? Tookie and I have lots of catching up to do."

I smiled broadly, but not for the reason Sarah must've thought. "Thanks, Isaac. It's kind of you."

He winked at me. "Not at all."

After a pleasant flight and shuttle bus ride to the hotel, check in of our contingent had to be handled carefully. On cue, Isaac suggested, "Ladies first," when our party massed at the front desk.

Room keys in hand, Sarah and I caught the elevator in the South Tower as I'd preplanned, getting off at the eleventh floor.

"Isn't this convenient being across the hall from each other?" she giggled.

"Sure is," was all I could get out. *Damn. Hope she doesn't leech onto me.*

I hurriedly hung my dress and slacks in the closet, placed my underthings in a dresser drawer, arranged my toiletries in the bathroom, and hid my tools out of sight, but handy for use. Before I could finish counting the different anatomically exaggerated satyrs on the wallpaper, I heard our secret knock at the adjoining door. I silently unlocked it from my side and whipped it open when I heard the confirming click from his side.

"*Tookie.*" The gleam in his eye told me he was as ready as I was.

I embraced Isaac and kissed his burning lips. "Not much time. Get naked now."

He complied. I was still unhooking my bra when I heard a knock.

"Tookie, we've got to sign up for our sessions now if we want to get what we want," said the all-too-familiar voice in the hall.

"Damn!" was my barely audible reply. "Sarah, I need to use the bathroom. I'll catch up with you," was all I could muster out loud.

I stopped stripping and threw naked Isaac onto my bed. I ignored the warnings about how unsanitary hotel bedspreads can be, telling him sadly, "This's all we have time for now." I lubricated my hands and went to work. "This'll have to do you until tonight." I finished him off with the happiest of endings, then slapped his butt and told him to get dressed. I locked the door after him and dressed.

My advance planning paid off. By having everything laid out in advance, Isaac and I got exactly those sessions we wanted. Sarah and I signed up for a bus tour of The Marriage Capital of the World while Isaac unsuccessfully attempted to emulate James Bond at baccarat. We sat on the open top of the double-decker tour bus to get a better view. It would have been great fun to make love to Isaac in front of the other passengers and all the tourists on The Strip.

Maybe it'd be smarter to do it when we were the only passengers. No one would interrupt us and we'd be more visible to onlookers, especially to those in upper-floor hotel rooms. Maybe we'd teach them a few things.

When we returned to the hotel, Sarah showed me her room. While she went into the bathroom to get me some water, I reviewed her session list. She was in enough sessions with me to not feel snubbed. I'd make a point of eating with her whenever feasible. She'd make good cover. Shit. Sarah would be in her room late at night, the one time I knew for sure I'd be able to get it on with Isaac. Damn. She'd hear me and would know what I'm up to if I really cut loose, and I really need to cut loose now.

"Have you ever seen anything as intentionally tacky as this room?" Sarah was such a prude.

"I especially like the Cupids over your bed, Sarah."

"I wish."

"Gotta clean up." I crossed the hall to my room, leaving Sarah standing in her doorway.

"Knock on my door when you're ready to go down for dinner, Tookie."

Just then a cute bellboy pushed a room service cart between us.

"Excuse me," I said to get his attention. He stopped and looked at me slack jawed.

"Excuse me…uh…" I read his name tag, "*Kevin*. I'm having a little trouble with my room key. Could you help?" I handed him my key and stood next to him to compare heights and check him out. He unlocked the door with ease then handed me the key. I vamped, "Thank you very much, Kevin."

Sarah and I stood there holding our doors open watching him as he pushed the cart to the corner and out of sight.

I gyrated my hips suggestively. "Grrrr."

"Tookie! You're incorrigible."

"I try. We can talk about him over dinner."

I tweaked my plan while I showered, then lounged in only a towel and plotted, waiting for Isaac to return from the casino. I liked my room. It was twice the size of what I usually got and I didn't think the gold lame wallpaper was so tacky. We could have dinner on the poker table if I figured out a way to be alone together.

"Knock, knock." I heard his quiet taps and flung my door open. "We've got time before dinner. Let's use your room. Mine doesn't have mirrors on the ceiling. Say, do you think you can borrow a bellhop's uniform?"

He stopped in his tracks. "What?"

I pulled him over to the bed. "Just do it. I'll make it worth your while."

"I don't understand."

"Take me. I'm yours." I spread-eagled on the bed. "By the way, ignore anything I might do with other bell-hops."

"Other bellhops?"

I pulled him down to me. "C'mon. Time's awastin'."

On the way to dinner, Sarah and I veered past the concierge stand. As I hoped, Kevin loitered there with two other guys, none of whom was twenty-one.

"Thanks for getting my door open…Kevin. You must work very hard."

The other bellhops barely restrained their giggles.

"Seven to seven, but I'm off tomorrow." He opened his eyes wide and looked straight at me as if to say, "I don't need any money, honey, if you've got the time."

"Enjoy your day off." I swished my ass for the bell-hops' benefit on the way out.

"I hope to," he said, leaving no doubt he'd like to jump my bones.

As we stepped into the revolving door, I distinctly heard, "Thank you, Kevin. You work very hard," in fal-setto followed by juvenile male laughter. *Success.*

"Have you no shame?" Sarah was a spinster for good reason.

"Not a molecule." *Perfect.*

Our group ate dinner at a large round table in a restaurant down The Strip from the hotel.

I don't remember the name or what I ate as my focus was elsewhere. I sat far across the table from Isaac, next to Sarah.

"I don't think it's a good idea, Tookie. He's kind of young."

"I'm not looking to marry him."

"He might get the wrong idea the way you flirt with him."

"I want him to get wrong ideas. Lots of them. I like men with wrong ideas."

"What'll people at Carver-Watkins think?" She looked genuinely concerned about my reputation.

"Nothing, unless you flap your jaws about it. You know the C-W motto, 'What happens on the road stays on the road.'"

I raised my menu to just below eye level, looked Isaac in the eye, and nodded. He winked.

I left the group immediately after dinner, yawning a few times, citing jet lag as the cause. Isaac reported that he hung around long enough to hear Sarah gossip about me to the others, including Carol, the executive secretary. Why she was along was unclear. It may've been a perk, or she may have been sent to spy on us, or both. Putting Isaac's wife's close friend/spy off my scent was an unexpected bonus.

Isaac drifted up after learning what he could. Other than him stuffing my panties in my mouth to keep me quiet when I felt like howling, I had an excellent night. Too shy to put mirrors over my own bed, I got the rare treat of seeing Isaac in action that night. I couldn't see much of myself, except receiving oral sex, from any position I tried.

The next day, I attended my sessions like a good girl.

At cocktails, the C-W group assembled to arrange dinner plans.

"Too tired. I'll just call room service," I said, setting our plan in motion. I headed toward the elevators.

Apparently thinking I was out of earshot, Sarah snickered, "I bet I know who she orders from room service."

Don't worry. I won't let you down.

Isaac caught a cab to a distant casino by himself—statisticians as a group aren't gamblers—they know the odds. Once out of view, he directed the driver to circle back and drop him off at the back of the hotel. He came up the back way and left his door ajar so room service could deliver our meal more quickly and quietly. While he put on the borrowed bellhop uniform, I pulled a transparent negligee over my black lace bra and panties. Isaac, the bellhop, tipped the regular bellhop twenty bucks to silently exit the back way. He then pushed the room service cart the short distance down the hall and to my door, knocking loudly.

"Room Service!"

I held the door open much longer than necessary so anyone in the vicinity could see my front and the bellhop's back, especially a certain spinster spying through her peephole.

"Please set it up on the poker table, Kevin." *Maybe I should call it my poke her table.* I closed the door loudly and spoke in my outside voice. "Now I need you to help me with something else, Kevin."

"Yes, ma'am."

"Please call me Tookie."

I signaled Isaac to start whispering.

"Tooks, want to play the bellhop and the showgirl?"

"I thought you'd never ask, young man. By the way. Your pet name is Kevin for now."

"Love it."

So started my first night of reckless abandon in Vegas. If Sarah didn't hear "Kevin. Oh my God, Kevin," a dozen times that night, she's deaf or can sleep through anything. To finish the charade, "Kevin" donned his uniform after our pre-breakfast coupling and noisily pushed the cart to the service elevator before taking a circuitous route back to his room.

I was ecstatic for the rest of the conference as everything went even better than I'd hoped. Our lovemaking was the best ever. Isaac showed his appreciation by always saying exactly the right thing at the right time. I concealed my feelings for him with great difficulty when we were in public, but I managed to maintain cover. I heard *Bolero* crescendo in my mind slowly the entire week, reaching its climax on the last afternoon of the conference. I strategically kept our schedules clear when everyone else attended the boring closing speech so I could give him the ultimate afternoon delight.

I alternated rooms and cleaned up any incriminating evidence afterward all week. I even placed towels strategically on our beds immediately before we joined each and every time. The maids who cleaned the rooms wouldn't look for evidence of our assignations on the white towels if other incriminating artifacts weren't left behind. I flushed everything else down the toilet. The maids had nothing to tell if his wife's spies bribed them. I was nothing if not thorough.

Isaac arrived the instant I was ready for him. "I never dreamed I could desire a woman as much as I desire you."

His eyes told me he was speaking the truth. By making each time better than the last, he lusted after me more than ever, even after he'd had me more times than I could count before this trip.

I kept him guessing so he didn't suspect what he was getting this last afternoon.

I snapped my fingers and pointed to the bed. "Sit there and watch me undress."

He drooled. He must've been imagining how good it might be after coupling with me that morning, the night before, the morning before that…

Having a couple of hours for the grand finale, I stretched out my performance to fill the time. By building up slowing and gradually, I created an anticipation designed to bring him close to cardiac arrest.

"But first help me get out of this." I backed up to him so he could unzip my zipper. His hand "slipped" onto my butt after pulling my zipper down.

"Patience, Kevin." I liked what he was doing, but needed him to slow down. I stepped over to my dresser and stripped down to my beige high-waisted panties and bra. Looking in the mirror, I asked, "What do you want me to wear?"

"Nothing."

"I'll compromise, but my privates have to be covered."

"Take off your bra."

"I consider them private, too."

"Oookay, I like you in black."

I picked my black ensemble out of the drawer and backed up to "Kevin." "Help me with my bra."

He did. But when he fondled my breasts my resistance evaporated. Both ensembles soon dropped to the floor as did any thoughts of putting them on. Isaac used his tongue to great advantage. I came to orgasm quickly because I was anticipating what I was about to do for him. As was my norm, my first climax was the most intense with those that followed decreasing in intensity as they washed over me.

I moaned and screamed without restraint each time "Kevin" brought me over the mountain. As loud as I was, probably just the maids on the floor heard me. Wild sexual encounters were so commonplace in Vegas, housekeepers paid little attention and continued with their duties. After I caught my breath, I gulped down half a glass of OJ. After resting a bit more, I ate a few apple slices and finished the OJ. Then it was his turn.

He was about to erupt. I expected eating me would arouse him but not as much as this. I needed to cool him down.

Should I have him take a cold shower? Better not, he might think I'm denying him and get angry. I could use one myself. I've got a long overnight flight in front of me. Better do that later. He might mess me, and few of my boyfriends since Tim have been fascinated by my body. Even Isaac's more interested in what I do to or for him with it. He doesn't delight in looking at me as Tim did. Shouldn't push my luck.

So, I gave Isaac a sponge bath to cool him down. There's nothing like ice-cold water on a man's balls to get rid of an erection. Under the guise of giving him attention, I washed his scrotum and pecker with a cold, wet washcloth and limp he went.

After drying him off with a hand towel, I started my slow, steady build up designed to blow his mind, to use the catch phrase of the day.

I prided myself on not being a prickteaser, but this one time I enticed Little Isaac at a most deliberate pace. When he started drooling with lust, I leaned back, poured myself another glass of OJ, drank a quarter of it, and suggestively ate three apple slices very slowly watching the clock out of the corner of my eye.

"Are you planning on leaving me like this?" he cried.

"Haven't made up my mind yet." I'd never made a

man wait like this before. My grand finale would show him I was worth the wait.

I wanted to finish with precisely enough time to shower, dress, finish packing, check out, and catch the shuttle to the airport without wasting a minute I could've spent better in bed.

When he thought I was about to go down on him to suck him as only I can, I straddled him and gyrated my scabbard down onto his waiting hardened-steel sword.

He thrust his hips upward, but I put my palms on his chest, signaling him to stop.

I remained perfectly still until my nerves calmed enough for me to have absolute control of myself, especially my love machine.

"What're you doing?" Expecting my great oral sex, he looked disappointed.

I loved confusing men, but I'd never maintained such self-control or stayed still as long as this. All of a sudden, I started squeezing him.

Isaac wriggled, with pleasure I assume. "Have you been hanging around a dairy?" He panted. "I've never felt anything like this before." He gasped for breath. "This feels like how farm boys described milking machines, but much better."

I laughed but remained still, not moving visibly up or down, backward or frontward or sideways. Everything I did I did internally and it worked perfectly. I flexed my newly toned vagina muscles up and down, down and up, creating a rippling sensation for him.

"Aawww. It feels sooo good. I can't stand it." His reaction became so intense his arms flailed wildly, knocking the lamp off the nightstand. Totally out of control of himself, he blurted, "Tookie, I love you! I love you! I love you!"

Caught completely off guard by his outburst of affection, I heard myself say, "Does this mean you want to marry me?"

"Yes! Yes! Yes! Whenever you want."

My vagina muscles operated at peak performance and milked every drop of his essence out of him and into me. Only one man had proposed to me and I didn't want him, so I counted Isaac's outpouring as close enough.

"It's too intense. Let me up."

Stunned by my unguarded response, I just squatted there until he pushed me off. We collapsed on the bed too exhausted to move until I noticed the time.

"We're going to miss our plane. Get moving and I mean *now*." I was accustomed to taking charge of men who didn't know their minds and pushed him toward his shower.

Having only enough time to put the lamp back on the night stand, I couldn't straighten up the rest of the room. I made a mental note to leave the maid a nice tip. Time allowed only a quick cold shower. It was fortunate I don't wear makeup because I didn't have time to fool with it. For a split second, I considered wearing a dress with no underwear but changed my mind and pulled on the first pair of panties in the drawer. I threw everything else unceremoniously into a suitcase or my garment bag before racing to the elevator and, at the ground floor, to the front desk to check out. Being the last two to catch the shuttle, Isaac and I sat at opposite ends of the bus in the only available seats. Some of the others gave us odd looks which I took to mean they noticed we both were late and disheveled, but they didn't comment about it.

CHAPTER 20

He Said All the Right Things

Isaac and I were assigned seats next to each other again, but didn't trade places with anyone for the trip home. Our side of the row only contained two seats, which gave us a measure of privacy and the opportunity to discuss our future together.

Carol couldn't have seen anything to report, but must've become suspicious. She slithered past our seats several times going to and from the restroom.

"Let go," I whispered. "Carol's coming again." I flipped through the airline magazine I'd previously used to cover our entwined hands.

Isaac failed to look innocent. "She's either got a tiny bladder or is spying on us."

"I want you to move in with me—today." I'd had enough of this sneaking about. I wanted our love to be public and Isaac proud to announce it.

He pondered whatever it is men ponder at such times, then asked, "Are you sure you want me?"

"So sure that I want you as soon as humanly possible. When we land, you go home—er—retrieve your belongings. I'll take care of our bags and get the apartment ready for you."

He kissed me like he meant it. *Isaac loves me deeply. I can tell.*

We went our separate ways upon landing. At home, I made room in the guest room closet for his clothes and cleared out a couple of dresser drawers by moving my gifts from Tim to the closet shelf. I couldn't help but notice our clothes from the trip smelled of sex, so into the washer they went. I may not care for fashion, but cleanliness and order are essential to me. The first load barely started to agitate when I heard someone at the door.

It was Isaac, disheveled and white as a sheet. "What happened to you? You look a fright."

"Let me in and I'll tell you." He staggered into my kitchen. "I need a drink."

"Sit down." I motioned toward the Formica table and got Isaac a glass of ice water from the fridge. He sat down, drank slowly, and took several deep breaths. I gently smoothed his hair.

"I barely had the front door open when she unloaded on me. 'You cheating bastard, I'm throwing you out.' She was irrational."

"Carol?" *That bitch.*

"Probably. She didn't say. I got my suits from the closet and laid them in the back seat of my car. When I came out with another load, she was throwing my things from the garage, helter-skelter. Some of my golf clubs landed on the lawn, others in the street. Two bounced off my car. Passing cars ran over a couple. One cracked my windshield. She sailed my tennis racquet into the neighbor's yard like a discus with a tail. She heaved my baseball, golf balls, football, tennis balls, and any other balls she could find into the yard. When she charged out of the kitchen, waving a carving knife, I jumped into my car and got the hell out of there, fearing my balls were next. I wasn't about to take any chances. She's crazy."

"You're safe with me. I'm not going to cut off your balls. I've got better uses for them."

"You're not funny." He was still shaking.

I hung up some of his shirts, ones that weren't wrinkled too badly in the hasty transfer from the house to his car, and staged the rest in piles in front of the washing machine. I refolded his clean socks and underwear and put them in his drawers.

"I have a couple of house rules. My bathroom is mine. The other one is yours. I don't cook or iron, but I'll do one or the other for you this one time, my love. Pick your poison."

"I'll live dangerously and do the ironing."

He looked in the cabinets, probably for booze.

"You're on your own in that department. I don't drink the stuff. Let's be perfectly sober our first night together. Okay?"

He acquiesced.

I picked up a few items for a simple meal as well as breakfast basics and prepared him a warm dinner.

"You're actually a good cook, you know?"

"Don't get used to it. This is for special occasions only. To us." *Clink.*

We talked for hours after dinner, making plans for the future. At bed time, we retreated to our respective bathrooms.

I washed my face and put on a night gown. Not wearing makeup reduced my bedtime preparation to that of a man.

Seeing I wasn't naked as usual, Isaac grinned oddly and patted my side of the bed.

"I don't want any sex tonight. I want to be held and cuddled. It's been a long, long time since someone loved me, although several claimed they did, at least for brief periods, and I need you to love me."

Isaac took me in his arms and whispered in my ear, "When does tonight end?"

"Noon tomorrow."

I got up early in the morning feeling the best I could remember, took a quick shower, and set out things for breakfast. We talked about our immediate future together over cornflakes. His lawyer took weekends off, so he had to wait until Monday to file for divorce. We decided to just enjoy each other's company, relax, and have some fun. We did. But all too soon, Monday morning dawned.

Before leaving for work, I put on a bridesmaid tiara for the awarding of the key ceremony.

"I accept this great honor with all due humility and will guard this key with my life." He kissed me passionately, too passionately.

I pushed him away. "Don't get me started. We've got to go to work. We drive separately and I get there earlier. Nothing is to look as if anything's changed."

"Everyone will know ten minutes after Carol gets there."

"We dare not flaunt it."

Sarah may have kept quiet about Kevin or no one believed her, but Carol surely told several people who told several others and before noon, we were the talk of the entire office.

No one, however, asked either of us anything, but that didn't keep me from noticing so many glances my way and conversations breaking off abruptly when I entered a room or cubicle area.

That night, I told Isaac, "Everybody knows."

"Are you sure?"

"Of course. How thick are you?" That was the first time I lost control of my tongue with him. I was glad it was one of my gentler retorts. "What says your mouthpiece?"

"He'll be talking to her lawyer tomorrow to see what she wants."

"What *she* wants?" Weak men frustrated me. After having had a run of them, I always seemed to pick another one.

Tuesday evening we ate at a diner around the corner from my apartment.

"Well, what did your lawyer say?"

"Bob said ours is a community property state. That means she gets half, if I'm lucky."

"I don't care. I've got you."

"Bob's seen cases where the wife gets the house and the husband gets the mortgage."

"That's a crock."

"We don't have no-fault divorce."

"So?"

"She might hire a private investigator to prove adultery."

I squeezed ketchup onto a napkin in the shape of a letter A and held it to my chest. I also unbuttoned the top two buttons on my blouse.

"That isn't funny, Took."

I'd never seen fire in his eyes before. He was really angry with me.

"We have each other. Isn't that all that matters?"

"Of course, darling." His words were right, but his tone wasn't.

Isaac dragged in from work Wednesday night, looking like he'd lost his best friend.

I kissed him. "Want me to give you a massage?"

"She wants the house, her car, the furnishings, our bank account, and my pension." His face paled and he hunched over like a defeated soldier limping home to his family.

"Your pension?"

"She won't get that, but she'll get the rest."

"What'll you get?"

"The mortgage, my car and its payments, her payments, and five years of alimony." He looked miles into the distance with glazed-over eyes.

"Ouch!"

"She's not leaving me much to live on."

"We won't need much. My salary covers this place and my car payments easy enough. You still have a great job with promotions in front of you and decades to build your pension."

"We'll have to economize in lots of ways."

"We don't need to belong to the country club."

"I forgot to mention—"

"Let me guess. She gets the country club membership and you get the dues."

"We'll have some pretty lean years to start."

"I don't mind. I'm used to not having anything. Now I've got you. That's enough." *Guess I'll have to put off starting a family.*

He smiled. "You really mean it?"

"Kiss me." *I have you. That's enough for now. I've got lots of time to have a baby.*

I felt especially close to Isaac that night. No man had ever sacrificed for me before. Our lovemaking was the best ever. He made my kitty purr quick, long, and loud. It was so good we were late getting up and had to hurry through breakfast to get out the door on time. It was a particularly busy day at work, even for a Thursday. After work, I hurried home.

He must be working late. Is that a note? It's his key. Oh shit!

He'd scribbled something on a sheet of yellow tablet paper and left it on the kitchen table. It read, *Tookie, You're a great girl but I*—and nothing else.

He had gone back to his wife. I couldn't believe it. We were in such perfect harmony. He was so attuned to my feelings. He always said exactly what I needed to hear. How could he have left me so easily?

The cold shock of reality struck me in the face when I opened his empty closet. Convincing myself that this was an aberration, I opened his dresser drawers. Empty too. She must've really put the pressure on him. No way would he have treated me this way without extenuating circumstances. I collapsed on the floor, crying like I'd never cried before. I sobbed uncontrollably.

After about an hour, I gathered myself enough to call Sybil. She'd dealt with some crumbs in her time but she wasn't home. Evelyn was as was Cynthia. My friends were, of course, quite conciliatory.

"Aren't men pathetic? The married ones are the worst and the single guys are dorks. All any of them want to do is get into our pants and leave immediately afterward. Slime," summed up their conclusions pretty well.

"You can spend the weekend with me," Evelyn said. "We haven't done a lot together lately."

She must have thought I was in no condition to be alone. "Thank you for your concern, but I'll be fine."

I was halfway through a pint of Haagen Dazs mint chip when my phone rang unexpectedly. I picked up the marble egg on the desk unconsciously when I lifted the receiver. Noticing it in my hand, I chucked it into the waste basket.

"Hello?"

CHAPTER 21

Goodbye Tim

I expected to hear Sybil's voice on the other end of the line but it wasn't. It was a voice that warmed my heart when I needed it.

"Like to have a houseguest this weekend?" I asked upon hearing Tim. *Why'd I say that? I haven't thought about him in ages.*

Probably shocked because of my less than civil treatment in recent years, he was silent for a few seconds. "Of course, Mary Louise. I'd love to have you."

"My car's acting up, so a friend will be driving me. Find her a date."

"Don't know many people here yet, but I'll try.

"Find somebody." I was firm.

Why'd I say date? Why the sudden change? Something's happening with me and I don't have a clue what it is. Tim's head must be swimming. Not sure mine isn't. Better call Evelyn quick.

With the brief exposure I'd had to Tim over the previous two years, I'd observed he was a considerably different person than the naive boy I'd rejected eight years earlier. He'd completed his bachelor's degree while working full-time and supporting a wife. When he called, he was operating a one-man office for his company out of his house a three-hour drive from me. His social skills, although far from polished, had improved considerably.

"I'm really glad you decided to get away this weekend," Evelyn said as we pulled onto I-287, "but you were vague about where we're going."

"Tim offered to show us around central Pennsylvania and I thought you might enjoy it."

"Tim, Tim? I don't remember you mentioning a Tim." Being confused was a not infrequent reaction for her because I didn't share my secrets with her for fear of disapproval.

"Didn't I? He was my very first boyfriend. We met in Milltown—the hick town where I lived before moving to Jersey—and broke up after he returned from Vietnam, a couple years before I met you."

"Vietnam? He's not a whack job, is he?" She looked concerned for our safety.

"Far from it. He's smart, stable, sober, and super-straight. He was married but that didn't work out. Proba-bly bored her." *And let her tramp all over him.*

"So, he was your first?"

"The exit for I-78's coming up in a mile."

Following Tim's precise directions, we pulled up to his house a little before noon. He waited alone on the sidewalk, looking as confused as the last time I saw him.

"To what do I owe this surprise?" he said as he helped me out of the car.

"Just lucky, I guess. You caught me at a good time." As expected, he was glad to see me and I couldn't help being a smart ass.

He carried our bags into the master bedroom and gave us a quick tour of the modest Cape Cod he'd rented from an anal army sergeant who was transferred to Ger-many. We strolled over to the rental garage where he stored his freshly restored sky-blue Thunderbird. He'd replaced the '56 rust bucket he had when we were dating with a very nice '57 model he bought in Alabama the previous year.

"Want to see some of the countryside after lunch?"

He didn't know what to do with us.

"You bet." What else was there to do in this backwater?

"Hop in," he said, opening the passenger door for me.

Just like old times, I slid across the bench seat to perch in the middle next to him. Planning on having a little fun, I put my left leg right where his hand'd fall if it slipped off the gear shift.

He looked at my thigh and the gear shift and back to my thigh. "Will you do the honors, Mary Louise?"

Curses, foiled again. He's spoiling my fun.

We lunched in a trendy place known locally as the G-Man in honor of their signature gingerbread dessert, not a law enforcer. All had soft drinks. Afterward, we toured the back roads of luscious Cumberland Valley. Evelyn and I enjoyed the beautiful scenery and the wind whipping through our hair riding top down in his gorgeous convertible.

Tim's new acquaintance, Sam, dropped by later to meet Evelyn before he'd have to leave to play bass guitar with his top 40s cover band. We four ate in one of the locals' favorite hangouts. I liked it because of its inviting rustic décor and good food. Afterward, Sam left for his gig and we returned to Tim's place. He didn't have a clue how to entertain two eligible women in their mid-twenties—or any other age, for that matter. We just sat in the kitchen, drank Cokes, and chatted.

"See this," he said, holding up a three-ring binder full of instructions, some hand-written and others typed, and manuals for all the appliances and equipment in the house. "I've never seen anything like it. He's directing exactly how I should do every little thing."

We laughed. The sergeant was anal to the point of being comical.

Tim looked me in the eye. "I still don't understand why you came."

"You caught me at a good time." He still loved me, as if I'd had any doubt.

"That's hard to believe, considering how you've been."

I gave him a sanitized version of my break up, finishing with, "But he said all the right things." *He really loves me but she bludgeoned him with debt.*

Tim seemed to have trouble processing this and excused himself.

This was my chance. I let him get away in that motel but not tonight. I posted myself a few steps from the bathroom door, directly in his path so he couldn't avoid me.

He stopped close to me when I didn't step away so he could pass. *Here goes. Lean in a little and see what happens.*

He bent toward me, as if pulled by gravitational attraction, until our lips met.

Success! He still kissed the same. No tongue. Just romantic.

I pulled my head back far enough to say, "You're still innocent."

He stood there as if in a stupor. I kissed him some more. He was so nice to make out with and still aroused easily. A little more kissing and I made my move, expecting to have great fun.

I didn't break his trance when I lowered him gently to the floor and deftly lowered his jeans. He wanted me as much as ever. It was now time for the coup de gras. I brushed the ends of my mid-back-length hair across his midsection.

He squirmed and breathed hard. His stomach muscles spasmed.

"Haven't you ever had oral sex?" *Bet you never guessed I'd be the Blowjob Queen.*

"Nothing like yours," he said, panting between words.

"You've probably never been with a woman with long hair." He was ready. "Let's go somewhere more comfortable."

I led him upstairs to the twin bed where he had planned on sleeping alone that night. I undressed him and laid him on the bed before picking up where I left off. He soon writhed and breathed even harder. I'd only touched him with my hair but he was more excited than any man I'd ever beguiled. No one had ever wanted me this much. *Show him what he's been missing. Wonder what his tastes like?*

I gave him very nice head, alternating among licking, sucking, and tickling his most tender spots with my tongue. I was at the top of my game that night. He said nothing but moaned quietly. He was still so shy he kept quiet so Evelyn couldn't hear us. He grasped the sides of the mattress so tightly, in an attempt to keep still, his forearm muscles bulged.

I stretched my pleasure out as long as possible, making sure to give Tim the best he'd ever get. I really liked his cum, too, all the better because he hadn't had any booze.

"Hold me and don't go to sleep," I ordered.

I could tell he enjoyed spooning me, especially since he could touch any part of my now naked body. "Don't fall asleep!"

He kissed my neck.

"Tell me." I hated it when guys weren't grateful and didn't tell me how good I was.

"My feelings are all mixed up right now."

"Not that," I snapped. "How did you like it? Did I please you?"

"I've had nothing that even comes close. For a while I thought I was having a heart attack. It was so intense."

"That's a little better." I let him fall asleep, emotionally exhausted, no doubt. I was too wound up and the bed was too small for me to sleep well. Finding myself wide awake at three, according to my Seiko, I amused myself by softly grinding my butt against him. He wanted me again. Rolling him onto his back without waking him was quite a trick. It was time for round two.

"Wha—"

A few hair drags and Tim woke. Enjoying what I was doing for him, he soaked it in, hanging tightly onto the bed again.

Getting tired myself, I brought him to climax a little quicker than before but kept the intensity level just as high. I swallowed and spooned him, ready to sleep. "Tell me," I demanded.

"You're the absolute best. No one could come close to you."

Better not giggle. Not only have numerous other men come close to me, they've come in me. I like him being so innocent he doesn't realize his double entendre. I drifted off to a pleasant sleep.

Woken by nature's call at seven, I grabbed my clothes and bounced downstairs to pee, delighted with how my evening turned out. When I came out of the bathroom, an angry Evelyn took me by the arm and pulled me into the kitchen, out of earshot of Sam, who dozed on the loveseat in the living room.

"What kind of friends does this Tim have anyway?"

Evelyn's face was red with rage. I've never seen her like this before or since.

"I don't understand." I was so pleased with myself I didn't want anything to disrupt my beautiful summer Sunday morning.

"After you went upstairs to do who knows what with Tim, abandoning me, I went to bed. The next thing I know, Sam's sliding in next to me, expecting me to do what you were probably doing upstairs with Tim."

"I'm sorry this happened."

Evelyn was so straight laced, she passed up an opportunity to get some experience and hone her limited skills with a guy who she'd never have to see again.

"And that's not all. He wouldn't take no for an answer."

Most ignore the first several nos. "Did he rape you?"

"Not that he didn't want to."

She was probably hysterical. He didn't seem to be a bad guy. "What happened?"

"When he whined about you going up with Tim, I told him that you and Tim go back a very long time and I barely knew him."

"Did he leave you alone then?"

"He poked me in the butt with his huge thing. I didn't know they came so large."

Evelyn was so prudish and inexperienced she might have been exaggerating. "Did he succeed?"

"He's so big he would've torn me open forcing it in. He left when I threatened to scream. It was horrible."

"I don't like oversized dicks either. Let's have breakfast. He won't be a problem today."

Tim toddled in, groggy and confused by the unfriendly looks we gave him.

He pulled me aside. "What's wrong?"

I responded in as calm a tone as I could muster, "We'll talk later."

He shrugged his shoulders, probably thinking it was nothing important.

Apparently hearing us in the kitchen, Sam awoke and stumbled in. "What's up?"

"Have some breakfast so we can do something," Tim responded. "Do you girls have anything in mind?"

We stared blankly. *Why're you asking us? We don't live around here.*

"How about Pole Steeple?" Sam piped up. "You can see across the valley from there."

A monument to your penis I bet. "How far is it?" *Can't stay long with Evelyn this upset.*

"Not far. It's just outside of town a few miles," Sam said. "The view is tremendous."

I'll bet. Better all stay together. Without considering the details, I said, "Let's take the Thunderbird. I don't get to ride in a convertible often." With that, we put away the breakfast things and walked over to the garage. It was there I realized I'd made a poor suggestion. The car had no backseat. Oh, oh. Actually, it would be worse for Evelyn if she got in a backseat with Sam.

Tim apparently had some experience squeezing people into his pre-seatbelt chariot. "Slide in, girls so we can see if there's enough room for the three of you on that side of the gear shift."

Not willing to surrender my position closest to Tim, I slid in first, followed by Evelyn and Sam. Tim slammed the passenger door, latching it.

"Ow. My ribs," Sam complained.

I hoped Tim cracked a few of them. It wasn't too bad. Sam couldn't get more than a free feel this way. She wasn't in any real danger.

Tim slid in. "You better shift gears again."

I smiled seductively. "No, your hand might slip."

"What a difference a night makes," Tim said, confused as usual, and aimed us toward South Mountain. Fifteen minutes later, we were on foot trekking up the trail to Pole Steeple. Tim tried to hold my hand but Evelyn pulled me away from him.

"Stay with me. Close," she said. "I'm afraid he might attack me behind one of those big rocks." She pointed to some house-sized boulders a short distance away.

At the top we were treated to a panoramic view of the valley below. Thinking Evelyn would be safe going to the restroom alone, I took Tim aside, watching Sam out of the corner of my eye.

"Do you know anything about Sam?" I was pissed and let him know in no uncertain terms.

"Not all that much," he said, looking befuddled by my anger.

"He tried to rape Evelyn."

"He what?" he said, shocked as if he couldn't believe what he'd heard.

"I'm keeping my eye on him and will scream bloody murder if he tries anything." I wasn't kidding but nothing unseemly happened. Soon, it was time to climb down.

Tim hovered all morning, probably because he'd always viewed me as a bit fragile, as someone to treat gently, to take care of. He was the only man who'd ever protected me. He didn't know if he was going to see me again or not. Neither did I.

Sam departed as soon as we returned to Tim's place. We three made some sandwiches and had a simple lunch, after which Evelyn and I put our bags in her car. Tim stood on the sidewalk, watching us leave. He waved a perplexed goodbye as we drove off.

⁓⁓⁓

I was at work barely ten minutes Monday morning when I met Isaac head-on in a hallway. He turned his head and rushed past me. My insides churned. I wasn't strong enough to deal with him yet and had to get out of there. I raced to the company library where I found a train schedule and made reservations. I dialed Tim, who answered on the second ring, apparently expecting anyone but me.

"Could I stay with you this week?" *It better be all right. I already bought the ticket.*

"Really?" He was even more surprised this time.

"I can't cope with seeing him at work."

"Of course." he said, clearly hearing distress in my voice.

"I'll arrive in Harrisburg on the four fifteen train.

"I'll pick you up." His voice was a mixture of elation and dread.

I hadn't eaten lunch, so Tim took me to a little café near the train station run by a recent acquaintance. "Hi, Joe. This is my first girlfriend, Mary Louise. She's visiting for a few days."

"Nice to meet you," he said, looking me up and down. "What'll you have?"

While walking to the ladies' room, I overheard Joe ask Tim, "Where'd you meet the Irish Setter?"

"That's not a very nice thing to say about a girl," said my protector.

"I didn't mean anything. I'm sorry." He went about getting our food.

I couldn't blame Joe too much because my dark red hair was close in color and wavy like the dog's coat. But comparing me to a dog was an insult.

I said little while we ate, due to hunger and out-of-control emotions. On the way to Tim's I opened up, "I couldn't deal with running into him at work, so I took the rest of the week off. I've got a lot of vacation saved up after not taking much time the last four years. Encountering him in the office is too painful."

"What'll you do next week?'

"I don't know. I've gone through all the guys in the office."

Tim obviously hated seeing me in such pain. "You can stay as long as you want."

"Thanks." I kissed him on the cheek. "He went back to his wife the day before you called."

"He was living with you?"

How can he still think I'm the innocent girl he fell in love with so long ago? "He said all the right things."

"And you believed him?"

Tim thought I was gullible. "He was so sincere and told me exactly what I needed him to say."

I was extremely vulnerable but Tim knew that, too. That's why I came to him for sanctuary. He still loved me and would never harm me. I was safe with him.

He opened the front door of his house and went in but stopped, standing still holding my bag.

He probably thought I wanted a room of my own. I led him by the hand to his bedroom. "Do you have any drawers I can use?"

"Any of them in the dresser. I use the chest of drawers." He put my bag on the dresser then started taking socks and underwear out of the chest.

"I'm not pushing you out of your room. I'm sharing it with you—if you'll have me." *I really don't want to sleep alone right now.*

Unpacking didn't take me long because I travel light. That task done, I shifted my attention to more pleasurable things and gave him oral sex.

As we lay on the bed in each other's arms, he asked, "Why did you seduce me all of a sudden?"

It never was clear to me why I seduced Tim, knowing he was still head over heels in love with me. Maybe it was out of guilt for imposing on his good nature or because I knew I'd be leaving him some time for someone more exciting. I might have seduced him in revenge for Isaac and the other men who'd used me. Maybe I was still angry at him for breaking up with me when I didn't have a replacement.

Better not let him think we'll be cuddling by the fireside after our children are put to bed. "Not sure. Could be ego. Have always wondered what you'd be like. I've always cared about you."

We fell asleep in each other's arms and slept soundly to the morning. I felt safe as always with him. After a simple breakfast of orange juice, cereal, and toast, it dawned on me that Tim had a job and must have work to do.

"Will you be leaving me alone much for your work?" As much as I liked alone time, I didn't want it then.

"Normally, yes. But I'm pretty well caught up now and have accumulated so much comp time I'll never use, I can focus on you this week. Most of the time anyway."

This was strange for me. I had nothing scheduled to do like I do on vacations and my friends didn't have Tim's phone number, so I wouldn't get calls from them. I decided to reward Tim for taking me in and distract myself by having sex as often as he could muster, within parameters of my making.

He soon seemed embarrassed to be receiving so much oral sex.

"I'd like to do something for you now," he said, reaching for my panty-covered crotch.

I pushed him away. "Don't bother. No point in trying."

His smile soured as if he thought I'd rejected him. "Intercourse?"

"Not yet." It was too soon since Isaac and I didn't get much out of screwing anyway. "What would you like me to do for you?" *See if he comes up with something interesting.*

"Would you put my balls in your mouth and hum? That's always sounded exciting to me."

"Stand up." *No one's asked for this before. Must not be very exciting.*

He hopped to his feet and I happily did what he asked. I didn't know what tune should I hum. I couldn't think of anything appropriate. Just humming random notes till he came made sense. Tim seemed to enjoy what I was doing, so I hummed and hummed for several minutes but he didn't come.

"Should I hum something different?" My mouth was getting tired—a new experience for me.

"I'm very sensitive there, so I thought I'd come quickly but it isn't working. How about putting them in a bowl of ice cubes? I've heard that's pretty exciting."

"No props. Whatever I do has to involve just you and me." *I won't resort to them until I'm older and need help to compete.*

"Would you suck on me?" he asked in a quiet meek voice as if he was afraid to ask me to do something for him.

"Sure. It's my fave." *No man had ever been so embarrassed about asking me for sex.*

"Thank you. Thank you. Every time is better than the last. I never in my wildest imagination you would be a sex goddess."

"When I started having sex, I decided to get really good at it." *I read. I studied. I practiced. Then I took on* any man I wanted plus a few I didn't. *Better not shock him with that.*

In the evenings Tim took me out for dinner and introduced me to the few people he'd met since moving there earlier in the year. I found it odd that he still seemed ill at ease with me, especially after seeing me naked so much. I needed to know more, so I got some information in bed.

"Did you divorce Zelda or did she leave you?" *She sure did a job on him.*

He looked away from me. "Technically, she divorced me."

I'd struck a nerve or something. He was always looking at my face or telling me how pretty I am. "Technically? What really happened?"

"To put it as briefly as I can, she ran around on me and rubbed my face in it, even brought drug dealers to my house.

"When I got laid off and had to take the job in Alabama, she stayed behind to sell the house. A week later, she said was pregnant and I couldn't be the father. Her period was so irregular I was skeptical. I knew I had to get out of what had become a sham of a marriage, but had to wait for the right time. She was behaving so erratically, I feared triggering her doing something harmful.

"A couple of weeks later when she called to tell me she finally had her period, I gave her the option of divorcing me. Not wanting her promiscuity and drug use made public, she took me up on it, but not without extracting a pound of flesh from me at every opportunity."

"Wow! She really screwed with your head." *No wonder he's so damaged.* "She's ancient history now. You can make love to me."

Apparently thinking I wanted something other than the squarest sex, he asked, "Doggie style?"

"No. I want to see your face." Nobody was going to butt fuck me anymore. Too many guys used me as a warm place to put it and I had put an end to that.

I spread my legs wide and helped him plunge himself into me as deeply as possible.

"Ouch," he said, wincing. "That thing cuts me."

Don't be such a wimp. "Nobody else complains. It's just my IUD string."

"Can't you remove it?" He remained inside me but didn't move.

"Not until you promise to get me pregnant and only then by my gyno." *How's that for an enticing offer?* I actually found giving myself to Tim in the boring missionary position pleasant. He was no stud by any means but he was gentle and considerate, if a little finicky.

☙❧

The next day he surprised me when he ventured into the bathroom while I was in the shower. I had just stepped into the tub and was about to turn on the water when I heard something behind me. I turned to see naked Tim looking at me with lust in his eyes, ready for another session.

"May I join you?" He seemed more confident this morning.

"Sure." What else could I say?

I stood motionless while he soaped me up, giving my slit copious amounts of attention.

"My girls need some, too." He'd had his hand on my muff long enough. He needed to spread the love.

Tim still didn't get it that my tiny breasts were my fondling spots of choice and the keys to unlocking my desire. Not wanting to get my hair wet by kneeling down and never liking to waste a perfectly good erection by jacking a man off, I did nothing—until we dried off.

I must've been getting stronger by this time because my Jersey girl smart-ass self was returning. When Tim finished drying himself, I laid on my back but kept my legs together.

"It won't work like this," he complained.

"Are you sure you were married?" *Let's see how he deals with this obstacle.*

He slid one knee, then the other, between my legs then guided himself into me with his hand. Not on the first try mind you. I didn't give him any help. Consciously, that is.

I didn't realize it at the time but, as constantly turned on by my mere presence as he was, just the thought of him wanting me got me ready for him. Without kissing or fondling, I soaked myself. Once he was in, I snapped my knees together, forcing his legs to drop outside mine.

How could he have been married and not known this position? Zelda must've been frigid. I grabbed his ass as hard as I could, holding him tightly where he did me the most good. I slowly gyrated my hips, giving myself a not unpleasant experience that was soon interrupted by him coming.

Feeling stronger and concerned he might be getting serious, I opened up with him the next morning on a stroll around his new neighborhood.

"Bet you didn't know I'm an exhibitionist." *Don't smile. Must say these things with a straight face.*

"Huh?" Shocked doesn't begin to describe Tim's reaction. Gobsmacked was closer to it.

"I like exposing myself." This was a good opener.

He tried to brush it off with a silly response. "I like it when you flash me."

"I got naked in my car."

His stomach audibly curdled. "Were you driving?"

"My boyfriend was driving my crappy Vega across Kansas and I got bored."

Still in denial, he asked, "That the only time?"

"Oh no. I had sex on a bus once. That was fun."

He started taking me more seriously.

"What's the longest you've ever gone without having sex?"

"Ten days."

He didn't specify with another person. Having my wrist in a cast was awful until I learned to hump the gear shift ball.

"Ten days?"

"Doug's wife doesn't like sex." I chuckled as if to make light of what I was telling him. "When I'm between boyfriends, I meet up with him."

His jaw dropped. "What's he do when you have a boyfriend?"

"That's his problem." I had him reeling. I was on a roll. Tim didn't know what to think. "I want to have a daughter and you can be her father." *Where'd* that *come from? Don't want to be pregnant yet. Might be fun to make him think I do.*

He turned white as a sheet. I thought he might faint. "What?"

"Here's the deal. I give you all the sex you want until I have the baby. If it's a girl, I keep it."

"What if it's a boy?" He looked like he thought he was talking to a madwoman.

"You keep it." *Maybe I shouldn't discourage him? I'd like to have his baby. She'd be smart and Tim has red in his sideburns and arm hair.*

He stood dumbfounded on the sidewalk until I took him by the hand and led him into the house. "Let's practice while you make your decision."

Tim wasn't the same after that. He still gave me sex whenever I wanted it and still loved me, but he was lost at sea when it came to dealing with me. He could easily have called my bluff. It wasn't really a bluff, I really did want a daughter. All he had to do was to tell me to get rid of the IUD he hated. But he didn't think quickly on his feet.

We both had to work on Monday and I needed a ride. So, he drove me home with the top down. Along the way, we stopped at a *Concours d'Elegance* for old Thunderbirds, where he parked amongst the over-restored cars, and entered the competition on a lark. I enjoyed being a couple with him. We closed out the fun afternoon driving the rest of the way to my place.

Not wanting to be alone just yet, I had him stay the night. Having him in my own bed was comforting.

I mounted him cowgirl style, the position I chose most often when I consented to having a man inside my baby factory. It gave me the most penetration, and I got to see his face. Falling asleep in his arms was particularly nice. Other than the girl above me disturbing our sleep with her moaning and bedsprings squeaking all night, it was lovely.

On Sunday morning, I showed Tim around Jamesburg and, after a light lunch, he drove home.

Work Monday was tough. Not as tough as the previous Monday but far from easy.

But I only had to make it through five days because, on Saturday, five of us girls from work were going away on a Windjammer cruise. Feeling needy Monday evening, I called Tim.

"Want to see me Wednesday?"

"Sure. But it's a long way for a school night. I now have work that has to be done."

I wasn't letting him off that easy. "We'll meet halfway. Make reservations at the Rustic Inn just off the King-of-Prussia Turnpike exit."

"I'll look for your car in the parking lot." He sounded more enthusiastic

Atrysting I will go. Atrysting I will go. Hi ho the derryo, atrysting I will go.

I waited impatiently in the motel's parking lot, fearful he might not come. The new Mary Louise might be too much for him. He pulled in a few minutes later, although it seemed like an eternity.

Upon entering our room, I set my bag on the dresser and started to disrobe.

"Please stop," he asked from the doorway.

"What?" Was he chickening out?

"I'd like to do it." He walked over and undid my top button.

"Okay, but I get to undress you." I felt vulnerable being undressed by a man who still had his clothes on.

"Fine by me." He smiled, enjoying any attention I gave him.

Working faster and having fewer items to remove, I had his off quickly. He, on the other hand, admired my body, part by part, as he methodically removed my shoes and socks, slacks, blouse, and bra. When Tim had me down to just my translucent green full-bottom panties, he ogled me from top to groin, pausing at wasn't clearly exposed. Impatient, I flopped on the bed face first.

"Have I put on weight?" He always liked my ass. If he lied I'd give him more of it.

He rubbed his chin and scratched his head then walked to the foot of the bed to get a different view. "Since when?"

"Since we were dating. Quit avoiding the question." I wanted a compliment and I wanted it then.

"You're just as gorgeous as I remember." He nibbled my ass through my panties, and we were off to the races.

಍಍

After ordering dinner, he went silent.

"What are you thinking about?" His being so quiet was unnerving.

"I'm reconsidering your offer."

"And…" Had he changed his mind? Was he holding my ovaries to the sperm?

"From the instant I first saw you, I instinctively knew you'd want children. You've done nothing since then to change that opinion. I've never had a driving desire to have children of my own but I've always known, and accepted, you wouldn't marry a man who wouldn't father yours. It's no surprise I'd be proud to father your redhaired kids, but I have ethical concerns about accepting your, let us say, unusual, offer." He took a deep breath and looked lovingly at me.

Here comes the letdown.

"Children need two parents. Girls need fathers as much as boys need mothers."

"Yours didn't do you much good." *Why do I have to be so mean and say nasty things without thinking?*

"I know all too well she doesn't love me. You don't need to rub it in my face." He gave me an angry look, something he'd never done before, and looked away.

After an eternity of silence, I said, "Go on, please go on."

"Are you finished eating?"

Shit. I'd done it this time. "Please tell me what you were going to say."

Even more serious than before, he started, "It's not fair to children to intentionally deprive them of a parent.

How would you like not having your father?"

I'd miss him terribly. He loved me so much.

Tim continued uninterrupted, "I cannot do that to any child, especially just to satisfy my sexual desires. I will, however, agree to father yours under certain circumstances."

"Which are?" *Here comes another stuffy marriage proposal.*

"We date for six months to see if we can tolerate each other well enough to raise a child. You have to swear on all that is holy to you to take every precaution to not get pregnant. I may even have you sign a legal contract by which you have to pay me a large sum of money if you renege on this part of the deal."

"But I don't have a chunk of money." I sure didn't like where he was headed.

"I'll have your wages garnisheed," he said as if he'd thought this through. "If we do get along well enough. I say well enough fully aware I'm not your first choice but I'm optimistic you'll grow to appreciate me."

Idiot. I've always enjoyed being with you. It's only when you get so serious that I get annoyed.

He wasn't finished. "We get married. We both vow to love, honor, and cherish each other and begin the extremely pleasant task of getting you pregnant—in a car outside the church if you want—on the honeymoon."

I couldn't keep myself from chuckling as I visualized me simultaneously struggling to get my pantyhose down while getting his trousers off in the backseat of a car filled by my poofy wedding gown.

"To make the deal more attractive to you, I promise to have sex any way you desire, whenever, and wherever, you choose, provided it only involves the two of us and doesn't put us at risk of being arrested."

I couldn't suppress a smile, thinking about some

things I'd always wanted to do but had never found any-one who'd do them with me.

"You have to make some compromises as well. Practicing to inseminate you has to be enjoyable for me, not painful. You must fix that. Change birth control methods or whatever it takes. Also, and this is the tough part, you must make love to me."

My temperature boiled. "I have. Several times. Do you have early-onset Alzheimer's?"

"No. You've given me casual sex. You've mocked me, ridiculed me, demonstrated your virtuosity, every-thing but loved me. You need to show me you actually care about me. This is non-negotiable. Let's go."

"You're not giving me a chance to answer." *You might be surprised.*

"I know your answer already. I'm tired and have work to do in the morning."

Getting things off one's chest usually lightened their load but not for Tim.

"Should I get another room?" It sounded like he wanted nothing more to do with me.

"Save your money. I won't molest you." He paid the cashier and almost ran back to the room.

Running's not going to get you away from me. We're staying in the same room, genius.

We parted quietly the next morning, both heading toward the Pennsylvania Turnpike. I waved at him as he pulled onto the westbound on ramp. Maybe he didn't see me. It was time to put Tim out of mind and focus on packing for the cruise. I was sure he'd call me when I re-turned.

⌘

Manning the rigging on the cruise kept us busy and

distracted me from Isaac and Tim. The quiet evenings helped me see things more clearly. The other girls complained when the crew didn't flirt with us. I got booed when I said, "They've got plenty of women with skinnier butts and bouncier boobs available to them. Quit complaining and enjoy the cruise. Didn't we come here to get away from that crap?"

"Speak for yourself," Jackie said.

I ridiculed Tim because he let Zelda damage him. I was twenty-seven and wanted my daughter more than anything. It was time to set aside boyfriends and one-night stands and get serious about finding a husband. It was good I didn't throw away those dresses Daddy got me. They might come in handy. Tim would be more reasonable when I returned. He still loved me. He always would.

About the Author

After a career of chasing, and being chased by, spies and assorted thugs across national monuments while being mistaken for Cary Grant, George Kaplan hung up his shoulder holster and used the money to buy a computer to serve as his word processor. Although well versed in writing after-action summaries, Kaplan had no experience with writing fiction, other than his expense reports.

Government repercussions about modeling characters after his cohorts and enemies would have been far too risky, so he fabricated a heroine who has qualities he's seen a few of on each of a number of women he'd rubbed shoulders (and sometimes more) with, during his long career undercover. Kaplan's first novel, *Only Tim Sent Flowers*, launches his Tookie series about an undiagnosed Aspie girl who perseveres through numerous unexpected adventures.